To hide her face, Akatsuki twirled at the water's edge. Her camel-brown coat flared out, and she was sure she was smiling. Shiroe turned back and waited for her for a little while.

Adventurer, you whose weight is borne by your winged soul! The mystical world of Theldesia is home to dragons and giants, magical beasts, and demihumans. Fragrant green winds blow across this new yet ancient land that opens before you like a blank page. Fill it with your life.

L⊕G HORIZON

Adventurer, you whose weight is borne by your winged soul! The mystical world of Theldesia is home to dragons and giants, magical beasts, and demihumans. Fragrant green winds blow across this new yet ancient land that opens before you like a blank page. Fill it with your life.

LOG HORIZON
6 LOST CHILD OF THE DAWN

MAMARE TOUNO ILLUSTRATION BY **KAZUHIRO HARA**

YEN ON
NEW YORK

CONTENTS

▼ CHARACTER INTRODUCTIONS

▶MIDDLE SCHOOL MIKO
MINORI

▶LOVELY ASSASSIN
AKATSUKI

▶MACHIAVELLI-WITH-GLASSES
SHIROE

SHE'S A VERY EARNEST, RESPONSIBLE GIRL, AND SHE ACTIVELY LOOKS AFTER HER ENERGETIC, RECKLESS LITTLE BROTHER, TOUYA. A MEMBER OF LOG HORIZON, SHE TRIES TO EMULATE HER TEACHER, SHIROE, AND SPENDS HER DAYS STUDYING IN ORDER TO CATCH UP TO HIM.

ALTHOUGH SHE FORMERLY HID THE FACT THAT SHE WAS FEMALE AND PLAYED AS A SILENT MAN, AFTER THE CATASTROPHE, SHE CHANGED HER BODY TO MATCH HER REAL-WORLD SELF. SHE IDOLIZES SHIROE, WHO SAVED HER, AND CALLS HIM HER LIEGE. AFFILIATED WITH LOG HORIZON.

AN INTELLECTUAL ENCHANTER WHO ONCE ACTED AS COUNSELOR FOR THE LEGENDARY BAND OF PLAYERS KNOWN AS THE DEBAUCHERY TEA PARTY. MENTALLY, HE WAS A BIT OF A HERMIT AND AVOIDED INTERACTING WITH OTHER PEOPLE, BUT AFTER THE CATASTROPHE, HE ESTABLISHED HIS OWN GUILD, LOG HORIZON.

▼ PLOT

IT'S BEEN HALF A YEAR SINCE THE CATASTROPHE TRAPPED PLAYERS IN A GAME WORLD.

THE ADVENTURERS OF AKIBA ESTABLISHED THE ROUND TABLE COUNCIL, AN ORGANIZATION OF SELF-GOVERNMENT, AND PERSONALLY HOSTED THE LIBRA FESTIVAL.

THOSE SIX MONTHS PRODUCED MANY TECHNOLOGICAL INNOVATIONS, AND SO THE FESTIVAL CELEBRATING THOSE INNOVATIONS BEGAN AS A GREAT SUCCESS. HOWEVER, IN THE MIDDLE OF THE FESTIVITIES, AN INCIDENT THAT TARGETED AKIBA'S "SYSTEM," THE ROUND TABLE COUNCIL, OCCURRED.

AN "INFORMATION WAR" UNFOLDED, AND SHIROE WAS HARD-PRESSED TO COPE WITH IT.

MINORI, THE ONE WHO'D NOTICED THE EMERGENCY, HELPED SHIROE BY DOING WHAT SHE COULD.

WITH THEIR HELP, RAYNESIA, PRINCESS OF THE PEOPLE OF THE EARTH, NAVIGATED A CRISIS OF HER OWN, AND TOGETHER THEY MANAGED TO BRING THE INFORMATION WAR SAFELY UNDER CONTROL.

HENRIETTA

▶ ABLE ACCOUNTANT

SHE BELONGS TO THE CRESCENT MOON LEAGUE AND HAS BEEN BEST FRIENDS WITH ITS GUILD MASTER, MARIELLE, SINCE THEIR DAYS AT AN ALL-GIRLS HIGH SCHOOL. SHE'S TERRIBLY FOND OF CUTE GIRLS, AND SHE PARTICULARLY ENJOYS PLAYING WITH AKATSUKI AS IF SHE WERE A TOY.

MARIELLE

▶ AKIBA'S SUNFLOWER

THE GUILD MASTER OF THE CRESCENT MOON LEAGUE, A MIDSIZED PLAYER-SUPPORT GUILD. A CLERIC WHO SPEAKS IN THE KANSAI DIALECT AND HAS A GENUINE "BIG SISTER" DISPOSITION. HER ATTITUDE OF TREATING EVERYONE EQUALLY HAS WON HER MANY FANS AMONG BOTH GENDERS.

RAYNESIA

▶ SLACKER PRINCESS

A DAUGHTER OF THE PEOPLE OF THE EARTH NOBLES WHO GOVERN THE CITY OF MAIHAMA. SHE MAY LOOK LIKE A FRAGILE, BEAUTIFUL GIRL, BUT SHE'S ALSO A NATURAL-BORN LAZYBONES WHO THINKS EVEN BATHS ARE TOO MUCH WORK. HER LADY-IN-WAITING, ELISSA, OFTEN SCOLDS HER FOR HER INDOLENCE.

MEANWHILE, AS A CONSEQUENCE OF AN INCIDENT AT THE FESTIVAL, AKATSUKI WAS CONFRONTED WITH MIDDLE-SCHOOLER MINORI'S QUICK WIT AND FEELINGS FOR SHIROE. THE REVELATION CAME AS A HUGE SHOCK TO THE NINJA.

AKATSUKI HAD DECIDED, UNQUESTIONINGLY, THAT SHE WOULD WALK WITH SHIROE. HOWEVER, MINORI'S PRESENCE PLANTED ANXIETY AND CONFUSION IN AKATSUKI'S HEART...

CHAPTER.

1

MURDERER

▶ LEVEL: **90**

▶ RACE: **DWARF**

▶ CLASS: **SAMURAI**

▶ HP: **13421**

▶ MP: **6710**

▶ ITEM 1:

[SMOKY QUARTZ GOGGLES]

FITTED WITH SMOKY QUARTZ, A SEMITRANSPARENT PRECIOUS STONE THAT BLOCKS INTENSE LIGHT, THEY GIVE BONUSES TO MANUFACTURING THAT INVOLVE FURNACES, SINCE TATARA TRIES NOT TO MEET ANYONE'S EYES, SHE OFTEN WEARS THEM WHILE SERVING CUSTOMERS IN THE SHOP AS WELL.

▶ ITEM 2:

[IRON-EATING RATS]

LEGENDARY MYSTICAL BEASTS SAID TO APPEAR TO MASTER SWORDSMITHS. THEY EAT RUST AND MAINTAIN TOOLS AND MATERIALS. BECAUSE THEY'RE CUTE AND THEY FIT IN THE PALM OF YOUR HAND, MANY PEOPLE WANT THEM, BUT SWORDSMITHS ARE RARE, SO GETTING ONE IS SAID TO BE INCREDIBLY DIFFICULT.

▶ ITEM 3:

[FIRE-RAT LEATHER GLOVES]

MADE FROM THE FUR OF A RARE VOLCANIC MONSTER. THEIR FLAME RESISTENCE IS SO HIGH THAT EVEN IF THE WEARER GETS ENVELOPED IN A RED DRAGON'S BREATH, THEIR HANDS WOULD BE UNSCATHED. EXPOSING THEM TO FIRE MAKES THEM CLEAN AGAIN, SO SLOPPY TATARA FINDS THEM VERY USEFUL.

<Matches>
An item that makes it
easy to light fires. Fire
is a milestone toward
becoming a civilized person!

► **1**

Just as she always did, Akatsuki passed through the narrow door to enter the shop.

The place was deep within the Production Guild District, set in a corner of a ruined building's remodeled basement. It was filled with stacks of crates.

This store "zone" was the sales area for the production guild Amenoma. As proof, Japanese swords were out on display, status set to *non-retrievable*. Among the many guilds that forged weapons, Amenoma was an eccentric one that specialized in Japanese swords.

Naturally, the members who ran this eccentric guild weren't normal either, and as a result of their enthusiastic manufacturing, tools and materials flooded from the relatively large forge at the back of the sales area. Swords and materials that were midway through the production process had overflowed into the sales area and were piled messily in crates, such that the place looked like a storehouse.

Still, as far as Akatsuki was concerned, this was all for the best.

Being greeted with a round of "Welcome!" when she entered a store made her feel pressured, and having products recommended to her by over-friendly salesclerks was a turnoff. Akatsuki was fundamentally shy. She'd grown able to talk quite casually with her guild mates Naotsugu and Nyanta, and she thought she'd managed to make friends with Touya and Isuzu and the others, but she was still pretty uncomfortable around other people.

In that respect, at Amenoma (even though it was because they just weren't concerned with sales), she was able to relax and size up the items on her own, and she was grateful for it.

"Okay…"

Relying on memory, Akatsuki made for a corner of the shop.

It was an area that held highly versatile Japanese swords.

In this other world, glass showcases weren't common.

Here, the swords simply hung from hooks on the wall.

Since the sales zone was controlled by the guild and many of the items were set to be non-retrievable, Akatsuki could touch the items, but she couldn't pick them up or move them anywhere. It was, however, possible to look at them and examine them carefully, so the item properties were displayed. The result was that customers who came to shop weren't inconvenienced, but there was also no danger of theft. It was a clever system.

It turned out that there were several dozen swords on display.

As it happened, a few of these were items that Akatsuki was keeping an eye on.

In *Elder Tales*, the conditions that made it possible to equip an item were set on the item itself. For example, the Green Steel Short Sword—Ornate Black Katana Mounting right in front of Akatsuki could be equipped by six of the main classes: Guardians, Samurai, Assassins, Swashbucklers, Bards, and Kannagi.

Samurai were able to equip almost all swords, but if the weapon's equip settings didn't include them, they weren't able to make an exception and equip it. Conversely, Monks weren't able to equip most swords, but if special permission was granted on the item's side, it was possible for them to equip that particular sword.

Major equipment for Assassins—Akatsuki's main class—consisted of bows, whips, and both Western and Japanese swords, but since Assassin was fundamentally a weapon-attack class, it was possible to equip many other types of implements as well, if desired. In the days when this had been a game, Akatsuki had used a short sword simply because it had looked kind of cool, but after the Catastrophe, she'd continued to make regular use of it for more practical reasons.

Akatsuki had experience in kendo, and it seemed like the easiest, most comfortable weapon to use.

Choosing weapons was a difficult affair. Akatsuki ransacked the familiar list in her memory, which she'd gone over many, many times already. *Elder Tales* might have tens of thousands—or maybe even hundreds of thousands—of weapon items, but it was common knowledge that, for a specific Adventurer trying to find the perfect weapon, there weren't all that many options.

To begin with, there were the weapon categories. These categories included one-handed swords, two-handed swords, spears, axes, pole-type weapons, bows, staves, cudgels, brass knuckles, throwing weapons, whips, and special weapons. Quantities varied by category, but if there were about a hundred thousand weapons in all, each category would, presumably, have about a tenth of that number.

There was also the issue of equipment levels. In *Elder Tales*, higher-level equipment appeared every ten levels or so. Furthermore, without exception, all Adventurers were compelled to update their weapons and switch them for new ones every ten levels, simply because if they kept using low-level equipment, they'd handicap their companions who were supposed to be on par with them. Skilled Adventurers tended to review their gear even more frequently because of that. In the end, with the level limit apparently set at 100 at current, if an Adventurer updated their equipment every five levels, that meant switching weapons a total of twenty times.

In addition, Adventurers were divided between twelve main classes. While it was possible for one weapon to be equipped by multiple main classes, different weapons would naturally fulfill different needs. For example, a Kannagi looking for a short sword would want one that provided magic power amplification and attribute defense, while most Assassins would want a short sword that focused on agility and attack power. In addition, even if a piece of equipment was geared toward Assassins, equipment choices could still vary depending on whether it emphasized the force of single attacks or attack speed.

These myriad conditions kept narrowing the field of weapon candidates for any one person by increments of one-tenth. By necessity, no matter how vast the total number of weapons was, the options that appeared as a result were limited.

Right now, for Akatsuki, there were probably about ten potential choices.

On top of that, there was an even greater problem:

Whether it was possible to obtain them.

In *Elder Tales*, powerful weapons were only granted as rewards during raids, almost without exception. Akatsuki had no raid experience. She flattered herself that, as an Adventurer, her level and skills were by no means low, but that was in terms of party Adventurers. In addition, 90 percent of the weapons from raids were nontransferable. In other words, it wasn't possible to trade ownership to someone else. Unless you participated in a raid and acquired one there, you'd likely never get one.

There were about ten weapons that Akatsuki wanted, but only two could be acquired without participating in a raid—or, in other words, could be purchased.

"...Welcome."

Hearing a voice, Akatsuki turned around.

A girl about as small as Akatsuki stood there. Of course, Akatsuki was a human whose height had been set to be short. The standard height for dwarves like this girl was about the same as a child to begin with, so the implications were a bit different. Since the race had unique abilities that were useful to several production classes, they were seen fairly often in production guilds.

Her name was Tatara. She was the guild master of Amenoma, a craftsman who'd mastered high-level Blacksmith skills, and one of Akatsuki's acquaintances.

In response to the voice, Akatsuki nodded.

She might be an acquaintance, but they weren't so close she could make small talk with her.

"Hmm..."

That said, as far as Akatsuki was concerned, Tatara was a pleasant person to deal with. The general opinion was that she poured all her affection into her swords, and as proof, her subclass was Swordsmith, a high-level Blacksmith class that was rare on the server. Possibly because she was indifferent about human relations, she wouldn't actively try to sell anything to customers even when they were standing in the sales area. She was one of the few acquaintances that Akatsuki never had to be afraid of.

…Not that that was the reason, but Akatsuki asked the question on her mind:

"Um, I know this is abrupt, but could I ask…? What happened to the sword that was on display here?"

Her voice had gone a little tense. As she asked the question, she thought to herself that people besides her guild mates really did make her nervous. Tatara had flopped her upper body down over the counter carelessly, and she answered from that position: "It sold."

The words astonished Akatsuki.

This was because, by that point, she'd been coming to Amenoma for two months.

The sort of high-level equipment Akatsuki wanted could get terribly expensive. This was particularly true of the rare raid weapons that were transferable. Some were displayed at Amenoma because they'd been reforged, but as far as Akatsuki knew, there weren't that many secondhand short swords. As a result, since it hadn't sold for two months, she'd thought that as long as she didn't buy it herself, it wouldn't sell for a while.

"Really?"

"Yeah, for real. They went all out and paid in full with cash…if I remember right."

"*Uuu…*"

Words failed her. She really hadn't seen this coming.

That said, when she looked at the swords on the wall again, the one she really wanted, Ringing Blade Hagane-mushi, or "Iron-Devouring Insect," was still there. Of the two short swords that had been for sale— Haganemushi and Hail Blade Byakumaru, or "White Snow Devil"—the latter was the one that had sold. That sword had a "proc," or programmed random occurrence ability that inflicted cold-air ranged damage. Attribute damage was effective against opponents with high physical defenses, but range damage could be difficult to use. In that sense, she might just have been lucky that the one she was really after was still there.

"…Gonna buy it?"

"*Uuu…*"

That question found her speechless, too.

Of course she wanted it. She wanted it so badly she could taste it.

In any case, as a weapon-attack class, compared to other classes, a larger percentage of Assassins' combat abilities depended on their weapons. In addition, Akatsuki was currently dealing with some personal circumstances.

She wanted a high-performance weapon.

However, high-performance weapons were expensive.

The remaining weapon, Ringing Blade Haganemushi, was the one she really wanted, and if things were like this, there was no telling when it would sell. That said, the figure written on its price tag was twice as large as Akatsuki's total assets.

She really couldn't say she'd buy it.

Of course, Akatsuki was going out to the fields day after day and battling monsters. It had been that way ever since Shiroe began shutting himself up in the guild house after the Zantleaf sweep. However, since the Catastrophe, this world changed as it pleased, and there were limits to how much money a player could earn alone.

For Shiroe, or possibly Marielle, or any of the other guild masters whose names were linked to the Round Table Council, the amount might have been something that they could pay on the spot. However, right now, for Akatsuki, the burden was too great.

Tearing her eyes away from the beautiful short sword in its black sheath, Akatsuki shook her head several times, communicating her intent.

Tatara didn't seem all that interested in boosting her sales, either. When she saw that Akatsuki wasn't going to buy anything, she lay down over the counter again, making noises that sounded like "*Mukyuu.*" Apparently this was where she slept.

As if to shake off her regrets, Akatsuki squeezed the handle of her current favorite short sword in its lacquered scabbard and left the Amenoma shop.

She wanted to improve her combat abilities as quickly as possible, and there was somewhere else she needed to go.

▶ **2**

It was December, and winter had fallen upon Akiba's landscapes.

Summer in Yamato had been cooler than summers in Japan in the old world, and apparently, as anticipated, winters were harsher than they'd been in the old world as well. Snow had fallen several times since the beginning of December. There hadn't been enough to stick, but every time, the wind had gotten colder.

That said, Akiba was an Adventurer town.

While the People of the Earth population had grown, Adventurers still accounted for two-thirds of the traffic in the streets. Adventurer bodies were tough; a little cold was nothing to them, and if necessary, one ring set with a small aquamarine gave them enough resistance to the chilly air to easily repel natural cold.

Akatsuki cut through the morning streets, walking rapidly.

She was headed for the outskirts of town.

At the southern edge of Akiba, Akatsuki blew her summoning pipe, leapt onto a swift black horse, and galloped off.

I want to get stronger...

Once again, Akatsuki murmured it to herself, silently.

Lately, it felt as if she thought this every day... No, several dozen times a day.

One more time, Akatsuki put a hand to her hip, tracing the sheath with her fingers.

It held a kiln-turned ceramic stained short sword. It was a high-level production-class weapon that Akatsuki had obtained before the Catastrophe. It certainly wasn't a weak short sword. Of the types that could be acquired when adventuring as a party, it was the highest grade.

Akatsuki thought that this weapon was exactly like her.

In a six-person party, her skills were high-level. She could carry out the role she was given flawlessly and efficiently. However, in *Elder Tales*, there was a world beyond that one: raids. Akatsuki had never taken part in a raid. She'd shied away from the long times spent on standby and the complicated human relationships.

In addition, no one had called her for the task.

However, no matter the reason, the fact was that Akatsuki had no raid experience. That meant she hadn't acquired the high-level treasure-class and fantasy-class equipment that could be obtained on raids. Akiba was home to major combat guilds like the Knights of the Black Sword and D.D.D. Their members probably included super-top-class Assassins who were more skilled than Akatsuki, and who had equipment she could never obtain no matter how much she wanted it.

Shiroe, Naotsugu, and Nyanta were like that as well.

They'd belonged to the Debauchery Tea Party, a group that hadn't been a guild but had once dominated the world, to the point where it had become a legend. They were super-top-class Adventurers who'd competed with the major combat guilds for victory.

Compared with friends like that, her own abilities seemed far too shaky.

She was a skilled Assassin, certainly: a modest top-class, or at least the very top of second-class. However, she wasn't a super-top-class Assassin.

That was Akatsuki's reality.

The very top of second-class.

She was a lot like the weapon she used.

As a result, she'd started going to Amenoma in search of a top-class weapon, even if it was at the very bottom of its class, but top-class weapons were—as expected—expensive, and they were out of her reach. The way she let her regrets accumulate and went back every day was absurd.

When she reached the Dovature Birdlands, Akatsuki dismounted. She wasn't planning to do anything bad, but from this point on, she needed to conceal her presence.

She advanced, slipping between the dense trees, and before long, her vision was blocked by a wall of greenery.

Of course there were trodden paths as well, but that sort of animal trail had inherited the game's design intent, and they meandered. It was a design technique used to make small places look bigger.

The Dovature Birdlands were a type of field dungeon. Although it was an outside zone, the small paths that ran every which way formed a labyrinth, and it had been designed to make it possible to fight lots of monsters.

However, after the Catastrophe, if you didn't mind losing some speed and taking a little trouble, you could skip the suggested routes and cut straight through the brush. You had to climb up and down small cliffs, and it did take work, but for the petite Akatsuki, slipping through the brush was comparatively easy.

This zone was located about forty minutes on horseback from Akiba. It was a zone designed for parties, and the monsters that appeared there had levels in the 80s. Akatsuki was level 91, and she wouldn't gain any experience points here, but in exchange, she could move in relative safety. On the other hand, although it was possible to defeat the monsters that appeared here safely, it took more than one attack to do so, which made it the perfect place for testing weapons and practicing. Akatsuki often came here for combat training.

The group she'd come here for was probably training right now, too.

After she'd pushed her way through the brush for a while, she heard the sounds of battle: clashing steel and a raucous noise that seemed to freeze the air; the sharp sound of electrical attacks... Apparently, the Knights of the Black Sword were going over their teamwork and equipment again today.

Akatsuki found a depression in the ground, then quietly sat down. From that cluster of trees, she could look down into the sunken clearing.

There, two parties from the Knights of the Black Sword were in the middle of a fierce mock battle. Akatsuki used her special Tracker skills to erase all traces of her presence, then began to watch their combat training.

Around the time of the Libra Festival, the word *Mystery* had begun to be whispered through the town of Akiba.

When it first appeared, it was a rumor a bit like an urban legend.

In *Elder Tales*, Adventurers' various actions were expressed as special skills. Special skills were granted to Adventurers according to all sorts of conditions, but the most common was through their classes. For example, Assassinate, the high-powered offensive special skill Akatsuki used, was one that could be acquired by Assassins once they reached a certain level. As Adventurers leveled up, these special skills were replaced by higher-level special skills. For example, Assassinate III, which was acquired at level 47, was weaker than Assassinate IV, which was acquired at level 57.

However, even with Assassinate IV, it was normal for its power to differ depending on who used it. The reason lay within the special-skill ranks. A special skill that had just been acquired as a result of leveling up belonged to a rank known as "Initiate." It could be used, but it wasn't very powerful. After that, by paying into proficiency or using specific items, it was possible to raise the power of the same special skill to "Elementary," "Intermediate," "Esoteric" and "Secret." To attain "Intermediate," you needed a scroll made by someone in the same class; attaining "Esoteric" required a scroll made with rare materials. Both were expensive, but could be purchased.

However, it was impossible to attain "Secret" without conquering a dedicated quest. In addition, that dedicated quest required participation in a raid. This difficulty in acquiring special skills was one of the reasons behind the difference in combat strength between super-top-class Adventurers affiliated with raid guilds and second-class Adventurers like Akatsuki.

According to the rumors, "Mystery" was what lay beyond "Secret."

It was a special skill rank that hadn't existed when *Elder Tales* had been a game, at least not before the Catastrophe. For that reason, some also called it Overskill.

Increased power in special skills due to a rise in rank manifested on several fronts.

Although this differed by special skill, Assassinate was an offensive special skill, so the damage inflicted simply increased. From what Akatsuki remembered, there was a power increase of about 22 percent between "Initiate" and "Secret." There was no knowing how much of a power increase to expect when you attained "Mystery."

As described, "Mystery" brought nothing but good things. However, its existence was no more than a rumor because the number of Adventurers who could declare categorically that they'd confirmed it was incredibly small. As far as Akiba's rumor mill went, half the people didn't believe in Mysteries or Overskills and half did, while even most of the Adventurers who believed in it thought it wasn't all that powerful. Akatsuki believed in the existence of Mysteries simply because Shiroe had declared they existed.

If I manage to acquire a Mystery, even I'll be more...

As she thought, Akatsuki hugged herself tightly.

Most of Akatsuki's own special skills were ranked "Intermediate" or

"Esoteric." Of course, for a party-level Adventurer, these ranks were more than sufficient, but she'd be no match for a member of a major combat guild. Even here, there was a wall in front of Akatsuki.

However, the Mysteries must exist.

Shiroe had said they existed, so they did.

And the ones who were most likely to have attained them were the strongest of the combat guilds, the members of the Knights of the Black Sword. Of course, there were probably Adventurers in guilds like Honesty and D.D.D. who'd attained "Mystery" rank as well, but the Knights of the Black Sword prided themselves on being elite, and it was more likely to exist among them.

No one knew how "Mystery" rank was attained, but in light of the fact that "Secret" was granted through special quests that required raid participation, it was logical that it probably involved some sort of quest. That just showed how little general knowledge there was about the way "Mystery" level was attained. In the current *Elder Tales*, where strategy sites no longer existed, information traveled slowly, and its value was through the roof.

This was why Akatsuki was huddled up in the brush in the bone-chilling December cold, watching the Knights of the Black Sword train. If another Assassin was using a "Mystery"-level attack, she wanted to see that skill and gauge how powerful it was. If they were going on a quest, she wanted to at least know its trigger.

They're tough… That was just one attack.

Even from here, she could tell the Knights of the Black Sword were strong: naturally, the Assassins who fought there, but even the other classes as well. They were so strong it was fascinating.

Heeey, cut in deeper.

Lame. That ain't enough damage, is it?

You've gotta step farther in!

The way they spoke might have been rough, but all the members of the Knights of the Black Sword were elites, in the top 1 percent on the Yamato server.

Their movements, their teamwork, the beauty of their equipment, their strength.

Just watching them made Akatsuki want to cry.

Even though fighting was all she could do…

She was weak in combat.

She remembered the profiles of her liege and her junior guild member on the night of the festival, illuminated by the bonfires. A pair of birds soaring to heights Akatsuki didn't understand.

She'd wanted to be by Shiroe's side. She'd wanted it very badly.

But she hadn't even tried to think about what Shiroe was seeing, and now she was paying the price.

I want to get stronger...

Once more, Akatsuki murmured it to herself.

However, she was keenly aware that that murmur alone would never make her stronger. She knew how foolish it was to be sitting here observing the Knights of the Black Sword. She didn't have the strength to accomplish one single thing.

Akatsuki, who had to protect Shiroe's secret, was the loneliest person in wintry Akiba.

▶ **3**

The glass bottle was big, so big it might have been better to call it a glass basin. Pale pink liquid circulated inside the glass vessel, and a man on a stepladder was casually tossing light brown leaves into it.

The fragrance that wafted up smelled like cocoa, but Roderick, who was frowning, knew it wouldn't taste the least bit sweet if you drank it.

This was a research facility known as "Roderick's Workshop."

It was a room in the Roderick Trading Company's guild tower.

"Guild tower" was one of the terms Adventurers used for guild halls. The term was often used when a guild bought up an entire building, as the Roderick Trading Company had, and used its interior as a guild hall. This was particularly true if the building was a tall one.

The Roderick Trading Company, one of Akiba's leading production guilds, had purchased a seven-story building on the north side of Akiba that it used as its guild hall. Inside, the laboratory that Roderick claimed as his own was overflowing with glass lab instruments.

There were small items for experiments, but the room also held enormous heating vessels like the one that was currently in use, and a pestle the size of a bathtub.

In order to create items in *Elder Tales*, all you needed to do was select the thing you wanted to make from a menu. If you had the materials and the machinery, it would be done in ten seconds. Even now, in this world, that method could be used the way it had in the game. However, if you wanted to create something new, as Roderick did, it was another story. You had to do everything by hand, right from the start.

If you wanted to produce in volume, you needed large equipment.

On the day the Round Table Council was established, Shiroe had pointed out the possibilities that lay within the new item-creation system.

These possibilities had first taken root in the field of food and drink, and had then spread to the disciplines of furniture making, smithy, and haberdashery. For the past six months, the artisans of Akiba had continued to discover and develop new items on a daily basis.

However, there were some artisans who were unable to apply manual skills from the real world. Roderick was one of them. His subclass was Apothecary. This was a production class that created the potions and balms that were staples of fantasy games.

Since there had been no "potions to recover 180 HP" in the real world where he'd once lived, there could be no techniques to use as models. Alchemists, Sigilmancers, Gem Engineers and other fantasy world–type production classes all had similar issues.

That didn't mean they couldn't create new items, however.

If they were unable to divert recipes and techniques from the real world, all they had to do was inspect the recipes that were already in this world, run experiments, and invent. Over the past six months, they'd created reinforcement-type recovery potions up to level 50, and sigils and gems had been continually improved.

One of Roderick's great personal achievements had been the development of a mass-produced Appearance Reset Potion. Unlike the real Appearance Reset Potion, it was simple: It only allowed changes to up to two parameters from the gender, height, weight, figure, hair color, eye color, and skin color options. However, thanks to the popularization of this potion, they'd nearly managed to eradicate cases of

Adventurers struggling with genders that were different from their old-world selves.

After that, Roderick had continued to analyze, mass-produce, and work out countermeasures for extremely difficult medicines such as Ambrosia, Theriac, and Netherworld Repast.

The Roderick Trading Company was counted as one of the three major production guilds, but its purpose wasn't quite production itself.

When *Elder Tales* had been a game, item creation had taken the form of selecting recipes from a menu. There were different recipes for different subclasses, and in order to become able to create a variety of items, artisans had had to collect countless Recipe Scrolls.

For example, even when speaking only of the types of medicines Apothecaries could create, there were instant HP recovery potions, gradual HP recovery potions, HP reinforcement potions, reinforcement potions for abilities, three types of poison antidote, antivenom potions, more than ten poisons for lacing weapons, movement speed increase potions, attack-speed increase potions...and so on. Because potions with stronger effects appeared every ten levels or so, even in the game, Roderick had been able to make over six hundred types of items. In other words, he'd had that many recipes.

That said, it was difficult for ordinary Adventurers, let alone beginners, to collect the vast number of recipes in their entirety. Even among Apothecaries, it took a lot of time and in-game assets to become able to make absolutely anything medicinal.

In an endeavor to counter that game situation, the Roderick Trading Company guild had been established with the goal of building a recipe library. If materials of corresponding rarity were used, it was possible to copy the recipes. In addition, artisans who worked at a guild that accumulated recipes naturally acquired many of them, and so were able to add more value to the cause overall than other crafters.

It was only natural that, following the Catastrophe, the Roderick Trading Company had been the production guild that shifted its focus to research and development.

At this point, most Adventurers who liked research and development had gravitated to the Roderick Trading Company.

In the same way, Adventurers working to apply technology from the old world to this one, to mechanize and mass-produce, were joining the Marine Organization, and Adventurers who liked selling the resulting items and doing business with the People of the Earth were affiliated with Shopping District 8. The Marine Organization ran its own guild shop, even so, but the Roderick Trading Company left its sales work to Shopping District 8 and several commercial guilds. All of its guild members were people who liked mulling over new experiments when they had time.

As a result, the Roderick Trading Company's guild tower was buried in pointlessly complicated lab equipment and bundles of record documents, and its atmosphere was disorderly. Many fans of MMO games were in high school or college. They'd been students to begin with, and the atmosphere of this research institution-esque guild was probably comfortable for them.

Internally, they often called the Roderick Trading Company the Roderick Laboratory, or the RoderLab for short. To them, it must have felt like an academy with a free and easy atmosphere, where they could immerse themselves in fun research every day.

Including things such as the popularity vote for the lunch delivery girls from Onigiri Shop Enmusubi, it was turning into a guild that was well suited to this other world in a different way from comfy, homey guilds like the Crescent Moon League.

In the heart of that guild hall, an enormous room with a high ceiling, Roderick turned around.

The voice that had spoken to him belonged to a young member of his guild. The companion, who was still young enough to be called a boy, went away, leaving a visitor behind. Roderick climbed down from the low stepladder and greeted his guest.

"Good afternoon, Nyanta."

"It's night already."

Roderick paused at that. ...*Hmm.* He'd been sure it was still before lunch...

"Even if mew skip lunch, night comes."

His question received an entirely natural response. Nyanta had been looking around as if he was deeply interested, but with a twitch of his whiskers, he took a letter from his pouch in a smart gesture and handed it to Roderick.

On taking it and skimming through, Roderick was left nonplussed.

The sender of the letter was Shiroe of Log Horizon. He'd known that from the beginning. The content was a request for research related to technology development, and he'd anticipated that as well. Such paper-based exchanges were occurring more frequently these days.

After all, this other world held all sorts of plant, animal, and mineral materials. Compounding them, verifying their effects, and searching for new items was incredibly entertaining. It was possible to look at the materials consumed in recipes from *Elder Tales'* game days and get a vague idea of the medicinal properties of the required materials. Collecting and analyzing this sort of knowledge and putting together ideas thrilled him.

The Roderick Trading Company attracted these so-called "research fiends." Although most of the members specialized in different fields, it was safe to say that, on some level, they all had that sort of temperament.

Roderick himself was aware that he had so much fun with this sort of trial and error that he tended to leave his Round Table Council duties to other guilds. The biggest victim of this was Shiroe. As a result, it was hard for him to turn down Shiroe's requests.

In addition, in most cases, Shiroe's letters turned out to be beneficial for the Roderick Trading Company as well: suggestions from Shiroe for new products, or introductions to promising guilds or people. At the very least, so far, they'd never been worse off for considering them.

However, this letter wasn't as easy to understand.

In any case, it held only a few lines.

"That's what it is, apparently."

"Nyanta, are you familiar with the contents of this letter?"

"No, not in the least."

Nyanta waved a hand at the dumbfounded Roderick. Apparently he really didn't know.

I want a catalog of all the magic items that are currently in circulation in Akiba, or are most likely in the possession of the large guilds. I'd also like you to investigate their abilities. In particular, could you append the flavor text to your survey material?

"Mmm, well... I don't have any objection to it. However, investigating this is going to take quite a lot of items that are higher than fantasy-class and secret-class. That's a lot of material. I expect that's why he came to us, but..."

"We don't have assets like that at Log Horizon, mew see."

"So you say, but I'd wager you do have quite a variety of things."

"Mya-ha-ha-ha. We've got lots of growing youngsters, and it's a drain on the wallet."

Nyanta laughed gently, showing a laid-back maturity. As always, he was neat and fashionable, a perfect gentleman.

Roderick sighed and let himself be convinced.

If Shiroe had sent him a letter like this, this sort of research would probably be necessary sooner or later. True, it was research which was likely to require a budget, but it wasn't an amount they couldn't scrape together.

It was true that the Roderick Trading Company was probably the best guild for a job that required investigating many types of items. After all, it had the largest recipe collection on the Yamato server, and it attracted obsessives who loved research more than anything else in the world.

"There are several things I'd like to discuss. Would you join me for lunch?"

"As I told mew, it's night."

"For ramen, then."

"I suppose I must."

He shrugged, and Roderick left the laboratory, in which he'd spent who knew how many hours, with his older friend.

Since it was winter, hot soup would probably taste wonderful.

▶ 4

It was a cold night.

The wind that stabbed her cheeks had a metallic chill to it. Kyouko sneezed hugely, then looked around. That had been a pretty impressive one. Really unladylike.

Thinking that Master Soujirou would probably be disillusioned with her if he found out, she rubbed at her nose, which had started to tickle again.

For Adventurers who'd reached a certain level, the cold air of winter wasn't a threat. They could use their equipment to shut out damage from the cold. However, saying they weren't cold would have been a lie. In particular, the information they got through their sight and hearing that told them "It's probably cold" convinced their spirits of the cold, long before they took physical damage.

As a result, Kyouko was hurrying to the guild house.

More than half the guild members were probably asleep there already.

While she'd been talking business with Shopping District 8—or rather, just chatting—it had gotten very late. However, it had been worth it: Kyouko's Magic Bag was stuffed with loot. She'd actually managed to get three salt-pickled salmon. Some of her companions would cry tears of joy if she fed them this. After all, it tasted like home.

If all goes well, maybe Master Soujirou, too—

Conjuring up sweet daydreams, Kyouko broke into a grin.

They'd eat lunch together. The menu would be onigiri, naturally, made with plenty of salmon. "Master Soujirou, you have some of your lunch stuck to your cheek." "I do? Which one?" "The right one." "Huh? Where, where is it?" "I guess I'll have to... There, I've got it." *Munch.* Heh-heh! Kidding!

In one of Akiba's back streets, Kyouko turned bright red.

Her twelve-cylinder maiden engine was going full throttle, repelling the midwinter's night wind.

Kyouko was an athletic type in any case, and her temperature rose easily. She had a good basal metabolism. If it had been Fragrant Olive, she would have gotten a nosebleed and collapsed. The anemic elf's ability to fantasize left Kyouko's in the dust.

"*Wachoo!*"

However, the mental lunch-date fantasy seemed to have made her careless. A sneeze that couldn't be called ladylike burst out. It really was a problem.

That sneeze had gotten her teased both in middle school and in high school. "What the heck, Kyouko?! You're like some old guy!" She could still remember it. One of her classmates in brass band had told her that. She'd actually liked the boy quite a bit, too. Calling a girl an old guy... That had been mean. She'd been pretty wounded by it.

True, she'd been a dedicated athletic-club type for ages, and in her class, she'd been less of a feminine type and more of a laughs-with-her-mouth-wide-open type, but even so, she wished he'd chosen his words more carefully. Such as, maybe, "Now there's a sneeze that hints at real greatness." ...No, actually, that would have been awful. Really terrible.

Kyouko thought about these things as she walked.

Even so, she realized—although it was a bit late for such realizations—that the way she sneezed was the same in this world, too. It had seemed only natural, but come to think of it, it was odd.

Although the fact that I'm in another world is odd enough to begin with.
She directed a verbal jab at herself.

Possibly because of the sneezing, she wasn't in top form tonight.

The greenery whispered. The air was cold and felt stiff somehow.

Night wind had blown through the spaces between the ruined buildings, rustling the trees. Then, by the time Kyouko noticed, there was a man standing in the darkness ahead of her.

He was about 175 centimeters tall, a man with long hair. A tight black tank top and leather pants. He wore sturdy jet-black armor on his arms and legs only, which gave him a strange silhouette, but strangeness on that level wasn't uncommon in Akiba, a town of Adventurers.

What made Kyouko stop in her tracks was the indescribable feeling of intimidation that rolled off the man.

Feeling as though her spine had frozen, Kyouko paused. She even took an involuntary step backward.

As if he didn't like the distance she'd put between them, the man came forward.

In the wan glow of the Bug Lights the Round Table Council had had installed, the man wore a black mask that resembled a blindfold. Although she had no idea when he'd drawn it, he held a sword that seemed to absorb the pale light.

The blade rose smoothly, as if pulled by a string, and Kyouko's body reacted to it before her mind did.

Kyouko was level 90, and a veteran Guardian too. The West Wind Brigade had a reputation for being a harem or girls' club, but in terms of achievements alone, it was among Akiba's top five combat guilds.

Kyouko was skilled enough to be the captain of the West Wind Brigade's second company.

However, that was all thanks to her Adventurer body.

As the silver light passed by, seeming to skim the surface of her eyeballs, greasy sweat broke out along Kyouko's spine. The first thing to surface from the midst of her fragmented thoughts was the feeling that she was about to be killed. The man in front of Kyouko was going to kill her. The next thing to surface—the word *PK*—was shattered by the words *in town*.

No, even in town, it wasn't as though murders couldn't happen.

It was just that the guards would teleport in and stop them.

In that case, if she hung on until the guards came…

In the worst possible scenario, she'd probably die. However, even if she did, she'd revive in the Temple. That was an Adventurer's prerogative. There was no need to be afraid. In any case, at level 90, there weren't many things that could kill her easily. Guardians had the greatest defense of all twelve main classes. Since she was in town, she wasn't wearing her armor, but even so, she was physically sturdy. *It's all right; I can get through this.* There was no need to be too afraid.

Thus, she tried to calm herself down.

…But it was no good.

The man had stepped in close enough that he could have kissed her, and when he smiled, showing the red, wet cavity of his mouth, the composure Kyouko had managed to scrape together fell to pieces.

He was too fast. Too fast for her to follow, even with level-90 kinetic vision. Or no, was it technique, rather than speed? When she stared at him steadily, he seemed to slip through the gaps between her thoughts with slimy invertebrate movements, closing the distance before she was aware of it.

She was only able to follow the first few silver flashes.

Kyouko saw the man grasp the hilt of a sword that had sprouted from her stomach.

No.

The sword the man held had run her through.

Expelling something from her lungs that was less a scream than a clot of damp air, Kyouko leapt backward.

However, when she landed, the sneering man was toying with a blade that had grown from her thigh.

Possibly the serial damage had hit her with a bad status effect: The blood that flowed from her wounds wasn't stopping. Kyouko ran through the alleys like a wounded hare. Her throat stung and wouldn't let her scream the way she wanted to, and her limbs felt limp, as if she had a fever.

The fact that, even so, she managed to maintain her agility and field several attacks was due entirely to her Adventurer body.

As she continued to raise wordless screams, Kyouko desperately kept trying to gather her thoughts and think of a way to escape.

Subjectively, a long time seemed to pass.

Far too long.

Shaken by her terror of the man, who kept sticking her with his sword any way he pleased, she'd almost lost her sense of time, but even so, too much time had passed.

"Ah, agh! Aie!"

Kyouko couldn't make the words come out. Stabbing her through the chest, the man warped the red cavern of his mouth into the shape of a smile.

"The guards won't come."

As she understood the meaning of those words, a doubt like roaring static filled Kyouko's mind. That was against the rules. She'd never heard of such a thing. The declaration had been far too unfair, and Kyouko slammed her raised fist into the man.

However, a blade sprouted from that fist.

The sight was almost comical. At some point, the man had jumped back, holding his sword out as if to thrust, and had stopped Kyouko's fist with it. Overwhelming speed and technique that surpassed Kyouko's, even at level 90. Soujirou might have been able to follow the

attacks with his Mystery, Clairvoyance, but she couldn't see through them.

Again and again, Kyouko struck out with her fists and her feet.

Kyouko had zero martial arts experience, but Adventurers' physical performance was fast and destructive enough to lead even a bear around by the nose. Those attacks fell prey to the man's blade, almost as if they were drawn into it. The single sword that hung from the man's right hand sliced Kyouko apart, protecting the man as if it had multiplied by a thousand.

She didn't understand.

She had no idea what in the world was happening.

Kyouko didn't know why the guards weren't coming, or why a PK had been allowed to run loose in the middle of town, or why a monster like this had infiltrated Akiba.

Kyouko couldn't even think straight anymore, and she kept fighting as if delirious with fever. However, if Kyouko seemed feverish, the man was lunacy itself. Smiling a sticky smile, the man ran his sword through every inch of Kyouko's body, as if tormenting her, toying with her.

The midnight battle came to an end in silence.

The late-night wind that blew between the buildings carried away the sound of their struggle.

Kyouko fell, still not understanding, and as if it had been promised from the beginning, the man stabbed his bright sword into her neck. As her vision dimmed, fading to black and white, Kyouko saw the blood that clung to the sword, her own blood, turn into frozen crystals and sift away.

Even though it was midwinter, they looked like pale pink flower petals.

Was the lethargy that lingered in her limbs frostbite? Tears that weren't from sadness fell from Kyouko's eyes onto the immobile remains of her arms and legs.

Kyouko had been on the brink of reaching something. However, in accordance with the laws of this world, she was sent to the Temple. By the time she woke and reached the guild hall where her companions waited, it was the next morning.

And so rumors of the murderer who threatened Akiba's winter spread like wildfire.

▶ **5**

A killer had appeared, one who dominated Akiba's nights.

The news spread even faster than the wind that blew over the town. On the first night, there had been three victims. The next night, just one. However, on the third day, a group of five had fallen.

Since several of these had been veterans from combat guilds, it seemed safe to say that the murderer's preposterous combat abilities had been proven to be far greater than those of level-90 Adventurers.

At first, people thought the incident would be easily resolved.

To begin with, this world had been modeled on *Elder Tales*, and in it, there was power in numbers. Even if the murderer was a bit stronger than an individual, if six people in a functional party formation surrounded him or her, it was assumed they couldn't lose.

The peculiar conditions of this world also gave them an advantage when it came to capturing the criminal. All the victims had been killed by the murderer, but they were still alive. Even if Adventurers died, they were shunted to the Temple and reborn. As a result, there was a wealth of eyewitness testimony regarding the murderer, and of combat information.

Enbart Nelles.

No guild affiliation.

Level 94, Samurai.

Long, dark hair with hints of indigo and a mask like a blindfold. Metal armor that encased his arms and legs.

With that many characteristics, they'd assumed that investigating would be easy. True, the incidents had occurred late at night, but that didn't mean they had to limit their search for the criminal to nighttime. As a matter of fact, guilds—particularly the West Wind Brigade and Honesty, which had suffered damage—were continuing to hunt for the culprit.

However, even now, a week after the incidents, they hadn't so much as glimpsed him, and the number of victims kept growing.

When Adventurers killed other Adventurers, the term for it was a "PK," or "player kill." It was one way of playing, and the act was currently restricted at the zone level by Akiba's Round Table Council. Yet, even though adventurers who committed PKs again and again were known as player killers—also abbreviated PK—that didn't mean they were automatically called "murderers."

To begin with, the town of Akiba was a zone under the protection of the guards.

If a violent act was committed there, a magical alert went to the guards' station immediately, and the guards—People of the Earth in special equipment—went to capture the offender... Or they should have. At this point in time, it was clear that something very strange was afoot.

Of course, in the process of their investigation, the Round Table Council had inquired at the guard station. As a result, they'd learned that, at the time the incidents had occurred, the guards hadn't detected any abnormalities. Apparently, at least as far as the *Elder Tales* game system was concerned, no PKs had occurred.

Rumors about the uncanny cutthroat spread rapidly through Akiba.

However, this wasn't because the incidents were an object of serious terror.

Instead, the stories were taken more as a morbidly fascinating urban legend.

After all, to Adventurers, death wasn't that great a risk.

It did have a certain disadvantage, of course: the danger of losing memories from the old world. Through a careful information disclosure maneuver by the Round Table Council, this fact had gradually become known to the town of Akiba. The dejection regarding this destruction of memory wasn't a small one, and it was particularly marked among the Adventurers who were involved in production classes in the town.

However, on the other hand, it was true that there was a certain mood of pragmatism as well.

This was probably due to the fact that Adventurers who had experienced death a dozen or so times said that the destruction of memory wasn't significant enough to feel like a problem; in fact, they were still participating in the town of Akiba without any trouble, just as their companions were.

Either way, the Adventurers lived in this world, and inevitable fates were inevitable.

Even if they were attacked by the murderer and became a victim, it wouldn't do them any critical damage.

In addition, although the Adventurers of Akiba didn't say it outright, it was partially because they placed great confidence in the Round Table Council, or RTC.

The RTC, which had been established less than a month after the Catastrophe and had handled Akiba's self-government ever since, had produced a variety of tangible and intangible achievements. The Adventurers shared a common experience that gave their community a clearer origin than any in the old world: the shock of the Catastrophe, and the following devastation; given that, the residents of Akiba were quite proud of the representative system that had risen out of the ashes. They'd even managed to pull together and hold the Libra Festival last month.

In other words, the term *monstrous* clearly expressed the strangeness of the incident itself.

Unfairness that deviated from the system. A monster that attacked out of nowhere, like a natural disaster.

—And yet, even so, the damage wasn't severe. On the contrary, the incidents seemed designed to cause only terror, and they were almost like a campaign tale. Most of the citizens of Akiba thought that, even if he behaved ferociously now, the matter would be resolved before long.

In any case, ever since the Catastrophe, all sorts of abnormalities had cropped up in the world and new incidents occurred nearly every day. And, too, as the largest Adventurer city on the Yamato server, Akiba was one big sieve of information. Mysterious incidents, mildly troubling incidents, hair-raising incidents, anxiety-inducing incidents—all *sorts* of things were here.

It was true that this serial killer wasn't the sort of problem that could be neglected, but Akiba had several other, bigger problems at the moment.

The two that could be deemed Akiba's main concerns were the Seventh Fall Subjugation Operation and the sudden rise to power of an enormous guild in Minami.

The Akiba expeditionary force, which had been victorious in the Zantleaf war, had finally begun its invasion of Seventh Fall, the castle of the Goblin tribe. The Goblin King appeared in the course of the Return of the Goblin King quest, and his strength changed depending on how active the Adventurers were during that event. In the confusion that had followed the Catastrophe, the Adventurers had ignored the Goblin King, and he'd developed to the point of plotting to send soldiers into the Zantleaf Peninsula. No doubt he was stronger than any previous raid boss.

No matter how high the difficulty level had risen, the enemy was fundamentally a Goblin, a midrange demihuman. Naturally, if this had been a game, he wouldn't have posed enough of a threat to worry about.

However, on the other hand, they couldn't ignore the fact that it was possible that common sense from the game no longer applied to the post-Catastrophe world. In addition, even if he was a threat the Adventurers could cope with, it wasn't hard to imagine that he might be lethal for the People of the Earth.

Due to these circumstances, Akiba's Round Table Council had dispatched a subjugation force composed of elites.

It had 450 members, with Krusty as commander-in-chief.

Of course, these troops were being dispatched to subjugate the Goblins and to bring stability to northeastern Yamato, but at the same time, the expedition was part of their exchange with Eastal, the League of Free Cities.

To that end, Krusty and Isaac, two of Akiba's most prominent heroes, had gone to the front with the subjugation army, and even Akaneya and Calasin had gone along as reinforcements.

That meant that the burden on the other Round Table Council guild masters would inevitably increase. There was a rumor that they were spending every day in the guild center or their own guild homes, fielding exhausting workloads.

This expedition operation was what was drawing the most interest in Akiba at the moment.

The 450 members of the expedition army had departed ages ago, and no one had any doubts about their victory, but the rear duties, such as supply transport and relief personnel, weren't going anywhere. There was also no telling when the Adventurers in Akiba would be asked to provide backup. Thus, there were reasons to pay attention, and no reasons not to.

The other subject that was attracting attention was information about Plant Hwyaden, which was said to have brought the West almost completely under its control.

At this point in time, many of Akiba's Adventurers had mixed feelings about the town of Minami.

To the players on the Yamato server, who were from modern Japan, the system of self-government established in Minami looked like a one-party dictatorship.

In the first place, in the *Elder Tales* game, having a variety of guilds crowded together had been the natural state of things, even where the game system was concerned. It had been only natural that the early confusion in Akiba had taken the form of guilds competing with each other.

It seemed somewhat high-handed that, in a short period of time, a single guild—Plant Hwyaden—had claimed supremacy and, on top of that, had absorbed all the other guilds.

However, could they criticize the move? That was hard to say. Instantly declaring that it was bad, just because it was a dictatorship, would have been too simplistic. In fact, according to the information that came in from Minami, trouble caused by Adventurers had dropped off dramatically, and although their policy was different from Akiba's, the Adventurers seemed to be advancing matters in harmony with each other.

In the first place, these were Adventurers who had played on the same server. It wasn't unusual for old friends and companions to live separated, some in Akiba and some in Minami. Sometimes Adventurers were invited to move to Minami from Akiba and did so, and sometimes they were invited to Akiba from Minami and moved that way.

In any case, Japanese people weren't good at bringing up politics in everyday conversation.

As such, Adventurers were conscious of the difference between Akiba and Minami and considered it high-interest news, but they also knew it was a slightly awkward topic to discuss.

In terms of the population difference between Akiba and Minami, there were comparatively more Adventurers in Akiba. However, Plant Hwyaden had more than twice as many Adventurers as Akiba's largest guild, the Marine Organization.

Even as they felt a premonition of trouble in the situation, people were hesitant to express clear opinions on Minami, and the mood was an uncomfortable one.

At present, Akiba was caught between these two major news items, and although the days passed peacefully, there was tension about them as well. As a result, although they knew the information about the murderer, most of the Adventurers didn't attach much importance to it.

On the fourth and fifth days, the murderer failed to appear.

However, on the sixth day... An arrest patrol squad from Honesty was completely wiped out.

The Round Table Council sent out a mild alert, requesting that people voluntarily refrain from going out at night. The Adventurers were one thing, but for a Person of the Earth, the situation would be irreparable. So far, all victims had been Adventurers, but that didn't guarantee the safety of other groups.

However, even at this point in time, no Adventurers predicted what the appearance of the murderer truly meant.

CHAPTER.
2
CRACKED WING

▶ LEVEL: **90**

▶ RACE: **FOXTAIL**

▶ CLASS: **KANNAGI**

▶ HP: **10771**

▶ MP: **10637**

▶ ITEM 1:

[SKETCHY DICE]

ORNAMENTS SHAPED LIKE DICE. THEY HAVE MAGIC THAT ATTRACTS GOOD LUCK, WHICH UNERRINGLY TRIGGERS CRITICALS, BUT AS THEIR RECAST TIME IS LONG, THEY CAN ONLY BE USED ONCE A DAY. IT'S POSSIBLE TO USE THEM AS ORDINARY DICE, BUT FOR SOME REASON, NAZUNA ISN'T ABLE TO ROLL ANYTHING GOOD WITH THEM, SO SHE'S SEALED THEM.

▶ ITEM 2:

[LIGHTLESS STRIKER]

A KATANA SPECIFICALLY FOR KANNAGI. IN ADDITION TO REINFORCING BARRIERS AND INCREASING THE SPEED OF SPELLS, IT ALSO MAKES RECOVERY SPELLS ACTIVATE CRITICALS. ITS STURDINESS LETS IT BE USED ON THE FRONT LINE AS WELL. SHE WON IT OFF A CERTAIN SWORDSMITH IN A BET.

▶ ITEM 3:

[MITHRIL UNDERSHIRT]

PRODUCTION-CLASS DEFENSIVE GEAR WOVEN FROM MITHRIL. IT'S DELICATE AND CAN BE WORN NEXT TO THE SKIN AND UNDER ARMOR. NAZUNA ALWAYS WEARS IT UNDER HER CLOTHES, BUT WHEN DRUNK, SHE TENDS TO PROWL IN UNDERSHIRT ONLY. AS A RESULT, SHE'S CAUGHT AND TOSSED INTO HER ROOM BEFORE SOUJIROU CAN SEE.

-190

-180

<FRYING PAN>
ADVENTURERS EAT OUT
OF THESE INSTEAD OF
DISHES. IT'S HOW THINGS
ARE DONE OUTDOORS.

"So, how about givin' up? G'wan, g'wan. Just give up and let me take care of you. I won't do anythin' mean."

"Mari. You sound like a lecherous middle-aged man."

"Ah, ah-wah-wah!"

Akatsuki sat on the edge of the sofa, shooting glances at the chaos in the middle of the room.

The wallpaper in this beautiful guest room was brand-new—a gentle pale pink hue. The interior decoration and furnishings were suffused with a feminine elegance. There was a delicate tea service on the coffee table. This, together with the women who had descended upon the room, made the atmosphere bright and cheerful.

Raynesia, the room's mistress, was smiling with as much composure as ever, but a subtle hint of bewilderment showed through. Well, that was only to be expected.

The outfit Marielle was trying to put on her was what people called a "nurse uniform."

Even Akatsuki thought that was too adventurous.

"That garment is a bit too...um...small for me..."

Raynesia shook her head in a little trembling motion that made her look like a rabbit, but *Oh*, Akatsuki thought, *that was the wrong reaction.* Sure enough: "Don't you worry! Our seamstresses made that custom, and it's just your size!" Marielle declared, catching her.

Refusing in a roundabout way like that didn't work on Marielle. On Henrietta…it probably wouldn't work either, Akatsuki thought. She shook her head again.

"Um, like this? This way, right?"

"No, that isn't it. Eek!"

"Mari… Really, you shouldn't use your hands like that…"

"Ah-wah-wah!"

The flustered one was Serara. That said, even as she dithered, when Marielle told her things like, "Grab me that headband," she did so obediently, making it clear what the hierarchies inside the Crescent Moon League were at times like this.

"You aren't going to rescue her?"

The Adventurer who sat across from Akatsuki, holding her teacup elegantly, was a woman called Riezé. An upper-class young lady with saffron blond hair, she was a Sorcerer affiliated with D.D.D. She was a slim, beautiful girl, and Akatsuki had heard that she was captain of the training unit.

In response to Riezé's question, Akatsuki shook her head slightly.

The Assassin was rather familiar with this sort of situation. After all, until just a little while ago, she'd been the one taking damage in the spot Raynesia now occupied. While the main aggressor at the time had been Henrietta, not Marielle, she'd experienced the situation itself in a general way.

She was fully aware that if she was foolish enough to attempt a rescue now, the result would be a secondary disaster, or rather, that the number of victims would double. Just like everyone else, Akatsuki valued her own life.

In short, at present, this room had turned into a dress-up chamber sponsored by the Crescent Moon League.

"I see."

Without particularly reproaching her for it, Riezé dropped her gaze to her tea.

Akatsuki picked up a bean jam bun from a plate and took a small bite. It was sweet and delicious. One of the perks of this mission.

It was strange to call this chaotic tea party a mission, but that was how Akatsuki thought of it.

In any case, she was here because Shiroe had asked her to come. It might have been a small request, but to Akatsuki, it was an unmistakable link to Shiroe. That had been a month ago, but still Akatsuki continued to attend this tea party.

At first, Akatsuki had been the only one.

She'd drunk tea in the midst of an uncomfortable silence, under Raynesia's dubious gaze, and had taken her leave after fifteen minutes. After a week, Marielle had joined them. Sometimes Marielle came by herself, and sometimes, like today, she brought friends from the Crescent Moon League. After that, starting with Riezé, who was drinking tea in front of her, women from several guilds had begun attending.

To be honest, it wasn't a mission she was very enthusiastic about.

She'd gotten used to Marielle, Henrietta, Serara, and the other Crescent Moon League women, but attending with members from other guilds was mentally exhausting. She was bad at conversing with relative strangers. She couldn't talk well, and Akatsuki thought the people she talked to must feel let down, too.

Unexpectedly, aside from the Crescent Moon League members, the first person she'd grown able to talk to was Raynesia.

In all, there were probably about fifteen female Adventurers who stopped by for the tea party. Marielle attended fairly frequently, but even then, it was only two or three times a week. Each of the other members belonged to their own guilds and had various duties.

Akatsuki was about the only one who attended every day... Although this was purely because she wanted to keep her promise to Shiroe to the greatest extent possible.

"Well, I'll be! What pretty skin. That's a princess for ya."

"M-Miss Akatsuki. Um, h-help."

"Ah-wah-wah-wah-wah..."

"Nah, nah. I'm tellin' you, I won't treat you rough!"

That said, it was because they kept seeing each other, not because they'd become friends or anything. She'd become able to make small talk with her, that was all.

...And so it was a problem to be asked for help like this. After all, until just a little while ago, she'd been prey herself. She huddled down, thinking that if she made herself small and stayed seated, the storm might pass over. However, maybe it made her look funny: She caught Henrietta's eye.

"Akatsuki, dear. ♪ Why are you huddling up?"

"!"

Akatsuki flinched, denying it, and Henrietta gave a pleasant laugh. However, for today, she seemed to have given up on the chase. Simply teasing her seemed to have been satisfaction enough.

Looking worn out, Raynesia came to take refuge next to Akatsuki. Even after having been toyed with so much, she sat gracefully, with her knees neatly together. Her expression was the same as always, too, but her lowered gaze seemed tired.

Akatsuki poured tea into Raynesia's cup as well.

She understood that fatigue perfectly.

The principal offender, Marielle, was rummaging through her Magic Bag, taking out new outfits and lining them up. Serara was being compelled to help.

Alarmingly, swimsuits and similar things had begun to appear in the parade of outfits... Even though it was winter. She began to feel sorry for Raynesia.

Raynesia was a truly beautiful girl. Her slender neck was delicate, and she must have been fine-boned: The line of her shoulders sloped gently, her face was small, and her long silver hair was as lustrous as silk thread. She was quiet and modest; she always had a faint smile on her face, and she never raised her voice in anger. She was a true upper-class young lady.

Oh, but she's a princess. Isn't that different from an upper-class young lady?

That was what Akatsuki thought, but she satisfied herself with the idea that "princess" in this case was like a higher-ranking class for "young lady," so it was more as if the grade had been raised.

Akatsuki and Raynesia's first meeting had been a barbarous one.

The day they'd resolved to make for Zantleaf, on Shiroe's instructions, she'd helped Raynesia change. —Or rather, she'd stripped her and made her change clothes. That had been their first encounter. As that was the case, Akatsuki thought Raynesia must think she was a very violent person. Just after the tea parties started, Raynesia had been rather frightened of her, and even now, she was a bit nervous around her sometimes.

However, even then, she didn't outright avoid her, and she paid attention to what Akatsuki said.

It was clear that she thought carefully about each topic and responded as thoughtfully as she could, to the extent that it made one think, impressed, *So this is what a well-bred princess is like.* All in all, she was pleasant company, and because her memory was good, once you'd spoken with her about a topic, she understood it. Akatsuki thought she could understand why she was popular.

"Are Adventurers generally able to wear outfits like this to good effect?"

Raynesia spoke up, sounding puzzled. It was a nurse outfit. With a miniskirt, no less. Raynesia wasn't tall either, but the balance between her head and body was good, and her bust curved prettily, so it suited her. Akatsuki shook her head, feeling rather awkward. No matter how you looked at it, only a sparse handful of Adventurers wore clothes like that on a daily basis. (The fact that there were a few who did was due to the influence of *Elder Tales*' game culture.)

Upon seeing that response, Raynesia looked even more dejected.

She was a beautiful girl who looked like a perfect picture no matter what she did, so even depressed, she was adorable. Akatsuki felt even odder.

If I was like that, too, would things with my liege have been…a little different?

That was what she thought.

However, on the other hand, Raynesia didn't have an Adventurer's body or an Assassin's abilities. She wouldn't be able to stay by Shiroe's side and guard him. *I wouldn't like that,* Akatsuki thought. It was unnecessary. She knew that. However, there was no way to stop the blood that seeped from the wound in her heart.

"…Yes… Yes. It's a nurse outfit… Pardon? Yes. A nurse outfit. In other words, the uniform worn by girls engaged in medical care… Hmm."

Riezé had abruptly begun murmuring.

A telechat.

Raynesia looked blank, but Akatsuki began to feel embarrassed.

"No, nothing so halfway. It's fifteen centimeters above her knees, if you can believe it."

Apparently Raynesia had registered her gaze as well; she tried desperately to pull the hem of the nurse outfit toward her knees. However, the cloth wasn't stretchy, and doing so didn't hide her legs. In fact, when it was pulled taut, the cloth only emphasized the lines of Raynesia's slim body.

"Um." At her wits' end, Raynesia looked to Akatsuki for help, with eyes that said, *Please do something*. However, Akatsuki wasn't used to this sort of situation either. Riezé was proper and ladylike, but she sometimes grew mischievous like this without warning. "Hrrn," Akatsuki grunted quietly, directing a reproachful gaze at Riezé.

Giving a light, pleasant laugh, with one hand set casually against her ear, Riezé feigned innocence: "I'm only joking. It isn't a real telechat." What awful taste. Raynesia was also gazing up at Riezé through her lashes.

However, Riezé made a small bow to Raynesia.

"My apologies. I was a bit jealous."

"What...?"

"Milord is infatuated with you, Princess Raynesia. So much so that when I'm sent over to play—I mean, to guard you—I'm released from training for the day."

A heavy ache.

It was probably true.

Akatsuki and Marielle had discussed it, and that had been their conclusion as well.

No doubt this People of the Earth princess would need to be guarded. That made perfect sense. As the Libra Festival incident had shown, there was a force that was attempting to attack Akiba, and it was clear that, in order to inflict damage on the town, that force wouldn't hesitate to involve the People of the Earth.

At the worst, even if Adventurers lost their lives, they could revive in the Temple, but that wasn't an option for the People of the Earth. Not to mention that, if Raynesia lost her life now, great trouble was sure to ensue. For example, their relationship with Duke Sergiad—Raynesia's grandfather in the city of Maihama, and the leading lord of Eastal—would sour, and in the worst case, break down entirely.

Naturally, Princess Raynesia was closely guarded by People of the Earth knights dispatched from the city of Maihama. However, People of the Earth were People of the Earth, and their levels were around 30. If an Adventurer seriously tried to kill Princess Raynesia, it would be difficult for them to guard her.

Of course, the town of Akiba had a guard system and a barrier that detected acts of violence. However, it was a function intended to capture or subjugate those who had committed violent acts, and although it might catch the culprit, if Raynesia had died, it had no function that would resurrect her.

Akatsuki thought Shiroe had asked her to do this job because he'd anticipated those circumstances. Marielle said she'd also been casually asked for help. Now, when Shiroe was unable to move a step, all Akatsuki could do was use everything in her power to comply with his request.

However, when she heard the exact same circumstances slip from the lips of the elegant girl who belonged to D.D.D., they brought pain along with them.

She stopped being able to look directly at Raynesia, the girl Shiroe was concerned about.

Even Akatsuki didn't know when she'd become so weak.

This isn't me. I'm not like this.

I know I wasn't like this.

She was happy Shiroe was counting on her.

Even so, here she was, comparing herself with Raynesia and the other women around her.

She wanted to get stronger. She wanted to comply with Shiroe's request.

She was doing her very, very best to do both. Even so, for some reason, Akatsuki's world was always dark and cramped. That hurt her.

Surrounded by bright laughter, Akatsuki was all alone.

▶ **2**

Sunset came early in winter, and by the time they left the manor, even the afterglow had faded completely.

Henrietta thought that nights in Akiba were beautiful. Compared to the old world, to her hometown of Tokyo, they were gloomy, but in comparison with the pitch-blackness of deep night in this world, they seemed quite dazzling enough.

A forest of buildings the color of darkness, towering in the indigo night. The spreading canopies of ancient evergreens. The scene was softly illuminated by magical lights that had been hung here and there. Henrietta thought those whimsical lights were much gentler than glaring neon signs, and far preferable.

"Dusk falls early these days, doesn't it."

"It really does."

Henrietta agreed with the blond girl who was walking beside her.

Her companion took a voluminous muffler out of her Magic Bag and wound it around her neck. From the way the extra at the ends hung down her back, it seemed to have been made for a man. "What is this, anyway? It's hard to wear. Bulky, too." The girl looked adorable in the getup as she grumbled, and Henrietta rearranged the muffler for her.

With the lower half of her expression buried in the scarf, Riezé replied to the assistance, "Thank you very much." She was quite possibly embarrassed; she kept her eyes averted as she spoke.

"No, no, it was nothing," Henrietta responded, giggling.

This new, younger friend of hers looked like a flawlessly perfect, proper young lady on the outside, and it was likely that the girl herself probably wanted to adhere to that image, but her true colors showed through here and there, and it was very cute. She was probably younger than she looked.

"You needn't work so hard. You're quite enough of a lady already."

"Pardon?"

She smiled at Riezé, who'd turned back to look at her, and pushed her shoulder.

"All right, come on. If we don't hurry, they'll close on us."

"True."

In this way, the two of them set off for the central avenue.

Henrietta was a member of the Crescent Moon League, while Riezé belonged to D.D.D. However, although their guilds were different, it wasn't unusual for them to go home from the tea party at Water Maple

Manor together like this. Marielle and Serara had returned to the guild a bit earlier to help with the dinner preparations, and Henrietta and Riezé planned to take a slight detour and buy a few side dishes.

Being able to enjoy delicious food every day was a happiness the Adventurers had rediscovered in their lives after the Catastrophe, but it was also a bit of a burden. In order to make food that tasted like anything, the subclass "Chef" was necessary, and as far as Henrietta knew, such players made up only a small percentage of the population.

Following the establishment of the Round Table Council, players had switched subclasses and the percentage had grown. However, it wasn't unusual for small guilds with ten members or less to have no Chefs among their members. Meanwhile, it was only natural to find Chefs in huge guilds with several hundred members, but preparing meals for several hundred people every day was a great burden.

At present, dining out and take-out meals prepared by People of the Earth were compensating for these circumstances.

"What will you buy, Miss Henrietta?"

"Fried chicken, perhaps. Mari has been whining that she wants some."

They'd reached the food stall mall, and, chatting, they began to make their purchases. The People of the Earth salesclerks were old hands at this as well. In terms of time, they were thinking of getting ready to close up their stalls, and they raised their voices, trying to sell off the day's remaining wares.

"Fried chicken? Did you say fried chicken, miss? Buy mine! It's garlic-flavored, and it's yours for three gold coins per kilo!!"

Henrietta, lavishly, purchased three kilos of the stuff.

There were forty hungry Adventurers at the Crescent Moon League, and an amount like this wouldn't count as a lot. They'd polish it off in no time flat.

Next to her, Riezé was buying quiches with hazelnuts. D.D.D. was a major guild with its own cooking unit, so this was probably a present or a snack.

The mall was fairly busy.

In order to weave their way through the river of Adventurers who'd come to shop, Henrietta and Riezé had to pay careful attention to their surroundings. In particular, groups which had returned from the subjugation wore rugged armor and carried long staffs, so they tended to take up more space than people in the old world.

By the time they'd finished buying their preferred items and had reached the mall's exit, Henrietta's impressions of the tea party had faded. Just walking through the mall was mentally tiring, and her feelings were focused on the meal ahead at the guild hall.

As a result, when Riezé casually murmured, "Akatsuki looks as if she's suffering," the words startled her. Still, Henrietta had been concerned about that lately as well.

"She seems that way to you, too, then?"

"Yes, she does."

Akatsuki had seemed listless lately. She'd always been rather shy and reserved, and she hadn't been the type to actively get involved with other people. Since she made things look all right on the surface, most people probably wouldn't notice, but Henrietta knew. After all, she'd been watching Akatsuki ever since the Catastrophe.

However, she found it a bit unexpected that Riezé had noticed as well. She'd only begun seeing Akatsuki frequently since she started to attend the tea parties held at Raynesia's manor. In other words, it had only been two weeks or so.

— Henrietta's opinion of Riezé improved a bit.

"Akatsuki has more experience at this than I do, doesn't she?"

When Riezé said "more experience," was she referring to age, or did she mean game experience? Henrietta didn't know, and she nodded vaguely.

"—I don't really know, either. I do hear she's a very skilled Assassin. As a matter of fact, I thought she probably was."

As they left the mall and walked down a road lined with greenery toward the guild center, Riezé continued to murmur. In the cold midwinter air, the girl's white breath seemed to enfold her words.

"She seems to have come to watch D.D.D. train once. Or rather, I'm not sure it was only once. I mean that I personally noticed her once. She watched us train for more than four hours."

"Did she…?"

It was the only response Henrietta could give.

She had picked up on Akatsuki's distress, indirectly. However, what had the few hours she spent watching a top-class combat guild train made that little girl feel? Henrietta could imagine that the pain had probably made her chest groan, but she couldn't say she understood the pain itself.

Henrietta was an ordinary Adventurer, one who'd never participated in a raid. This world aside, when *Elder Tales* had been a game, she'd never been among the top-class Adventurers whose names were listed in the rankings.

"At first we thought she wanted to join the guild. It rather sounds like bragging for me to say this, but we aren't too shabby of an outfit. When it comes to challenging raids, we have the best environment in Akiba— Or at any rate, we work diligently to make it so... Although our staff is composed entirely of morons. As they are morons, when it comes to combat, they're just like children. No, they *are* children. More than children. Über-children. They're high-maintenance children, and they strike out for raids like Americans flocking to a barbecue... And so we thought she wanted to join."

"I doubt that's the case."

"—You're right. We understood that almost immediately."

As Henrietta pointed this out, Riezé nodded, with her gaze still turned to the ground.

"We did report it to Milord, just to be safe. Some thought she might be a spy. But his response was 'Leave her.' He said to let her watch, unrestricted."

For a short while, the sound of boots walking over damp fallen leaves continued.

"It appears this rather upset our proud, childish members. I doubt he had misgivings about it, but later on, Milord gave me a special mission..."

The beautiful blond girl's expression was embarrassed, yet somehow proud. At the sight, Henrietta gave a furtive sigh. Wasn't having feelings for Krusty almost an act of barbarism? When she remembered the big man who scattered around unreasonable demands with a nonchalant expression, she couldn't help but feel sympathetic.

However, she pointed out to herself, Akatsuki—who'd fallen for Shiroe—was no different.

In comparison, things were quite peaceful for Henrietta herself.

True, when she thought of Shiroe, she did feel a faint, sweet ache, but the emotion was well within the permissible range. In this world, where there wasn't much in the way of entertainment, being able to watch Shiroe and Akatsuki—or Shiroe and Minori—being close and savor the ache in her chest was an act similar to reaffirming her own happiness.

Quiet, unreciprocated love from a safe distance. Since she was satisfied with that, it would have been impertinent of her to feel appalled at Riezé and Akatsuki.

"According to Krusty... I mean, Master Krusty, he owes Shiroe a debt of some sort. That's why he's allowing Akatsuki to observe without restriction. He also said to accommodate her if anything happens. We aren't allowed to be aggressively kind to her or to recruit her, but..."

Paying no heed to Henrietta's thoughts, Riezé stopped speaking.

"Is that how it was...?"

Henrietta thought that that sort of thing could happen.

Even Shiroe probably wasn't aware of Krusty's thoughtfulness.

Men seemed to be quite tedious, or rather, roundabout. If he was going to be considerate, why hadn't he simply spoken to her and heard what she had to say? However, considering Akatsuki's current position, she thought being spoken to might only have troubled the Assassin.

In any case, I think what dear Akatsuki wants is...probably confidence.

That was difficult.

For a certain type of person, having it was only natural, and they never thought about how to acquire it.

Marielle was like that. Like a golden sunflower, Henrietta's good friend illuminated her surroundings with boundless light. Henrietta didn't have the confidence to smile that way. She thought she'd probably never have enough conviction to embrace her surroundings like that, not as long as she lived.

That was something unique to Marielle, something most people, including Henrietta, didn't have.

On the other hand, Henrietta knew there were people who could never have anything resembling confidence, no matter what they did or how they struggled. For that sort of person, time spent living was probably terrible torture. Henrietta had seen people with frightened, subservient eyes. By the time you were old enough to graduate from college, you'd met several people like that. No matter where they were, that sort of person was either tired and afraid of not fitting in, or they aggressively threatened those around them.

When she considered herself, Henrietta thought she probably fell somewhere in the middle.

She wasn't able to have unshakeable conviction, the sort of confidence that allowed her to believe she could never lose what was precious to her. However, as a result of hard work and experience, she could anticipate what she would be able to do.

For example, she'd probably be able to stay on good terms with a handful of friends.

She'd be able to do her job well enough that it wouldn't cause problems for the company.

Marriage… Now that this uproar had occurred and arranged marriages were no longer an option, she honestly didn't think she'd be able to manage it, but even so, spending her time as her guild's accountant while poking fun at her friends' romances would probably make for a surprisingly pleasant future.

It wasn't likely that she'd find herself playing a heroic part in their endeavors to return to the old world, but she could use the techniques she'd learned so far to protect the younger members.

That was how Henrietta pictured herself.

She couldn't do what she couldn't do, but she was able to do what she could.

It was nothing special: an ordinary conclusion drawn by an average person.

"It's only natural to have wishes that won't come true," Riezé murmured, with her face half-buried in her menswear muffler.

Yes, it was only natural.

To ordinary people, it was far too routine.

To most people, living meant getting used to the reality of not being able to have what you wanted. Henrietta was completely used to it. Riezé probably was as well.

That didn't mean the pain went away.

There was probably no way around getting used to not having things. However, that wasn't the same as growing numb to the pain of being unable to have them. That was stasis. If you didn't get used to it, you couldn't live, but if you grew too used to it, you might as well be dead.

To Henrietta, there was something dazzling about Akatsuki.

That awkward girl had an easily wounded weakness, one Henrietta had numbed in herself on the pretext of growth. It might be a weak point, but it was also an asset.

At the same time, she knew that that tenderness was causing Akatsuki pain.

Henrietta loved Akatsuki, and she didn't want her to feel that anguish.

However, she thought there really might be no help for it.

She didn't know how to help her, and in any case, it seemed as though it might not be the sort of thing other people could help with... To the point that, when she looked back at herself, she didn't know how she'd become the person she was now.

"It looks as though all we can do is simply be with her."

"...You're right."

Riezé probably understood that as well. That was why her response had been a short one.

Honestly, that pitch-black Master Kuroe!

Henrietta heaved a great sigh, being careful not to let Riezé notice.

That young man was too clever by half, but his closest confidante was in distress, and what was he doing? She'd thought Shiroe had the insight to see through anything, but apparently he was blind when it came to this sort of situation.

Or maybe it isn't that his eyes are good. Maybe he's simply wearing a telescope he can't take off.

Thinking something that was just a little rude, Henrietta smiled wryly.

She wanted to be kind enough to Akatsuki to make up for it. Tomorrow she'd bring clothes for Akatsuki as well and make it a dress-up day. Once she hit on that idea, Henrietta's mood brightened in an instant. As she made a list of the clothes she was mentally pulling out, she excused herself by thinking, *This is for Akatsuki's sake.*

The indigo night was still peaceful.

▶ 3

There was a force that was attempting to recolor that same night with phenomenal determination.

It was the guild known as "the showiest guild on the Yamato server," "the harem group," and "the young ladies with iron discipline": the West Wind Brigade.

Rumored to have the highest proportion of girls in Akiba (although not all its members were female), as its nickname indicated, the guild always radiated a showy atmosphere. In a first-floor hall, several dozen guild members were enthusiastically making preparations.

Of course, most of the members were girls. However, there was nothing soft about the atmosphere. All sorts of beautiful women and girls were there, briskly tightening wrist guards and leggings, dressed as if headed for a showdown. As they exchanged whispers in low voices, all were indirectly watching Soujirou, their guild leader, in his Japanese-style *haori* coat.

Soujirou, whose face still held something boyish, looked out over the hall. Twenty-four members were planning to sally forth into Akiba tonight: a team composed of four six-person parties, the same scale as a full raid. Of course, every one of them was skilled and at least level 90.

"Everyone."

At Soujirou's voice, the tension in the hall increased. Although twenty-four members were participating in the sortie, others must have been there to help with equipment or see them off: There were more than twice that many members gathered in the hall.

"I know I've said this several times already, but we don't know what the enemy really is. Whatever you do, please don't get careless. Understand that his power is greater than yours…and mine. Don't fight him one-on-one. I also forbid independent action. Make sure to move as a team, and report in as necessary. Nazuna will stay here as a contact."

"Yeah. I took the job, so I'll do it, but… Don't do anything reckless, people. If you end up engaging with the target, use top-class combat formation and fight a delaying battle. This time around, we organized

things so there's two healers per team, so you won't have enough attack power. Don't think you'll be able to do anything with just one team. Your duty is to pin 'im down, then call in. That's it. Okay?"

Nazuna, who wore a loose dressing gown, spoke in a leisurely voice. The team that was about to head out was tense, and that was enough. Things would be fine. She believed in her guild mates.

The West Wind Brigade was smaller than D.D.D. or the Knights of the Black Sword, but it had managed to stay in the fierce struggle to be the first one into battle thanks to its firm unity and strong sense of purpose.

Now the West Wind Brigade was talking big about apprehending the criminal.

Nazuna, whose abundant black hair was bound together at her back, gazed at each and every one of the members who were preparing to head out. There had been no oversights, either in equipment or in strategy. Nodding to the guild members, who were all raising cries of "Understood," Nazuna continued:

"All right, you'll switch in two hours. We'll organize the second strike unit and get them ready here. There'll be a midnight snack waiting when you get back, and it'll be a good one. Of course, you'll be heading out again two hours after that, so don't relax too much. Like Souji said, the other guy outranks us. Be careful about that. Okay, Souji, it's all you."

"Hmm. Let's see. I think you said everything I was going to say. All right, then, just one thing: The target killed one of us. —Cut him down."

Soujirou was a young man with an atmosphere like spring sunlight.

His vaguely good-natured smile was the same as ever, but those words—which he'd spoken without raising his voice—froze the air in the hall. As if drawn by that cold air, the shoulders of one female Cleric trembled, and she screamed out her determination to get revenge in a voice that seemed to have been wrung from her stomach. It was already completely dark outside, but none of the members paid any attention to that.

The four teams valiantly burst out of the guild hall.

The West Wind Brigade's guild hall was built to feel rather Japanese.

It hadn't been that way originally; the change reflected the guild members' taste and Soujirou's preferences. Similarly, the first floor was a spacious place, to allow for troop inspections before sallying forth. It was empty, with no furniture.

Pulling a wooden chair into that great hall, Soujirou sat down.

For the moment, he was on standby, but apparently he couldn't bring himself to withdraw to the dining hall or his own room.

"I hear they're making miso pork in the dining hall."

Nazuna spoke to him, thinking she should try, but Soujirou's only response to her proposal was to smile and shake his head.

Nazuna pinched the tip of her chin and thought.

She'd been this way in the old world as well, and for a woman, she was relatively tall and full-figured. It wasn't the sort of glamour an idol singer would have, but her figure was good. Although she'd been told she was "easy on the eyes," as far as she was concerned, her body was a bit too much for her. Apparently, when she stood with her feet apart at shoulder width and crossed her arms, she looked more self-possessed than her age would suggest.

She was the type who was good at looking after people, and since she was also one of the guild's founding players and one of its longest-serving members, the people around her trusted her completely. As a result, half-inevitably, Nazuna was viewed as the sub-master of the West Wind Brigade. Nazuna herself was aware that she handled more of the practical business than Soujirou did, who led by exercising his charisma.

All the members were good kids who idolized Nazuna, and Nazuna thought they were adorable as well. The West Wind Brigade was Nazuna's tribe. After living together here since the Catastrophe, she thought of them all as her family.

However, sometimes, when Soujirou let a practical expression show through a crack in his usual mild-mannered mask, it made her remember her old comrades, and then she wanted to lean on him.

Naturally, logic was on Soujirou's side this time.

Their opponent was a murderer who threatened Akiba's nights. As one of the eleven guilds on the Round Table Council, the West Wind Brigade bore a certain moral responsibility for the safety of Akiba. Nazuna also acknowledged that the major combat guilds had a duty to patrol the town.

Furthermore, this murderer had killed a West Wind Brigade member.

Of course Kyouko had revived in the Temple. What she'd lost from the incident, memories included, hadn't been serious. Although Kyouko was afraid of the murderer, even she wasn't so frightened that she wouldn't be able to face him again. She'd said so herself. However, an assault was an assault. The murderer had struck at Nazuna's—and Soujirou's—family.

That was unforgivable.

Nazuna thought so as well.

She thought Soujirou shared that anger. However, even so, his decision had been a bit too smooth. That was in his personality; he'd been that way ever since he was part of the Debauchery Tea Party. When you called it "carefree" or "unhesitating," it sounded good, but on the other hand, it leaned toward relentlessness and cruelty.

Nazuna thought Soujirou wasn't anywhere near as gentle and good-natured as the women of Akiba thought he was. Well, no, he was a gentle, good-natured boy, but it wasn't because the individual in question was exceptionally good.

He was like that because he was like that. That was all.

Soujirou was kind to women. Almost without exception.

However, it wasn't because he liked them personally. He was simply "that kind of boy."

He was giving orders to retaliate against the person who'd struck a girl in his family, not because he had any particularly deep attachment to Kyouko. He was merely "that kind of boy."

It was a certain type of rule, a mechanical decision, and Nazuna was unable to influence that part of him. She could probably get him to postpone such a decision temporarily, or to cancel it for something else—for example, she could tell him, "Let's meet up with the Knights of the Black Sword first" or "We should let the Round Table Council handle things this time."

However, she couldn't admonish Soujirou, or guide him to grow.

The only ones who could influence Soujirou on that level were Shiroe and Kazuhiko.

Because Soujirou was overly conscious of women as beings who must be protected, Nazuna's words about certain things would never reach him.

Soujirou was kind to girls. It wasn't a virtue; it was one of his flaws, and it couldn't be corrected.

In the West Wind Brigade, people assumed Nazuna was one of Soujirou's lovers.

However, to Nazuna, Soujirou was something like a little brother.

He was awkward and unsteady, and she couldn't leave him alone.

The fact that Soujirou was able to present himself as guild master, as if that was normal, was just a fortunate coincidence, with no guarantees and nothing to support it. Nazuna thought the boy named Soujirou Seta was someone who could easily destroy his own guild at any moment.

I mean, I love him. Of course I'm absolutely nuts about him. But.

Unconsciously ruffling Soujirou's black hair, Nazuna found herself caught up in her thoughts.

She did love him, but—speaking without fear of being misunderstood—the boy was abnormal.

…To the point where he was about on par with the murderer.

If he hadn't been, he'd never have been able to hold together a guild that consisted of over ninety women. Not only that, but it wouldn't have been possible to use that system to aim for the top of the server in raid clearings.

"What's wrong?"

Soujirou spoke to Nazuna; his eyes were round. He'd probably gotten worried because she'd been quiet for so long. But even with her concerns, Nazuna smiled back at him… He was family, so there was no help for it. She'd just have to use what she had to make up for what Soujirou lacked. And they'd have to avenge Kyouko, another family member who'd fallen to the murderer's blade.

▶ 4

The moment a white mist began to gather at her feet, the scent of the wind seemed to soften.

The night shook off the heaviness it had worn like a thick curtain, growing gradually lighter and more transparent. It was a premonition of dawn.

The town of Akiba was still shrouded in darkness, but the chest-crushing pressure of late night was already gone.

The sky was slowly turning a limpid deep blue. Although the silence was unchanged, time flowed on.

Akatsuki had just finished a night of patrolling, and she was tired.

One all-nighter wasn't enough to affect Adventurer bodies in the least, but scouting had kept her nerves under constant strain, and it had tired her mentally more than physically.

I'm hungry...

She wanted to drink hot potage.

Nyanta's special potage soup, with lots of corn.

However, right now, she was up on a crumbling elevated track. At Log Horizon, her friends were probably sleeping the deep sleep that came just before dawn. She couldn't pester them for warmth.

In any case, these late-night wanderings were a secret from her guild mates. She was jealous of the young girl who was her friend, and she wanted to become as strong as the Adventurers in raid guilds, so every night, she slipped out of her home and pursued the murderer. She couldn't tell her friends about something like that.

As she looked down at the town, which was gradually growing brighter, Akatsuki heaved a deep sigh.

The reason she couldn't tell, and the reason she felt this tired, was that she was aware that this quest was, at heart, nothing more than her own selfishness. The wish to get stronger was simply her ego. Neither Shiroe nor Naotsugu had asked her to do it. Even Akatsuki knew that chasing the murderer was a bit like trying to grasp at clouds.

True, if she pursued the murderer, she might be able to witness high-ranking guilds in combat.

If that happened, she might get to see the Mysteries they used.

If all went well, she might even find a hint about the rank.

All these things were hypothetical. Haphazard action plans based on "maybes."

Akatsuki knew this acutely. That was why she couldn't tell her friends.

Crossing over the main drag, Akatsuki walked along the elevated track toward the center of Akiba.

By now, the darkness had left Akiba, and early morning had come. The cold, cutting wind peculiar to winter mornings stole the warmth from Akatsuki's cheeks. She'd spent the whole night in her ninja clothes so that she'd be ready for combat at any time, and she'd gotten cold. It had been all right during the night, when she'd stayed on high alert and moved around, but once day had broken, while she'd been gazing vacantly down at the town, she seemed to have gotten chilled.

Her mood wasn't very cheerful.

Akatsuki thought that was only to be expected. She'd prowled around town all night long, and she had nothing to show for it.

She clambered up onto a big, mossy chunk of concrete, then reached out farther, finally arriving at the top of the rubble. In the old world, this place had probably been a platform on the Chuo Line, but now lots of trees grew here, turning it into a hanging garden. The air was cold, but because the wind was blocked, she could breathe a little easier.

This huge structure wasn't a separate zone; it was an open, freely accessible object set up in Akiba. That meant there was no set entrance or exit, and if she'd wanted to, she could have jumped down off the elevated track.

Akatsuki thought absently about going down the central staircase and cutting through the guild center square...but then sat down on a decaying bench.

She didn't think she was that tired.

It was only that she didn't want to move anymore.

Once she sat, the area around her stomach felt heavy. It felt as if something had curdled there, and she couldn't stand it.

Akatsuki was surprised at herself.

Why was she sitting on the bench, and why was she staring at the ground? She was forced to face the fact that she'd simply been tormenting herself that much.

She kicked a pebble with her toe. The pebble rolled across the hanging garden which had once been a platform, and was now cracked and crumbling here and there and bristling with ancient trees. She saw a small bird take flight; apparently she'd startled it.

Feeling terribly depressed, Akatsuki found her thoughts meandering. About the guild. About Shiroe. About vulgar, stupid Naotsugu.

About Nyanta and his delicious cooking, about her juniors, about the Crescent Moon League, about the enemies she'd fought before now.

And about Minori.

She thought she was a very feminine girl. She was tidy. She was conscientious, cheerful, not timid, and polite… None of those things were anything special on their own. She was cute, but only on a level that would have made her mildly popular in class, and she tended to be a bit too direct.

She couldn't cook, and she was a middle schooler, so she certainly didn't know all the fashionable shops around town. Akatsuki thought Minori's taste in pouches was childish. When she talked to Shiroe, she frisked around and her voice went high-pitched, and it must have made Shiroe feel fed up with her.

Akatsuki bit her lip hard.

What was she thinking?

Shameful.

Even *she* thought she was being disgustingly narrow-minded.

The self Akatsuki had seen in the mirror had been ugly, drawn out, and warped. The bitterness of jealousy had accumulated like sediment, and it tortured her. What had Minori done, anyway?

At the very least, she'd probably never held any ill will toward Akatsuki. Even so, privately, she looked down on Minori, thinking of her as a cheeky little kid… Even though she knew that wasn't really the case. Even though she knew Minori was her lovable, hard-working junior. Even so, she couldn't hold back the feeling that the girl was just an uppity, annoyingly precocious middle schooler.

As she brooded this way, all alone, she couldn't take it anymore. The jealousy she was normally able to forget when she was in a crowd flooded her heart. She couldn't hold the torrent back even if she tried, and it seemed about to swallow her up.

Akatsuki took several deep breaths.

She relaxed her clenched fists.

The deciduous trees had dried up for the winter and lost their leaves, but the conifers were still deep green; it was their shadows that fell over the damp garden.

Somewhere, she heard a twitter, as though someone were shaking a small bell.

It was the little bird she'd seen earlier.

In the winter air, this deserted ruin from the Age of Myth had a bright, crisp beauty to it. Even the clear air, which froze the white breath she exhaled, was an important, irreplaceable element that highlighted that beauty.

In the midst of light that was simply white instead of bright, Akatsuki felt she was a black stain. A black stain that would only spread if scrubbed. Even her dark hair, which she'd been proud of until now, became loathsome at the thought.

When she thought that Shiroe might not like her hair—that he might prefer hair of a brighter color, like Minori's—she felt as if her stomach had been packed with stones.

…This, even though Akatsuki knew very well that Shiroe wouldn't base his likes and dislikes on a thing like hair color. Shiroe wouldn't show favoritism over something as material as tresses.

Even so, all because of her jealousy, Akatsuki had found herself asking: *Doesn't he prefer lighter hair?*

She'd spread the filthy jealousy inside her to Shiroe, someone she respected as her liege.

Even as she sat there, Akatsuki's jealousy was compromising Shiroe. *And I call him "my liege" with this mouth?*

Akatsuki finally understood why she'd sat down on this bench.

In short, Akatsuki didn't want to return to the guild hall.

She was just like an elementary schooler who'd skipped after-school lessons.

That thought struck her as ridiculous, and she laughed. It was a childish escape.

Akatsuki was cold, in pain, and in a wretched mood. It had been her precious, precious place to belong, and she'd been really happy there, but in order to protect that happiness, she'd stayed up all night, chasing after power, and now, after all that, it was hard to go home. Reality, in which she'd gotten her priorities backward, reproached her.

Minori and Touya and the rest of the younger group were out on an overnight hunting trip, so they weren't there.

If she went back to the guild house, she wouldn't have to see them. She was well aware that Nyanta would give her a warm welcome.

…And so, not wanting to go back was not Akatsuki's choice, but her ego's.

Even *she* knew that not wanting to be seen in this jealous state was vanity.

However, she couldn't throw it away.

I want to see my liege.

That was what Akatsuki desired. The wish was so strong it made her chest tight.

She wanted to see Shiroe. She wanted to talk to him, even if it was only a little. She wanted to go up close to him and tug on his white coat. She wanted to pour Black Rose Tea into his teacup from a canteen. She wanted to sit on the sofa with him and look out the window. She wanted to stand beside Shiroe as he looked at complicated documents and made an equally complicated face, and then imitate that complicated face herself.

But that wouldn't happen. Selfish and vain as she was, she didn't think she was qualified to set her mind at ease near Shiroe. Not only that, but if she went back there now, she'd never be able to run off again. From this point on, she'd live as a sort of free bonus that came with Shiroe.

She'd thought that wouldn't be so bad.

She'd thought it would make her happy to be her liege's ninja, as if she was sunbathing beside him.

However, that had been cheating.

Minori had taught her that she'd only been leaning on him, because it'd made her happy.

A swallow that lost its ability to fly would stop being able to follow Shiroe someday. When that happened, they'd have to part ways.

She'd been thinking the same things for a while now, over and over. In all of them, the subjects were "I" and "mine." Even she thought it was too self-centered, and it disgusted her.

There probably wasn't anyone who'd like a girl like that. Akatsuki herself wouldn't want a friend who was so self-centered that she could only talk about herself.

…And so, she couldn't see Shiroe now.

It was also an order she'd received from Shiroe, her liege.

"...I'll stay at an inn today," she told herself.

Akatsuki forced her heavy body to its feet.

She really shouldn't have been tired, but she felt oddly listless. It had to be the emotions.

This strange land, caressed by the winter wind, was vast, and no voice answered her call.

▶ 5

Raynesia shut her eyes tightly, against the cold.

Naturally, simply closing her eyes did nothing to take the edge off the chill.

It was rare for her to be out in the streets of Akiba like this.

Even if she was at a new post (or rather, being left to her own devices), Raynesia was the second daughter of the House of Cowen, the leading family of Eastal, the League of Free Cities, and a successor to one of the two remaining dukedoms in Yamato. Due to security issues, she didn't go out much. Even if she did go out, it was usually only to perform inspections from a carriage, and she almost never walked around town in her everyday clothes this way.

If Marielle from the Crescent Moon League hadn't suddenly stopped by and said, "Let's go get brunch somewhere else today!" she probably wouldn't have gone out at all.

Generally, Elissa or the guards would have put a stop to this sort of sudden outing, but this was Akiba. If a few skilled Adventurers were protecting her, she'd be safer than if she'd stayed shut up in Water Maple Manor. On top of that, although she didn't know what her motives had been, Elissa had made the preparations for the outing so quickly that she hadn't been able to talk her way out of it.

"You're all fluffy, aren'tcha!"

"I suppose you should wear a hat, too."

As a result, Raynesia was walking toward Akiba's main avenue, flanked by Marielle and Riezé.

For today's outing, she was wearing a hip-length coat trimmed with fluffy fur.

To begin with, Raynesia wasn't very familiar with the contents of her own wardrobe.

Because daughters of the nobility had their ladies-in-waiting select their clothes for them and changed several times a day, this wasn't unusual, but on top of that, Raynesia wasn't much interested in fashion, so hers was an extreme case.

After all, she was lazy. Changing clothes didn't bring her much joy in the first place. If they'd left her to herself, she was confident that she could have spent a whole year in a linen dress.

Of course, Raynesia had received more than enough aristocratic training. Everything had its own time, place, occasion, and etiquette, and she knew quite well what sort of clothing she needed to wear.

It was a pain, but Raynesia was aware that her long silver hair was unusual. Clothing that suited that hair was also unusual, and unfortunately, pajamas weren't on the list.

As a result, Raynesia didn't know what sort of clothes her wardrobe held, or how many of them there were. She only thought, vaguely, that there were all kinds of things in there.

"There just isn't much low-level cold endurance equipment, is there?"

The group was walking along in a close huddle, with Raynesia in the middle. The girl who'd spoken to her from behind was named Mikakage.

She was a sociable, cheerful girl, another of the people who attended the tea parties.

"No," Raynesia answered, briefly.

She'd answered obediently because Mikakage was one of the people she felt indebted to. It wasn't because she was an Adventurer. The woman was a Chef. Since she brought over all sorts of snacks at every opportunity, going against her was out of the question.

Raynesia didn't really know the details, but apparently there were two types of Chefs among the Adventurers.

These were Chefs who had high skill values but were personally quite bad at cooking, and true Chefs whose cooking techniques matched their skill values...or so she was told. Skill values expressed the individual's cooking prowess, and so Raynesia didn't really understand why people talked about "letting treasures go to waste" or, on the other hand, "being well-matched."

However, even if she didn't understand that aspect of Adventurer culture, she knew that Mikakage was known as a "real" cook, and in fact, the snacks she brought were delicious.

These were cakes and candies so delicate she had no idea how they'd been made: truly jewel-like sweets. On the other hand, while they were brought over far less frequently than the sweets, Raynesia liked her pork miso soup and rice with mushrooms as well.

According to Mikakage, sweets were art, but other dishes were entertainment. Raynesia could only wonder about that. She thought they were delicious, with mellow flavors.

Mikakage took the muffler that Raynesia had wound around herself and hung an odd accessory from it. The little spirit that always followed Mikakage around stretched up on tiptoe, insistently trying to see. It was a little stuffed animal, a puppy, and really cute: It was roly-poly, and it looked sleepy.

"The percentage isn't much, but what do you think? Is that a little warmer?"

"Yes. It is warm."

The People of the Earth probably couldn't make tiny stuffed animals this elaborate. The best they could do would be wood carving. That meant this was the first time Raynesia had worn a stuffed animal as an accessory. She thought it made her outfit much more like the Adventurers' than wearing jewels or ribbons would have.

"Excellent."

Mikakage nodded. Marielle, who'd peeked in from behind her, said, "Isn't that nice!" and gave a dazzling smile.

This Marielle woman was another of the people who often came to Water Maple Manor.

She always brought all sorts of clothes to change into, so she'd thought she must be in charge of clothing and accessories for some guild somewhere, but when she listened closely, it turned out that she was one of the Round Table Council eleven. The leader of one of Akiba's eleven governing clans.

At first, Raynesia had been very tense, but before long, she'd gotten used to her.

On hearing that she belonged to one of the town's governing clans, she'd begun conversations as if she were talking to a member of the peerage, but every time, she found herself turned into a dress-up doll and regaled with town gossip, and it became a bit of a performance.

Marielle was thoroughly cheerful, loved parties, and was always smiling.

She'd been the first one to call Raynesia "Sia." Raynesia had been called "Reisi" by her family, but she'd never been called "Sia" before. At first, it had bewildered her, but she'd soon grown used to that, too.

Her tea parties with the Adventurer women were already part of Raynesia's daily routine.

And while Raynesia might be "the winter rose of Eastal," Sia was just an inexperienced People of the Earth girl who'd been posted to the Adventurers' town. She was a noble, of course, and a fledgling diplomat, and sometimes she played at being a merchant. But whatever she was, she wasn't "the winter rose of Eastal."

Raynesia realized that the girl with honey-colored hair who was walking ahead of her, matching her pace to Raynesia's unsteady steps, had turned back. She was a girl called Riezé, and she managed the knights in D.D.D., another of the eleven guilds. She supervised Krusty, Raynesia's archenemy. Her rank within the guild was probably high as well.

Riezé frequently attended Raynesia's tea parties, too, and Raynesia thought she was a very clearheaded young lady. Her demeanor was the most aristocratic of all the attendees. However, even so, she was far more enlightened than the hidebound members of Eastal's high society.

Riezé was even the one who'd taught her that word *enlightened*.

It meant, "Wearing clothes that don't constrict your stomach, and being able to eat custard *dorayaki*," which were little custard-and-mini pancake sandwiches.

It was a very, very good word.

From Raynesia's perspective, all the Adventurers seemed like unprecedented beings.

This was probably true for all People of the Earth, not just for Raynesia. Even Elissa sometimes sighed, let her shoulders droop, and lamented, "Come to think of it, they *are* Adventurers, aren't they…"

Adventurers were far too different from their people, and Raynesia and Elissa didn't understand them.

Raynesia met many of People of the Earth these days, and almost every day, they asked her:

"What are the Adventurers?"

"How should we handle them?"

Since she'd been posted to the town of Akiba and was serving as an intermediary with the Adventurers, Raynesia met with People of the Earth nearly every day, and then mediated trade with the Adventurers, looked for Adventurers who would take on job requests, and often gave them advice. Personally, she didn't think she was managing to do the job properly at all, but even so, since there was no one else, she had to do it.

Even though she was asked about the Adventurers, Raynesia didn't know the answers either. In fact, there might be many things Raynesia knew less about than any other given Person of the Earth. And what's more, because she was in closer contact with the Adventurers than anyone else, as the days went by, the number of things she didn't understand kept growing.

However, she'd managed to understand a few things.

Adventurers were Adventurers.

Raynesia thought that the most fundamental mistake the People of the Earth lords had made at the lord's council in the Ancient Court of Eternal Ice was attempting to treat the Adventurers like nobles.

The Adventurers weren't nobles; of course trying to treat them according to the rules of the aristocracy wouldn't work well. In the same way, Adventurers weren't lords' subjects or knights, either. They weren't even People of the Earth. For that reason, it was a mistake to treat them according to People of the Earth rules, or to try to adapt them to fit their convenience.

Raynesia thought that had been why the conference had failed.

Adventurers were only Adventurers. They shouldn't be classified as anything else.

However, come to think of it, Raynesia's surroundings were bursting with people who could be labeled. Counts were counts, barons were barons, knights were knights, chamberlains were chamberlains, citizens were the residents of a city, and villagers lived in villages. Hunters hunted and woodcutters cut down trees.

People had roles, and they lived within those limits. That was only natural. Before Raynesia was Reisi, she was the granddaughter of a duke, and the winter rose princess. She'd never had a single doubt about that. Even now, she didn't hate the idea, and she thought it was only natural.

However, she'd realized that it wasn't possible to use those rules to understand the Adventurers. All she knew was that, even if she didn't know the correct answer, she mustn't try to fit them into a framework or look at them in terms of their class or role.

It would certainly have been easier if she could have gotten along with the Adventurers by putting them in broad categories, such as "members of the Crescent Moon League clan" or "guild members with cooking skills." Like the knights in the Knights of Maihama, or the ladies-in-waiting that came to the castle to serve, or the critical young male aristocrats.

However, Marielle and Riezé and Mikakage were all too remarkable for that, and she couldn't do it.

Every single Adventurer was like a special jewel, polished carefully by the gods. Each was unlike any other, and they sparkled and shone.

"Hmm? What's up?"

Marielle turned back and looked at her closely, seemingly worried.

Raynesia smiled and replied, "I'm fine." Seeing this, Mikakage asked, "Are you hungry already?" and the whole group laughed. *Do I really look that hungry?* Raynesia worried. The Adventurers always had little sweets in their pockets or bags, and they were constantly trying to feed them to her.

Once they were on the wide avenue, Raynesia and the others turned north.

"This way?"

"Yes, that's right."

Marielle and Riezé, who'd spoken to each other, were dressed comparatively lightly.

Unlike the People of the Earth, the Adventurers preferred activewear. Apparently this was true even now, in midwinter. Marielle was wearing a short skirt that exposed her tight-clad legs. She thought she really had to be cold, but the person in question didn't seem bothered by it.

Riezé was wearing a coat and muffler, but underneath, she wore the same sort of white blouse and tight skirt she always did. Raynesia and Elissa, who was just behind her, were far more bundled up.

It was sheer coincidence that Raynesia spotted Akatsuki just then.

Because Marielle had asked Mikakage, "Is Milky Margaret over that way?" and Mikakage had trotted ahead to show the way, the two who'd been paying attention to Raynesia had moved away from her. As she gave a small, relieved sigh, she happened to look up and see Akatsuki, leaving a building through a door that seemed to lead underground.

Akatsuki was biting her lip.

The slight figure walking on the other side of the road looked like a lost child.

Suddenly, all sorts of feelings flooded Raynesia. It was the sort of mood that came from a night spent gazing up at the ceiling of a dark room for hours on end.

Raynesia tried to say something, but before it became words, it stopped, as though something had gone wrong in her throat.

She didn't really know what it was she would try to say.

Raynesia felt like a vine that had collected rainwater in its leaves and was slowly bending. The expression Akatsuki had worn was the sort of expression that drained the strength from you and made your heart feel heavy. It was an expression she'd never seen before.

She looks like a child, somehow, she thought, out of nowhere.

Raynesia had thought of that black-haired girl as a dagger made of obsidian.

As beautiful as a jewel, with a strength she couldn't comprehend.

Using the head even she didn't think worked very well, Raynesia considered her next move, then gave up. Either way, Akatsuki was gone, vanished into the crowd. She hadn't noticed Raynesia and the others. She'd just passed right by.

The thought gave Raynesia a slight, if painful, feeling of trouble in her chest.

…But this wasn't particularly unusual.

All sorts of feelings were constantly drifting through Raynesia. Most of them weren't guests she could welcome, but she'd known since she was small that if she curled up under a warm comforter and closed her eyes, they would melt into the darkness. She was rather confident in her ability to curl up under a comforter.

Raynesia shook her head, trying to switch gears.

This was the town of Akiba, and she was a fledgling negotiator. She had more than enough motivation and necessity to switch gears.

"Heeey, Sia! Whatcha doin'? This way!"

At the call, Raynesia broke into a delicate run on unsteady feet.

▶ 6

"Princess. Priiiincess."

Elissa called her mistress's name.

She'd called to her because things had seemed awfully quiet. Raynesia was on the sofa, looking down.

She seemed to be at a loss. Her spun-silver hair spilled over her small, rounded shoulders, flowing down like a waterfall. The beautiful girl wore a disconsolate aura that would have made even a stern-faced corporal whom orcs feared want to speak kindly to her and comfort her: *You mustn't get so discouraged. I'll help you.*

Madame Henrietta would probably have said she looked "like a puppy in the rain."

In any case, she seemed fragile, lonely, and filled with melancholy.

She was the very image of the sort of frailty that made you want to run to her and hug her.

However, Elissa knew very well:

This was her "I'm tired and I don't want to do anything else" pose.

"Prin-*cess.*"

"Elissa?"

Raynesia raised her chin, her gaze upturned.

Framed by cheeks as smooth as a boiled egg, her damp eyes shimmered.

Make no mistake: Her eyes weren't damp because she'd been thinking sad thoughts, or because she was moved, but because she'd been biting back a yawn.

"Yes, yes. You're tired, correct? I'll prepare your bedroom shortly, so wait just a little longer, please. Would you like tea? Or perhaps something sweet?" Elissa asked.

Raynesia had a better appetite than her appearance suggested, and it had been quite some time since she'd eaten brunch with the group of Adventurers. It wouldn't be at all strange for her to start feeling hungry soon.

She had no idea whether it was due to her constitution or something else, but no matter what or how much Princess Raynesia ate, she never gained weight. Not only that, but even when she ate meat or cake, her skin stayed as smooth and soft as a baby's. She couldn't fathom how rough skin could be a concept for anyone. Elissa was extremely jealous that she could eat without paying attention to her diet.

After the Catastrophe and the reformation in Akiba, an abundance of flavors had been rediscovered in foodstuffs of every variety. Now, half a year later, the reformation had permeated People of the Earth society as well, and everyone, from the aristocrats at the top to the commoners below, was enjoying that new experience.

The revolutionized food had a true depth of flavor, and people often ate too much. At this point, many People of the Earth nobles were afraid of gaining weight, but Raynesia was the exception: She didn't gain any at all. Elissa had complicated feelings about this. Elissa carefully limited herself to one piece of cake every three days. She was fundamentally different from superhumans like Raynesia.

"No..."

Raynesia shook her head slightly, then turned to the side, resting her cheek against the back of the sofa as though she couldn't bear it any longer. A young apprentice knight whose heart burned with longing probably would have gotten a nosebleed from that gesture alone.

Not me, though.

Casually approaching Raynesia, Elissa lifted her slipper-clad feet and shifted them onto the sofa, bending her knees. Raynesia didn't resist; she sat sideways on the sofa, lethargically.

For a "lovely princess of Maihama," the position was a rather ill-mannered one. If a man had been in the room, it might have given him the wrong impression. Internal aspects aside, Raynesia had learned very well how a noble princess should carry herself, and as a rule, even her family didn't see her in poses like this one.

Elissa was the only one who was able to see Raynesia like this.

Not that I particularly want to, mind you.

Having confirmed that Raynesia's feet were up, she took out an indoor broom and swept under the low table and the sofa.

"Princess."

"Hmm?"

"What did you eat today?"

"Cream stew."

"My, my… In the style of the Adventurers?"

"They said it was Flame Boar. It was good."

"Things have been lively lately, haven't they?"

"They really have."

As they conversed, Elissa continued briskly cleaning the room.

This was a guest room that was kept immaculate, as a rule. It didn't take much work. Even if she was cleaning, there was technically no need for her to go to the lengths of lifting her mistress's feet up onto the sofa. If she'd been dealing with an ordinary noble, no doubt they would have struck off her head. She was able to do these things precisely because she was dealing with the absentminded—or rather, tolerant—Raynesia.

Lately, they were hosting tea parties nearly every day. If she swept up immediately like this, it would make work easier for the person in charge of early mornings. Tomorrow, the Adventurer women would probably come to call again. In particular, the small black-haired girl—Akatsuki—had come every day for the past ten days or so.

"You look very tired today."

"Yes."

Raynesia wasn't saying much.

She really must be tired. Elissa couldn't blame her. Madame Henrietta and Madame Marielle had done just as they pleased with her. After returning from brunch, Raynesia had been subjected to yet another dress-up tournament. Remembering her mistress's voice—which had pleaded for mercy in a truly pitiful way—Elissa chuckled a little, deep in her throat.

It was Elissa's job to dress her mistress in such a way that she could present her anywhere without embarrassment.

Yes, meticulously managing Raynesia's clothes was her duty as well.

After all, due to her mistress's appearance, people noticed her. Thinking of outfits day after day was a monumental task.

For example, if she had a conference with a merchant, and she wore the same dress to the conference after that, she'd probably be held in contempt for "always wearing the same dress, even though she was the daughter of a dukedom." As a result, Elissa and one other of the ladies-in-waiting's jobs was to keep types of dresses on hand every day whenever she changed clothes, morning, noon and night, and to keep a careful record of the accessories she wore each time.

If they were dealing with People of the Earth nobles and merchants, that sort of conventional treatment was enough. It was a troublesome duty, and it required puzzle-like planning abilities, but if she thought about it as being a time-honored job, it was nothing.

When dealing with the Adventurers, though, she had trouble. After all, there was simply no precedent. If it was an audience or some other formal occasion, it was possible to design outfits according to the topic of the audience or the requirements of etiquette. However, these recent tea parties were considered purely private affairs. An overdone outfit risked incurring the Adventurers' displeasure. Still, even if it was all right to wear casual clothes, she didn't know what sorts of clothes were considered "casual" according to Adventurer common sense.

After all, Adventurers wore all sorts of clothes. Most Adventurers seemed to distinguish between clothes worn for battle and ordinary clothes for around town, but for some, the line between the two was blurry, and it wasn't unusual to see individuals who spent most of their time in plate armor.

There was another problem as well. In an attempt to learn the Adventurers' preferences and customs, she'd examined dresses and outfits which it would have been hard to call dresses in Akiba beforehand, and the prices had been all over the map. Though imperfect, the House of Cowen was a great noble family. That meant that, although the Adventurers' equipment was expensive, it wasn't as if they couldn't purchase casual clothes. However, even if that was so, the pricing was far too incomprehensible. It was common for a silk shirt to have a price fifty times higher than the practically identical shirt hanging next to it.

The shopkeeper had explained that the materials were different.

The longer she listened, the more astounded she was, but Adventurer shops sold boots made of tanned Gorgon hide and bustiers made with Falnat down, as if that were only natural. Clothes made by subjugating and using such high-level mystical beasts were so expensive that even the dukedom, which had one of the People of the Earth's greatest fortunes, couldn't afford to buy them up one after another.

Truth be told, the dress-up tournaments that were held day after day were, in part, the result of Elissa having asked Marielle for advice. "Just relax and leave everythin' to me," Marielle had declared merrily, and thanks to the clothes she brought in, Raynesia's Adventurer-compatible wardrobe was gradually being filled out.

For the sake of that project, Elissa felt no hesitation about offering up her mistress for a dress-up doll party. In any case, if she didn't do something like this, Raynesia wouldn't budge an inch. Elissa thought it was good medicine for her.

She loved and respected Raynesia nonetheless, of course.

When she'd spoken sharply during that conference, Elissa had felt like applauding: Even if it was her own mistress, that had been splendid. However, Raynesia was a fundamentally indolent, cowardly, thoughtless, feather-pillow girl (meaning her head was stuffed with down).

Elissa respected and loved her, but if asked whether she could constantly *serve* her with respect, she'd have to say it was doubtful.

Well, this is for Raynesia's sake, after all.

As she folded up a lap robe, Elissa pondered.

It wasn't just the clothes.

Having friends of the same gender who were her own age, or marginally older or younger, was a rare experience.

It was one thing for Elissa, who was the daughter of a low-ranking noble, but for Raynesia, who'd been born the granddaughter of the Cowen dukedom, they might be even harder to find than a good husband.

Elissa remembered the perfect smile her mistress had worn in the palace at Maihama, and at the Ancient Court of Eternal Ice. Aristocratic society was strict. A single bad rumor could be fatal, particularly for young women.

In order to survive surrounded by the watchful eyes of the gossipy sparrows at court, Raynesia had acquired elegant manners. The mask she'd chosen to protect the honor of her grandfather and her family was so perfect that it had won her legendary renown and the name "Eastal's winter rose."

However, for that very reason, Raynesia had never had a real friend. Her relationship with Elissa might be relatively close, but even so, a lady-in-waiting was a lady-in-waiting.

"Still, although it may not be my place to say it, you looked as if you were quite enjoying yourself."

"Pardon…?"

"I think it's good that you've made friends."

This was really true.

Elissa thought that, over the past two weeks, Raynesia's expressions had grown quite varied.

"They aren't friends."

—However, the words that came back weren't what she'd expected.

"Hmm? Then what are they, pray tell? When you spoke with them… Well, sometimes you seemed to be at your wits' end, but you looked as though you were having fun."

"They're Adventurers."

Raynesia answered Elissa's question without any particular enthusiasm.

"I wasn't having fun while we talked. The Adventurers are different from us. They're much too different. The etiquette I've learned doesn't work. Unless I put my feelings into words and communicate them properly, they won't understand, and if they don't, we can't talk to each other."

That was probably correct.

The Adventurers weren't particular about social standing. When they held tea parties, they even invited Elissa. Similarly, since being posted to Akiba, Elissa had acquired a few acquaintances: Madame Henrietta, who worked in a way with which she could sympathize; Riezé, who bore a very slight resemblance to her little sister back in her hometown; and Serara, who was so domestic she would have loved to have her as a fellow lady-in-waiting.

Of course, as Raynesia said, Adventurers and People of the Earth were very different. Sometimes their views conflicted, and sometimes they couldn't tell what the other was saying. However, it wasn't so bad they couldn't join hands.

Elissa thought Raynesia had taught her more about that than anyone else.

For that reason, at the same time, she asked a question, as though urged on by her doubts:

"But you were so…"

"If I had even a little fun, I have to tell them I had fun. If I'm sad, I need to say I'm sad, and if I'm happy, I have to express my gratitude. If I don't, they won't understand, so I do it. You know, too, don't you, Elissa? I'm really more idle and cowardly and…irresponsible. To be honest, I couldn't care less about fashionable society and the nobility. If I could take naps every day, that'd be enough for me. In any case, I don't really understand that sort of thing."

Raynesia's murmur sounded somehow bored.

"It's a job."

"—Is it, then."

"…"

Raynesia looked away, leaning limply against the back of the sofa. Spelled out in words, it looked as if she'd grown tired of it, or had given up or, at the very least, as though her attitude was irresponsible. However, beautiful girls had it good from start to finish, and even that careless pose was as pretty as a picture, which made it impossible to deal with.

Elissa was the only person Raynesia showed this sort of pose to.

In the presence of People of the Earth nobles, she acted like the perfect lady, and naturally she did so with princesses her own age as well. Even with the Adventurer women, although she was genuine, she was meek as a lamb. It might have been Raynesia's armor, designed to keep her innermost heart hidden.

—*I suppose there was that individual as well…*

Elissa remembered the big sandy-haired man. True, Raynesia did seem to have opened her heart to that young man. However, the elements of not being able to lie or deceive him figured largely into that Raynesia hadn't had the freedom to choose in the first place.

Hadn't she ever wanted that?

If I had even a little fun, I have to tell them I had fun.

That was what she'd said.

Still, didn't the fact that she was thinking that way mean she was confessing that she *had* enjoyed herself?

Even if she was tired enough to nap on the sofa before dinner, Elissa thought that if she looked forward to each day enough to wake up the next morning without any help from her maids and be thinking about what to wear, then surely they *were* friends, and it wasn't simply a job.

Hadn't Raynesia been enjoying life a lot more since coming to this town full of Adventurers?

However, her princess turned her gaze to the window, which had already begun deepening to indigo, and she didn't seem to have realized this simple fact of friendship. Either that, or she was avoiding the word *friends*. Elissa didn't know whether she'd given up on those somewhere along the way, or whether she'd never hoped for them in the first place.

Elissa felt something like mild pity.

This girl, Raynesia, who'd been blessed with beauty and acclaim and wealth and even status, sometimes seemed to have abandoned something once and for all. It would be sad if the heroic courage she'd shown at the lords' council had been born from resignation like that.

As the princess gazed out the window, naturally her expression was beautiful and fragile, but it also held a trace of boredom. At the sight, Elissa heaved a sigh.

She wanted to help her mistress, but she knew that lukewarm advice wouldn't reach her.

Raynesia's excellent lady-in-waiting was well aware that Raynesia was just as stubborn and unreasonable as she was lazy.

CHAPTER.
3

FALLEN GUARDIAN

▶ AGE: **90**

▶ WEAPON: **HALF ALV**

▶ CLASS: **SORCERER**

▶ HP: **8758**

▶ MP: **13137**

▶ ITEM 1:

[PRIDE OF QUEEN]

A MAGNIFICENT STAFF SET WITH A MYSTERIOUS CRYSTAL THAT CHANGES COLORS IN RESPONSE TO ACCUMULATED MAGIC. A TROPHY FROM THE "QUEEN OF ANTIQUITY RAID" QUEST. IT HAS AN EFFECT THAT BOOSTS THE THREAT OF MAGIC WHEN SEVERAL SPELLS WITH THE SAME ATTRIBUTE ARE USED IN A ROW.

▶ ITEM 2:

[SMALL POLARIS BOTTLE]

A SMALL, BEAUTIFULLY CRAFTED BOTTLE WITH COLD, SHINING BLUE AIR SWIRLING INSIDE. WHEN OPENED, FRIGID POLAR AIR RAGES ACROSS A WIDE AREA, STOPPING ENEMIES FOR A SHORT TIME. ONCE USED, IT TAKES A FULL DAY FOR THE COLD AIR TO FILL UP AGAIN, SO USE WISELY.

▶ ITEM 3:

[GOOD JOB CARD]

A SCRIBE PRODUCTION-CLASS ITEM KNOWN AS A MESSAGE CARD. THIS IS SOMETHING D.D.D. HANDED OUT TO ITS MEMBERS AS A REWARD, BACK WHEN THIS WAS A GAME. MISA DREW A DEFORMED VERSION OF RIEZE'S CHARACTER ON IT.

‹Magnifying Lens›
A favorite item of monomaniacal
observation fiends who don't let
the smallest detail escape
them. Occasionally contributes
to science.

► 1

Although there was no particular rule about it, people at the RoderLab who had the same subclass and were doing similar research formed fixed groups, becoming communities that called themselves "sections" or "departments."

For example, Mikakage and the other Chefs performed experiments to test the limits and properties of new cooking methods and the act of cooking on a daily basis. In order to do this, they needed an abundance of clean water, ingredients, and fuel, as well as facilities such as kitchens, ovens, heating equipment, items with refrigerating and freezing functions, knives of all types, a variety of containers, mortars, mixers, and more.

The value of the groups known as guilds lay in being able to jointly possess large-scale facilities which would have been difficult for any individual to scrape together. Of course, since they were owned by the group, it wasn't possible to use them by yourself, but even so, the idea of being able to use a top-of-the-line kitchen if you contributed a small amount of money to the guild was appealing. Lately, exemptions were often given even for these contributions. This was because their joint development projects with Shopping District 8 was proving profitable.

The RoderLab held a dozen or so kitchens of varying sizes with all sorts of facilities, and they were used by the roughly seventy members of the cooking section. It was only natural that members of the same class would connect with each other to draw up schedules or adjust the equipment they planned to use.

"Allie!"

When the carefree young man appeared in the small kitchen, it was late afternoon. The light that streamed into the room seemed to have had a hint of orange diffused into it, but it was still too early for sunset.

Startled by the sudden visitor, Allie the Alraune, a petite plant spirit, shivered and leapt up. Grabbing that chance, he caught her easily.

This young male Cleric with awful taste (he was wearing three shirts with loud patterns layered over each other) was Aomori. Both Mikakage and this colleague of hers—who, in spite of being an Adventurer, wasn't very dependable—were Chefs, and in terms of affiliation, they both belonged to the cooking section.

Allie, who was holding a potato in each hand, flinched, then began to struggle, twisting and wriggling.

"Don't torment Allie, Aomori."

"I'm not tormenting her. Am I, Allie?"

The struggling spirit, who was only as tall as a girl who'd just entered preschool, was wearing an outfit that was identical to Mikakage's. She was a shy girl. To Allie, Aomori was like a scary uncle who seemed to approach to shower her with affection, but always teased her instead. Below the macaron cap that matched Mikakage's, her big eyes were wet with tears.

"A-o-mo-ri!"

When Mikakage scolded him, Aomori responded as usual, muttering—"It's not Aomori. It's 'Blue Forest'"—but he put Allie down. Still holding her potatoes, Allie ran around behind Mikakage and crouched down, huddling by her feet.

"Got anything to eat here?"

Aomori pulled a nearby chair over and sat down, asking a question that was pretty irresponsible for a Chef. Without rushing, Mikakage pointed at the pot. Aomori shambled over to it. Then, with bizarre cheers of "Yo-ho" and "Wahoo," he began filling his plate.

Paying no attention to Aomori, Mikakage kept peeling potatoes with a small petty knife. Every time she peeled one, sweet Allie handed her the next one. Since Allie was so short, the way she stood on a special stand, leaning out over the kitchen table with ears twitching, was adorable.

Mikakage was a Druid, and Allie was one of the nature spirits she could summon, but there was no time limit on that summoning. In other words, unless told to go back, Allie would be there forever. Mikakage thought of her diminutive attendant as a little sister, and she lived with her, without sending her back. The miniature cook's coat and pastry chef hat matched Mikakage's, and had been specially ordered from the RoderLab's clothing section.

Mikakage had spent the period of chaos and confusion that had followed the Catastrophe with Allie and her other small attendants. Her little-sister helper Allie. The Myconid who carried her belongings. Orchis, the lullaby songstress. If they hadn't been with her, she probably would have been crushed. Mikakage was glad she was a Druid.

"So, this." At Aomori's voice, Mikakage turned her ears (and nothing else) his way.

"What is it?"

He probably meant the contents of the pot.

She was pretty sure that was… Searching her memory, Mikakage answered.

"Horned Yakuu shank and chickpea stew. It's seasoned with salt and pepper, cream, butter, and several kinds of herbs."

"Is that right. I don't get it."

At Aomori's frank response, Mikakage shrugged.

Hearing things like that would only cause her trouble. Mikakage wasn't good at cooking to begin with.

People might ask, "What are you talking about? Your subclass is Chef," but Mikakage thought of herself as a confectioner, and she didn't feel like a cook. It wasn't that she was completely incapable of making food for meals, but as a rule, she left everything to the pot. Pressure cookers were wonderful: All you had to do was put in the ingredients, add the seasonings, and heat it, and most of the time it turned into food of some sort. Mikakage considered them a great invention and used them all the time.

"By the way: cheese."

"Huh?"

Aomori, who'd been eating thick potage-style stew, looked up, tilting his head to the side in confusion. When she asked for cheese again, he said, "Oh! Oh, right. Yeah, it's done, it's done," and pulled something that looked like badly shaped tofu out of a refrigerated tote at his feet.

Accepting it, Mikakage sniffed it, checking the smell. It was definitely ricotta cheese.

This would broaden the range of sweets she could make. Should she go with cannoli? Or keep it basic and make a cream cake? She could pair it with pudding, too. If she was going to make something, she wanted to surprise people.

"Thanks."

"Yep."

Aomori drank water as he answered. He wasn't a regular Chef, either.

He was an odd one who'd switched over to Brewer and, although he worked to create all sorts of ingredients, he didn't do any cooking on his own. That being said, in a way, that was only natural.

If you wanted to cook normally and serve the food to customers, your best bet was to join Shopping District 8 and set up a shop. You could also get financing as one of the minor guilds affiliated with them. If you wanted to produce in volume and aim for the markets, the Marine Organization was the recommended route. They were currently creating a meal distribution system, and you'd be able to do business in a big way.

This was the RoderLab, a place that attracted oddballs who liked researching and developing new things.

In that sense, there wasn't much difference between Mikakage and Aomori.

"Are you making something else?"

"Uh-huh."

As she carefully lined up potatoes in a baking dish, then sprinkled them with granulated sugar, Mikakage responded absently. Compared to cakes made with wheat flour, potatoes, and other raw ingredients tended to produce different results depending on the day. Moisture content, sweetness, and the flavors inherent to the ingredients were more pronounced, and they varied. In adding sweetness with sugar, she was only supplementing the ingredients. When she thought of it that way, she had to be careful.

"A present for someone?"

"Uh-huh."

"Take me with you."

"No."

Mikakage answered instantly as she poured in cream. Aomori had an ulterior motive there. After he'd heard it was a girls-only tea party, he'd made the same request dozens of times. Aomori—or most guys, really—truly didn't understand: Chatting was important.

Really irreplaceable.

There were several things Mikakage had learned after coming to this world.

One of them was the value of time spent with friends. Here, there were no televisions. No cell phones. No movies or manga. Almost anything that could be termed "entertainment" had disappeared. Calling things "entertainment" made it sound as though they weren't necessary, but Mikakage could declare categorically that this wasn't the case. It was likely that most Adventurers could.

That miserable atmosphere in the town just after the Catastrophe. Even if they had immortal bodies, it didn't really seem like "living" when they spent their days in a despondent mood, listlessly eating food that had no flavor. She thought that human life was something better, something more fun. To that end, it was absolutely vital to have something that would console their spirits.

Like sweets. Or friends who'll eat those sweets.

Come to think of it, Mikakage thought the time she'd spent talking with friends after school had been the best time ever.

She remembered stopping by the hamburger shop almost every day on the way home from club in middle school. They'd order hundred-yen milkshakes and tirelessly tell dumb, funny stories until it got dark. At the time, it had seemed only natural to her, something she'd have limitless access to. When she started high school, she'd drifted apart from those friends and had begun going straight home. Manga and games had filled those hours for her, but after coming to this world, Mikakage had reconsidered, and now she thought human warmth was really important.

Mikakage had been rather shy, but now Allie was here. Mikakage's small partner was a lot shyer and more timid than she was. Strangely, when she was with Allie, Mikakage was able to be proactive. She'd thought that, for Allie's sake as well, she needed to actively greet people. When she was trying not to embarrass herself in front of Allie, she was able to manage without being tense, even in front of Princess Raynesia, a peerless beauty... Although maybe she was able to avoid being tense because she'd seen her profile when she'd been caught off-guard.

Besides, sweets that made Allie happy made everyone else happy, too.

Creating new sweets and serving them to her friends was Mikakage's greatest pleasure now, and it was the center of her daily life. Luckily, she was able to make enough to live on by selling sweets and submitting recipe logs. In that sense, of all the time following the Catastrophe, these days felt the most fulfilling to Mikakage.

The new facts she'd discovered in the cooking section... They did make her feel a bit uncomfortable, but the investigation looked as if it would yield a modest harvest. Investigations were fun, once you got used to them.

"What, the get-together's that important or something?"

At Aomori's petulant question, Mikakage took a moment to think. Of course it was important. How could it not be?

Making sweets.

Having people eat those sweets.

Telling pointless stories.

Nothing was as important as these things. The problem with guys was that they wanted set results from everything. But it wasn't okay to rush any of these elements. Proper heat, proper timing.

Mikakage put on a big oven mitt, took the potatoes baked in cream out of the oven and served them to Aomori. She was experimenting with a new dish. Aomori was emitting whoops of delight, but since it was a prototype, she couldn't serve it to everyone at the tea parties yet. This was just a couple of steps above tasting for poison. That was why Aomori was good enough.

"Yes. It's really important. Really-really. I bet there's nothing more important."

"Huh? Not even your relationship with me?"

"That's less important than scorched, failed jam."

Ignoring the dejected Aomori, Mikakage began to put away the cooking implements she'd used.

After all, even as Aomori sniffled, he'd probably polish off the potatoes, and Allie—who, though shy, was a busybody—would probably comfort him.

▶ **2**

When the young man's visit was announced, Raynesia felt something unexpected.

Of course she knew him by sight, and he was an important person, but she realized she had never imagined him visiting her, or indeed anyone.

In aristocratic society, visits were announced several days to several months in advance, but for better or worse, this was Akiba, and the servants at Water Maple Mansion, Raynesia's residence, had grown accustomed to abrupt guests.

This time as well, the visitor had been shown into the drawing room before Raynesia had even been informed.

With Elissa's help, the princess tidied her hair a little and changed clothes. Although the young man was someone from "her side," he wasn't a noble, and, most important, they were both People of the Earth who lived in Akiba. Deciding there was no need to dress as formally as she would have for a soirée, she'd chosen a long-sleeved one-piece dress with slim lines.

The dress was pink, as misty as a light snowfall. It had been a gift from Marielle of the Crescent Moon League. Of the clothing she'd been given, it was one of the most demure pieces, and Raynesia secretly liked it.

When she trotted into the drawing room, hurrying just a little, the guest stood to greet her.

"It's been a long time since we last spoke, Lady Raynesia."

The visitor, who bowed his head politely, was a young man. His name was Kinjo. He was the young leader of the Kunie clan in Akiba.

"I'm terribly sorry to have kept you waiting."

Raynesia gracefully returned the courtesy.

While Elissa prepared tea, an odd silence flowed between them.

Raynesia didn't know much about this young man. On the contrary: The fact that he was the young leader of the Kunie clan was nearly all she knew about him. The Kunie were an unconventional clan, even for the People of the Earth, and it was safe to say that, in a sense, they had special influence in Yamato.

Yamato was roughly divided into five territories.

The Ezzo Empire, which had been founded in the wastelands to the north. The Nine-Tails Dominion, a merchant shipping nation far to the south. The Duchy of Fourland, which had already collapsed and was now a dangerous island where monsters ran rampant. The Holy Empire of Westlande, which had inherited the blood of the Westlande Imperial Dynasty. Finally, Eastal, the League of Free Cities, which had put down roots in Eastern Yamato and included the city of Maihama, which was governed by Raynesia's grandfather.

The same currency was in circulation in all five of these territories. The money was divided into halves, quarters, and whole coins, but these were ordinarily referred to in general terms as "gold coins." Raynesia had heard that the exact same currency was used, not only in Yamato, but even on the continent.

These gold coins had been used since ancient times, and the members of the Kunie clan were the ones who controlled their circulation, or in other words, the banks.

They had inherited a few of the ancient alvs' technologies, and they were able to send and receive articles across long distances using a method that was different from the intercity gates. The Kunie clan used these technologies to operate the financial institutions scattered across the country.

However, they weren't a banking clan.

Their mission was to maintain the magic technologies from the time of the ancient alvs.

The bank was the most typical example, but in Eastal, they were also in charge of maintaining the barrier cities' magical defensive circles. There were roughly thirty barrier cities in Eastal, and ancient facilities that transmitted magic had been built underneath them. This magic prevented monsters from invading, and it also powered the mobile armor.

With the exception of the cities belonging to the Holy Empire of Westlande, which had been afraid its nobles would rebel, almost all the barrier cities in Yamato were supported by the Kunie clan.

That was how heavy the clan's responsibility was. In a way, you could say their clan was more important to Yamato than the nobles. Even when Raynesia had been posted to Akiba, her grandfather had duly sent word to the Kunie clan.

However, on the other hand, since antiquity, the Kunie clan had been known for its curious lack of interest in fame or power. Among Eastal's nobility, the unanimous impression was that they handed their mission down orally and cared only about its accomplishment.

In general terms, ordinary People of the Earth nobles—and Raynesia herself—were conscious of the Kunie as an eccentric People of the Earth tribe that was strange and mysterious, but that had lent its strength to maintaining the world since antiquity.

"Please, do have some tea."

However, for that reason alone, Raynesia didn't know how to speak to him. For the moment, because it seemed safe, she offered him the tea Elissa had made. What she'd set down on the low table was green tea they'd recently purchased.

Kinjo softly lowered his half-closed eyes, then brought the cup to his lips.

She'd heard from Elissa that he was young, and even now, when she was facing him, there was no other way to describe him. However, even when she gazed steadily at the young man—who had violet eyes and black hair, and was dressed in a formal suit with a stand-up collar—his age wasn't clear to her.

Naturally, he was older than Raynesia, but what would he be compared to Krusty the warrior-menace? The smooth contours of his cheeks made her think he might be much younger, and his sinewy hands made him seem much older. Raynesia had never seen anyone whose age was this unclear to her before.

"I apologize for my sudden visit today. A grave incident has occurred; I've come to explain it to you, and to apologize."

Kinjo had returned his cup to its saucer, and he grimaced as he spoke.

"What might that be?"

"A suit of mobile armor has been stolen from the guards' station."

"What…?"

"We believe the thief was one of the guards, a member of the Kunie clan."

Raynesia didn't usually think of herself as being quick on the uptake, but this time she truly missed his meaning.

She was also keenly aware that the blood was draining from her head.

A vicious dizziness assailed her, and her vision seemed to darken.

Mobile armor was one of the relics from the ancient alvs, special armor used in order to protect a specific zone. The greatest difference between it and ordinary armor lay in the magic that was externally supplied to it, and that function greatly improved the physical abilities of whoever wore it.

Currently, the People of the Earth's combat abilities weren't that strong, comparatively. Not only were they no match for the Adventurers, they couldn't stand up to any monster that was midlevel or above. Even so, they were able to protect their living space in the world because they had help from several quarters.

One was the legendary People of the Earth heroes known as the Ancients, as well as the Adventurers, who acted as guerilla fighters and put down the world's enemies. Another was the barrier technology that protected the big cities and major highways from monsters.

The organization of guards equipped with mobile armor was an element just as important as the previous ones.

Depending on the situation, People of the Earth who'd been strengthened by mobile armor gained abilities that surpassed those of high-level Adventurers. In addition, although their abilities were limited to the cities, they could teleport and put people in prison. The guards employed these abilities to keep the peace in town.

Of course, the use of these abilities wasn't unrestricted. Mobile armor required a vast amount of magic just to operate, and she'd heard it could be used only in certain cities.

"Yes, that's correct. Mobile armor can be used only in a few major cities. Without a constant supply of magic from the enormous magic circle constructed under the city, the wearer finds it difficult even to move. That's one of the armor's distinguishing characteristics. In addition, mobile armor is tuned to the magic wavelength of its specific city, so if removed from Akiba, it would be nothing more than rubbish."

Raynesia was dumbfounded. Watching her steadily, Kinjo kept speaking.

"However, that doesn't change the gravity of the situation. Even if it's only papier-mâché if taken outside, within the city, its strength is unequaled."

Depending on how it was adjusted, mobile armor could greatly amplify output. In the town of Akiba, its abilities surpassed level 100. Its purpose was to control Adventurers who committed violent acts in town, so this was only natural, but its combat abilities were set to surpass even those of Adventurers at the highest level.

In fact, part of the reason Raynesia, a woman, had been posted to this town governed by Adventurers was the fact that her safety was guaranteed by the mobile armor and the guards. Of course, the official stance was that she was taking responsibility for having touched off the battle for Zantleaf by making reckless statements, without permission from the lords' council. However, it did mean that her grandfather had had that much foresight when it came to posting a defenseless People of the Earth princess to an Adventurer city with only a handful of attendants.

However, the combat abilities that served as a guarantee had been leaked to an outsider. That news indicated a variety of things, all at once.

"But then... You can't mean... The murderer..."

Raynesia had gone pale. In response to her question, Kinjo nodded.

"Yes, the Kunie clan is involved in those crimes. As embarrassing as that is, I'm forced to admit it."

The scandal was enough to freeze Raynesia.

The Kunie clan—and a guard, at that—must not cause a situation like this. It was the sort of thing the People of the Earth hadn't imagined even once in the space of several hundred years.

However, if that was the case, it did explain several mysteries.

The failure of Akiba's guard system to detect the murders was only natural. The surveillance network was designed to detect harm Adventurers or People of the Earth did to each other. When the guards did battle, it wasn't a crime: They were keeping the peace.

In other words, there was no way the murders *could* have been detected.

While wearing the mobile armor, the criminal had combat abilities greater than the Adventurers. Raynesia had no combat strength, and she didn't know just how much higher "greater" would be, but from the rumors she'd heard over the past several days, she knew there had been quite a few victims already.

Moreover, the fact that the Kunie clan had a hand in the incident was lethal on two points.

The first was that the clan's existence was far too transparent, as natural as air. The teleporting guards that protected the peace of the city and the banking network that stretched across all of Yamato... The systems were too much a part of society, both for the People of the Earth and for the Adventurers. Their convenience and safety were solid components of the social infrastructure.

However, didn't that make the fissure in their foundation all the more terrifying? Raynesia hadn't received expert training, and she couldn't even imagine exactly what sort of disaster it might cause, but she felt an unease at the idea, like black clouds on the horizon.

The second was more direct: The Kunie, although eccentric, were People of the Earth, and they had killed Adventurers.

Adventurers were completely different beings from People of the Earth. Their physical appearance was similar, but the difference between their biological potentials was as great as the difference between heaven and earth. Adventurers increased their abilities dramatically by engaging in harsh combat over and over again, and when they were high-level, they had combat abilities that would allow just one of them to fight a band of a hundred knights.

Up until now, the Adventurers of Akiba had protected Raynesia. They'd supported her as well. However, wasn't that because Raynesia and her people were weak? Even if that hadn't been all of it, Raynesia felt this was part of the reason.

When that crumbled, the relationship between the Adventurers and the People of the Earth might suffer a fatal collapse.

Why is this happening...?
Raynesia's mind filled with regret and resentment.

There really was no other way to describe her mood. Why had this unnecessary trouble occurred *now*, when she'd been posted here, when she was standing right out in front? This incident hadn't needed to happen, had it? The Kunie clan hadn't had a single scandal in centuries, and she was at a loss to understand why they'd misbehaved *now*, of all times, and in Akiba no less, the town where Raynesia lived.

"This incident is due to our carelessness. I'm truly sorry."

"Can't... Can't the Kunie clan, um...do something about it?" Raynesia asked.

She'd had a hunch even before she asked him, but she'd had to ask.

"I'm sorry, Princess Raynesia. Of course, if we cut off the supply of magic, the mobile armor will stop functioning. However, if we do that, the city's defensive magic circle will also lose its abilities, and it will take decades to bring it back into operation. I can give you no other answer."

In order to protect Akiba from the monsters outside, the magic circle could not be stopped.

The fact that that magic circle was giving the murderer strength shattered Raynesia.

▶ 3

Akatsuki, who'd been let into the anteroom, was warming a cup in her hands, a quiet expression on her face.

She wasn't particularly cold. There just hadn't been anything else to do.

She didn't know how much of it was an accident and how much it had been a plot on the part of Elissa the maid, but her sharp Tracker's senses were letting her hear nearly all of the conversation in the next room.

No matter how she thought about it, though, it was too much for Akatsuki to deal with alone. Akiba was in crisis: It was the sort of thing no one but a big guild like the West Wind Brigade or D.D.D. would be able to cope with, the sort of thing the Round Table Council might have to move for.

Akatsuki thought she should probably pretend she hadn't heard anything and leave.

That beautiful princess, a girl like moonlight, had been worrying about whether or not to tell the Adventurers. Akatsuki felt as though, if she heard part of the murderer incident before Raynesia had made up her mind, it would have had too great an effect on the state of things.

As a result, Akatsuki thought she'd get a look at Raynesia's face, but when she thought about it later, she realized it might have been too capricious of her. Because of what her liege had said, she'd thought she'd at least check on the princess's expression; the reason she even attempted it was the mission Shiroe had given her, and nothing more than that. In any case, right now, Akatsuki didn't have a shred of mental leeway to worry about other people.

She slipped out onto the balcony through the window of the anteroom. In combination with her drab everyday clothes, she probably looked like a creeping shadow. For a high-level Adventurer's physical abilities, jumping across to the balcony of the drawing room—three meters away—was even easier than stepping across the border of a tatami mat.

Raynesia was there, in the shadow of the elaborately sculptured window frame, beyond a lace curtain that looked like foam. The young man who'd been speaking with her a moment ago must have gone home: She was sitting all alone on the drawing room sofa, burying her face in a large cushion.

How strange, Akatsuki thought, absently.

Raynesia had always been calm, cheerful and genuine, and she'd held her head high. She was the sort of beautiful girl you couldn't help but envy. Even more than her beautiful silver hair and her slender neck, her constantly modest, gracious manner created an atmosphere that was decisively different from the Adventurers. The girl Raynesia had the power to persuade any Adventurer that upbringing really did determine who you became.

…And now Raynesia was leaning forward as if her strength had run out, hugging a large cushion and burying her face in it. She didn't look like Raynesia at all.

"It's useless."
There was glass between them, but she'd heard that voice.
The faint voice had been like a silver bell, but reckless bewilderment clung to it.
"It's really no good."
Every time she shook the cushion, her smooth silver hair rippled like a waterfall.
"…Why now? …Why me?"
It was as if Raynesia's body had wilted.
A long, long sigh escaped the princess, and she became a fragile little girl.
"Things are not going my way—"
On the wintry balcony, Akatsuki nodded. She understood that feeling all too well.
There were too many difficult things in the world, and too few things she could do well with her own hands. It was a very frustrating, miserable feeling.
"Could you make this a little easier on me? …Would you give me a bit of extra help? Would you hold back…just a little, perhaps?"
Akatsuki had wished these things as well.
Was there anyone who hadn't?
But they wouldn't come true.
She didn't think there was anyone who hadn't been let down. No one ever got everything they wished for. The things you'd thought you'd gained, the things you thought you'd made, the things that were yours alone… Before long, they all faded, slipping through your fingers.

It was too trivial, and sometimes she wanted to think that maybe wishing itself had been a mistake. It was so bad it made her think that spitefulness was the chief element in the world.

"What should I do?"

Raynesia sounded as if she was at a loss, and so Akatsuki answered her.

"Discuss it with the Council?"

"But if I do that, won't we find ourselves at war with the Adventurers?"

"Still, you can't keep it a secret. It's hard to say we know enough about the situation, but even so."

The window had been opened ever so slightly, and Akatsuki had slipped in through it, not even disturbing the curtain, to stand in front of Raynesia.

She felt something just a little nostalgic. She'd looked down on her liege when his head had been bowed like this. That time was very distant now. The one in front of her wasn't her black-haired liege, but a silver-haired princess.

"I really will have to tell, then...?"

"I don't know."

"Why is that menace gone at a time like this? He always turned up when he had no business here, and now... He's truly useless."

"Krusty left for Seventh Fall, the Goblins' castle."

"I know. Still, that doesn't mean... Oh, no, that isn't it..."

"..."

"That isn't...it?!"

Raynesia's head came up as though she'd been stung. The corners of her drawn lips were trembling, and she was trying desperately to compose her expression, but the corners of her eyes were very slightly red.

"Um, oh. I..."

Raynesia hastily resettled herself, sitting up straight. Akatsuki stood in front of her. Since the tall princess was dealing with the petite Akatsuki, even when she was sitting down, if she sat up straight, there wasn't much difference in their eye levels. Possibly because she was uncomfortable, Raynesia lowered her gaze. Akatsuki felt bad for making her feel like that.

Akatsuki hadn't meant to eavesdrop either, or to come into the room like this.

"Wh-what— You, um… You heard…?" Raynesia peeked up at her through her lashes. Akatsuki nodded. Raynesia acknowledged, "Of course you did…" letting the end of the sentence fall in resignation.

Both seemed to be at a loss for words, and time flowed between them.

With no help for it, Akatsuki took a sweet red bean bun she'd bought for lunch out of her bag and handed it to Raynesia. The two girls sat on the sofa, side by side, and for a short while, they quietly savored the sweetness they'd torn apart.

"The criminal's a Person of the Earth?"

Raynesia answered Akatsuki's question, haltingly.

"Yes, that's right. A suit of mobile armor has been stolen from the Kunie, a clan that is responsible for guarding the town. Apparently, since the mobile armor is guard equipment, incidents it causes in town won't be reported, and it's able to bestow great combat abilities. I'm really…terribly…sorry."

"Why?"

"Pardon?"

"Why was it stolen? Who stole it?"

"The person who stole it also seems to be missing. We don't know whether the person who's currently using it is the member of the Kunie clan who stole it or not. We don't know his goal or where he's hiding, either."

"I think he's hiding in the sewers."

"In the sewers?"

Akatsuki filled her in on what she thought.

"From what I heard, I doubt he's hiding outside Akiba. In that case, the sewers are about the only place that hasn't been searched completely, and where he'd be out of sight."

From what she'd heard, the murderer seemed to have acquired the power of a guard.

Akatsuki had been startled when she'd first heard that, but, if true, it did explain a few things.

The murderer's combat abilities had probably surpassed level 100 and were close to level 110. The Adventurers of Akiba were mostly around level 90, so of course they'd be no match for him.

At the same time, if he was using the guards' power, he was very unlikely to leave Akiba. After all, if he left, he'd lose his combat power. Considered that way, the number of places he could hide was limited.

However, capturing him was likely to prove extremely difficult.

In order to bring crimes committed in town under control immediately, the guards had a teleportation function. When used to punish PKs, this function was reassuring, but when a criminal was able to use it proactively, there was no better escape method.

Even if one of the big guilds formed a raid force and surrounded him, if all he wanted to do was run, he'd be able to get away for sure.

"I see…"

Akatsuki looked at the girl in front of her.

A daughter of the greatest noble family in eastern Yamato: the House of Cowen.

A legendary beauty whose name was known throughout Eastal.

The intermediary between the People of the Earth and the Adventurers, and the central figure in the Zantleaf war.

The "mystic princess of the silver moon."

The girl before her didn't seem like any of those things. She looked ordinary.

She wore an expression of depressed anguish, but even so, she was nibbling at her sweet red bean bun. This was a regular girl, the sort you could find anywhere. Not only that, but Akatsuki thought she was probably the same in the other women's eyes.

"That's a problem for you?"

"It's a problem."

As the two of them nodded, it was likely that neither had the leeway to cope with anything but their respective problems. At the very least, Akatsuki saw herself in this beautiful silver princess.

Akatsuki's liege had said something:

Protect Raynesia, the People of the Earth princess.

Akatsuki had taken those words to mean "guard duty." However, just now, she'd realized there was a possibility that that hadn't been it.

I wonder what my liege wanted me to protect…

If it had been about physically protecting Raynesia, there wouldn't have been any need to come to these tea parties, would there? If the other girl had only wanted to be physically protected, there wouldn't have been any meaning in hosting the tea parties, would there? Wasn't she overlooking something important? Something Marielle and Henrietta and the others noticed a long time ago?

The words Akatsuki wanted to say to Raynesia were, *It can't be helped.*

Lots of unfair things happened. There were lots of things you couldn't handle, lots of wishes that wouldn't come true.

There really was no help for that. Akatsuki didn't have the ability to draw a miracle to Raynesia, and so the only words she could say to her were *It can't be helped.*

If she were able to add one more thing, it would probably be, *You're doing your best.*

Akatsuki had seen the great achievement she'd pulled off at the lords' conference. She'd also heard Shiroe's evaluation of her. And, for a while now, she'd hidden close to her, watching over her. As a result, she could say, *You're doing your best.*

However, was she qualified to say those words to her? The girl was a daughter of the nobility, the representative of the People of the Earth, and she was shouldering a heavier responsibility than the eleven guild masters on the Round Table Council. Akatsuki was uneasy about whether those were words she could say to her.

When she'd thought that far, Akatsuki realized she personally felt just a little respect for this silver-haired girl. That was why she'd come here every day and watched over her from nearby.

Even now, when she was frantic to get stronger, when it was hard for her to go home to her own guild house, she'd been on her mind.

"I'll go find him."

Akatsuki stood up.

If the one she was looking for was a Person of the Earth, and if he had a special teleportation item, that would give her ways to look for him. He probably spent the day lying low in the sewers, and at night, he used teleportation to infiltrate a place where he could see across the whole town—a place ordinary Adventurers couldn't get into—and watched the streets.

"What?"

"I'll carry out my duty. I saw that you're giving it your all."

Raynesia's outstretched hand closed on empty space.

Having found a clue, Akatsuki had departed through the open window, sortieing into the streets of Akiba again.

▶4

Ten eyes were gazing at silver light.

The crossing blades drew trails like shooting stars, light bursting forth, only to vanish.

As if through an agreement, they slipped past each other or struck each other, with a noise of rejection that was more like shards of crystal than metal.

As Nazuna and her companions watched, the murderer and Soujirou were locked in mortal combat.

The strikes Soujirou's weapon, an *uchigatana*, paid out were incredibly smooth, without the slightest hint of intimidation. However, Nazuna knew that each strike held an unavoidable terror for its target: The slashing attacks seemed slow only because they were so graceful. Soujirou's attacks saw through his opponent's evasions, and in contrast to their appearance, were perfectly lethal.

Yet the murderer repelled Soujirou's attacks with his grotesque gauntlets and armor.

It wasn't proper swordsmanship. His movements were instinctive, his fighting style nearly animalistic. It was colored by a clear joy for murder that only humans felt.

Almost before the sparks from one deflected attack had vanished, the murderer's sword struck from a slipshod stance.

Unlike Soujirou's, his attacks didn't follow the etiquette of swordsmanship. In a sense, they were rough strikes.

However, precisely because they were so haphazard, they were fast and hard to predict.

In fact, Nazuna's companion Kyouko had fallen victim to them, and Kawara, whom Nazuna was cradling now, had sustained a serious injury.

"The boss is amazing..."

The murmur that slipped from the form between her arms mirrored the thoughts of all the members who waited behind Nazuna.

They really should have surrounded this opponent and fought as a group.

Enbart Nelles.

Level 94, Samurai.

Nazuna no longer thought that this demon, who was one level above Soujirou, was an Adventurer. The idea that he was a Samurai was ridiculous.

Nazuna had been watching a Samurai (Soujirou) for a long time now. True, the special-skills system in *Elder Tales* was diverse, and there were lots of special skills that the Samurai class could acquire. Level changed most skills into more advanced ones, and there were about forty series. It wasn't possible for a single Samurai to master all of them, but the difference between the skills the murderer in front of her was using and the ones Soujirou used was just too great.

The stranger wasn't a Samurai. The way he fought was too different from Adventurers.

Even so, at first, they'd faced him as a party.

It had been directly after one of the West Wind Brigade search teams had encountered the murderer and failed to capture him. Soujirou's group, which had been waiting back at their headquarters, had sortied and engaged the murderer in this narrow alley.

However, Nazuna's group's battle plan—to surround and obliterate him—had fallen apart easily.

In this alley, in the gap between two ruins, it hadn't been possible to put together a decent formation. On top of that, there was no one in Nazuna's party besides Soujirou who could pin down the murderer's uncanny swordsmanship.

Kawara, the second vanguard, had been sliced up in the blink of an eye, and Nazuna and the spell casters had taken damage as well. If Soujirou hadn't dashed forward in one sprint and put pressure on the murderer, one or two of them would probably have been sent to the Temple by now.

Nazuna quietly gave her thanks.

*　　*　　*

Not because Soujirou had saved them.

And not for the good fortune of having gotten by without sacrificing any girls in front of him.

Attacks that would have cut people with sound, if that had been possible, came together over and over. It was evening, and the winter wind was growing dryer, becoming cold enough to crack. The murderer's sword raced as if to slash that air apart.

In the midst of a landscape where white mist leaked out even if you tried to hold your breath, Soujirou repelled the attacks.

It was Soujirou's Mystery, Clairvoyance.

Nazuna didn't understand it completely, but Clairvoyance was a defensive Mystery. Soujirou had told her it saw trajectories that ran through the air. It was a new power he'd acquired. Making free use of it now, Soujirou continued to deflect the murderer's attacks.

Soujirou's usual composure was absent.

Ordinarily, he wouldn't have deflected the attacks. He would have let them slip by him, or parried them.

The fact that he couldn't do this showed just how fast and sharp the murderer's strikes were.

Then a strike he couldn't fully parry came along, and one of the large sleeves of the armor Soujirou wore, which made him look like a warrior from the Warring States period, flew off.

Her other companions probably couldn't tell, but Nazuna bit her lip.

That attack had burst the defensive barrier she'd been providing to Soujirou. It was a defensive spell that prevented damage to HP by setting barrier magic in advance. In a way, you could say it was invisible, additional HP. Ripples ran across the surface of the pale blue, mirror-like effect, and it shattered. Even if those around her could see it happen, Nazuna, the spell caster, was the only one who could know specifically how much damage it had taken before it fell away.

The Purification Barrier Nazuna had used had been equivalent to slightly less than 20 percent of Soujirou's total HP. In other words, in that moment, if the barrier spell hadn't been there, Soujirou would have lost 20 percent of his health. The attack power was equivalent to that of a raid boss, and it made Nazuna anxious. If he took attacks like that one after another, Soujirou really wouldn't last.

Of course she was preparing to chant another barrier into existence, but it wasn't a spell she could use back-to-back. Kannagi like Nazuna fought by combining barriers and subtle recovery to fully protect their companions from danger.

If she blindly stuck with barriers, she'd lose more MP than she had to, and before long, the battle would begin turning against them. Even without that, it felt as though she was walking a tightrope. If the murderer in front of her sensed that she was casting defensive spells like this, his blade might turn on her.

However, if she turned her back on the fight, she wouldn't be able to protect or heal Soujirou.

All she could do was watch him, gauge her own powers, and continue to entrust everything to barriers, even if they were like tissue paper.

What is *this guy? As if a gamble like this could exist!*

There were some things she understood precisely because she was a Kannagi.

She was the main healer of the West Wind Brigade, a guild which yielded to other top-class groups in terms of size yet kept challenging raid after raid anyway and was one of the top guilds on the server.

Yet defeat in this fight seemed almost certain.

Because the tank who was drawing the enemy's attacks was Soujirou, they were managing to preserve a balance by the skin of their teeth, but if it hadn't been him, Nazuna was certain they would have been trampled, and that would have been that.

Even Soujirou wasn't able to parry all the attacks.

Of course, even if this had been a raid, it wouldn't have been possible to negate all the attacks from a giant dragon or murderous golem. In most raids, combat moved forward with at least three, and sometimes as many as ten, healers supporting just one vanguard player. Then, while the vanguard kept the powerful enemy pinned, the attackers shaved its HP down to nothing.

However, right now, they didn't have enough healers or attackers. In any case, in this narrow alley that was like a gap between furniture, they couldn't use a raid formation.

Nazuna and the others had thought that if the enemy was an

Adventurer, or possibly an average monster, they had nothing to be afraid of. They hadn't thought the murderer would be such a demon.

And again—

"Ghk!!"

The enemy slipped through Soujirou's attack.

The murderer had gotten around to Soujirou's right side before they were aware of it. His weird silhouette moved like an insect as he took a swipe at Soujirou's shins. Soujirou leapt, evading the attack, but his usual dance-like grace was gone. He didn't have that sort of breathing room.

Soujirou would link several attacks together and break down his opponent's stance, working diligently to create an opening for an attack, but this monster would use his strange martial arts to negate the blow. It had happened again, just now.

He slipped through Soujirou's attack and caught him in the back.

If they could only hit him with an attack, she doubted he'd respond like an actual raid monster, but they just couldn't hit him. Even if Soujirou was able to stay this active, if things kept on this way, Nazuna's MP would run out and the front line would crumble.

And it was likely that…

As long as we're here, I bet Soujirou won't run.

She was sure of it.

"…Master Sou."

"Boss."

"It's no good, I can't see!"

She heard murmurs that held hints of pain. It was Nazuna's companions. They were covered in wounds, and it was technically Nazuna's job to heal them, but right now, she couldn't even do that properly. She wanted to hang on to even the slight amount of MP it would take to heal them.

On a separate circuit from her increasingly anxious heart, Nazuna put together a plan for retreat.

Soujirou couldn't run. This was partly because he would never abandon his female companions, and also because he was already being pushed hard by the murderer: Running would leave him open to attack from behind.

In the same sense that Soujirou couldn't run, Nazuna couldn't run either. If Nazuna ran, the barrier would fall in a few seconds at the earliest, and thirty seconds at the most. If the barrier fell, the damage would be dealt straight to Soujirou's HP. In order to keep Soujirou alive—in other words, to delay the pursuit for even a little while—Nazuna couldn't run.

But what about the other girls?

She could let Kawara and Olive and the others go first. That was probably the only right answer.

However, she needed an opportunity to do it. If they began running away pell-mell now, the murderer might shift his target from Soujirou and lay waste to the girls. It was Soujirou's role to keep that from happening, of course, but there was no guarantee he'd be able to prevent it entirely. The demon was simply that skilled.

If they had some sort of chance... Even as she thought this, time was slipping past her, and it was growing darker. The murderer's blade danced, shining with a phosphorescent glow. The twilight stretched out, longer and longer.

Glimpses of uncertainty were visible in the way Soujirou swung his sword. The battle was a contest. Even if this was Soujirou, she couldn't presume that mental agitation wouldn't trigger his collapse.

Just then, a swallow swooped down.

▶ **5**

She ran along the branch of an ancient tree that surrounded the guild office building, then launched herself from its tip.

The thinner the branch, the better. Branches that seemed thick enough to sit astride felt secure, but when using flexibility to "fly," they were a bit inconvenient.

In movements she'd repeated over and over, Akatsuki ran through the town of Akiba.

There were corridors in the air, just as there were roads on the ground. Branches and roofs that were easy to jump to. Balconies and crumbling signs. In the Adventurers' town, which held the ruins of old buildings and ancient trees, there were routes specifically for those who raced through the sky.

When had she become able to travel through the air along those routes without thinking about it?

When this was a game, it hadn't been an option.

She didn't think she'd been able to do it yet when the Round Table Council was established. By the time they returned from Zantleaf, she'd already been doing it unconsciously. She wasn't clear on when she'd become able to do it, but by now, she couldn't imagine traveling through Akiba without this method. Even in zones she'd never visited before, she felt herself unconsciously observing the flow of the wind, the placement of the buildings, and the positions of trees and the walls of structures.

Her long hair fluttered through the layers of the air.

If her hair was heavy, that meant the air was damp and rain was on its way.

If it tugged at her, the wind was strong, and some of the routes would be unusable.

Having acquired even this sense, Akatsuki had begun to gain physical skills that were far and away the best among the Adventurers who used these corridors in the air.

She was only doing what she always did, but her body felt hot deep inside, and her limbs were light.

Akatsuki watched for the instant her weight came down on the tip of a branch, then flung herself into the air. When she caught the wind, her awareness of her body's movements was sharper than usual. She'd repeated these motions dozens of times, but why was it that she was able to land on the next branch using half the strength she normally used, then let her mind skip ahead to the next leap, which would use the shift in her weight?

Her short conversation with Raynesia spun around and around in her mind.

Akatsuki wasn't good at thinking about herself in relation to other people, and she couldn't organize her thoughts well. How Raynesia had looked. Raynesia's words. Her own feelings. Her responses. They floated up inside Akatsuki like rising bubbles, brushing against her, then burst and vanished.

Because they disappeared before becoming words, Akatsuki didn't really know what it was that had pushed her into motion.

Raynesia was working hard.

Those words alone smoldered in her heart.

…To the point where she thought she should be rewarded.

The evening sun was retreating into the west. As she watched it out of the corner of her eye, she strained her ears, spreading her senses wide and thin. The presence-sensing skill she'd used over and over again picked up miscellaneous murmurs from the town of Akiba.

Let's go back to the guild and make onion soup.
Where should we hunt tomorrow?
Want to go get dinner with me somewhere? I, um… My treat!
Y'know, I've been thinking about a new business.
I swear, our sub GM is so strict!
I wonder if I could get a date somehow.
The Adventurers eat twice as much as we do, don't they…
Nah, three times as much.

The conversations were truly trivial, nothing important. Ordinarily, she probably wouldn't even have registered the exchanges. However, for some reason, Akatsuki's ears picked them up with unusual clarity today.

These were their secrets.

Everyone lived through the activities of their day, and in the evening, these were the modest plans to spend the night with the people closest to them. Either that, or the little private wishes each had for themselves, about what sort of day they wanted the next to be. Of course these weren't the kind of secrets that would cause them trouble if anyone overheard, but in the sense that they were the individuals' feelings about themselves, the whispers counted as secrets.

Akatsuki didn't really know, but it was likely that the murmurs were very important to each of those people. Today, she understood that importance.

Without knowing what it was she'd touched, Akatsuki brushed against something big and extraordinary.

*   *   *

Possibly because she'd been thinking these things, by the time she spotted the fight, she'd already leapt into it.

It was about two minutes from the time her ears caught the rasp of sword guards in close combat and she changed her course, to the point where she spotted the battle from a deserted fifteen-story building. The instant she detected it, she flung herself lightly into the canyon between the two buildings.

She didn't simply relax into the free fall: She kicked the walls of the buildings on either side, trying to accelerate.

Putting a hand to the hilt of the short sword bound to the small of her back, Akatsuki held her breath and plunged into a tailspin.

As she felt the kickback from cutting through the membranes of air that were automatically deployed by magic equipment, Akatsuki finally recognized the situation.

A single party was fighting the black murderer. There was a Samurai vanguard, and a rear guard composed of just one healer. They rest had been partially wiped out.

The vanguard was Soujirou, guild master of the West Wind Brigade, one of the eleven guilds that made up the Round Table Council.

In MMO games, what Akatsuki had done was called "kill stealing." It meant a situation where one party was fighting an opponent, and an Adventurer who wasn't a member of the party attacked that opponent without permission. Since the action was very closely related to stealing experience points or treasure, it was considered poor etiquette and frowned upon.

On top of that, the other party was from one of Akiba's leading combat guilds. Since Akatsuki was bad at dealing with other people, ordinarily, she would have been at her wits' end and probably wouldn't have approached in the first place.

However, this time was different.

Her consciousness was saturated with everything that had happened since that morning.

Her mind felt as though she was delirious with fever, but even so, the world Akatsuki leapt through looked dozens of times clearer than usual.

An Accel Fang, sweeping sideways from the right.

It didn't reach. She'd known it wouldn't. She kicked the wall, danced through space: Stealth Blade.

She flipped, dodged: Quick Assault.

As she'd felt on that first charge, the murderer was strong. Akatsuki probably couldn't win.

Even so, she didn't stop.

In an attempt to gain even a small hint: Venom Strike.

She stepped back as the enemy's sword bore down on her. Not enough. She forced herself backward with Gust Step. Still not enough. Even as the pale blade slipped through Akatsuki's zone of defense, freezing her spine, she stepped forward with blazing composure. Not caring that her right bangs had been cut away: Accel Fang.

Too shallow. One more! Carefully changing the trajectory, as if scooping it up: Accel Fang.

Faster, faster, faster still.

At some point, Akatsuki noticed that pale blue ripples were shimmering around her.

It was a Kannagi's barrier spell. She could tell it was a high-level spell, several times stronger than the one Minori used. No doubt it was support from the healer she'd seen a moment ago.

However, Akatsuki knew that even that was no more than slight insurance. The murderer's blade was still turned on the Samurai in front of her. That was why he hadn't made many counterattacks on Akatsuki, which was why Akatsuki was still alive. If it had been one-on-one, Akatsuki's life would have been long gone.

Although she hated to admit it, the round-faced boy—who wore his hair in a ponytail even though he was a guy—was one of the top-class vanguards on the server, West Wind Brigade leader Soujirou Seta. He was a tough guy with a war record and fame that made Akatsuki's pale in comparison, and even *he* wasn't able to restrain the black murderer.

"Run!"

Akatsuki saw the corners of Soujirou's lips rise in response to the words she'd screamed.

An intense, penetrating gaze struck Akatsuki. Even though he looked younger than she was, it was a man's expression, and a threatening one, and Akatsuki anticipated that it would frighten her.

However, in fact, she'd ignored that premonition and was still fighting like a small-scale storm.

"Why?"

Soujirou's question was quite natural, and it left Akatsuki at a loss for words.

She'd only yelled on reflex, and even she didn't know why she'd said it. This Person of the Earth, who was far stronger than Akatsuki, was a monster.

Come to think of it, that was probably only natural. His level was higher than any Adventurer's, and his abilities were being augmented with mobile armor. Another look showed her that the swollen silhouette of the murderer's limbs was due to the fact that he'd forcibly fixed parts of the guard armor to his body. The bits that looked like light-emitting diodes—proof that magic was still being supplied?—formed a defensive membrane, blocking the Adventurer's attacks.

Akatsuki probably couldn't win. It was likely Soujirou couldn't either. No one could defeat the murderer in this narrow alley. The only way to do it would be to surround him with far more Adventurers and put pressure on him...but was that why she'd yelled? Did she want to use herself as a decoy to save Soujirou?

Amid Akatsuki's saturated thoughts, she saw Shiroe, looking up at the sky, his face troubled.

"Why?"

"Because defeating him and resolving this are two different things."

A grotesque strike bore down on Soujirou, ready to rip through him, and Akatsuki intercepted it with all her might:

Assassinate. It was an Assassin's fastest, strongest special skill, dealing over ten thousand in instantaneous damage, and even *that* could only knock the murderer's thick, black, enormous gauntlet off course.

"So run!"

"I can't agree to that."

At her repeated warning, Soujirou's smile deepened. He'd had his sword raised over his head, and he brought it down.

The murderer dodged, then released a superhuman kick that Soujirou evaded, letting it brush against the right side of his bangs. As he lost hair in the exact same place as Akatsuki, Soujirou stepped in to cross swords, slashing up at the blade that had been on its way down.

Soujirou was strong. Probably several times stronger than Akatsuki.

Even from an exchange that had taken no more than a fraction of a breath, she could tell.

However, precisely because of that, Soujirou must have known he couldn't finish off the monster here and now... And yet he wouldn't run. Why? *What a stubborn boy*, Akatsuki thought. Come to think of it, all the men in this world were stubborn. Touya and Rundelhaus—the younger boys in the group—were exceptionally stubborn. Naotsugu was more stupid than stubborn, and he couldn't mend his ways. Sage Nyanta was also more stubborn than he appeared. The fact that he put cucumbers in salads was proof. Akatsuki felt as though the only one who'd listen to her suggestions was her liege, Shiroe.

"On your left!"

Akatsuki stopped abruptly, and a violent mass of metal flashed right past the end of her nose.

She'd just barely avoided that side blow, and Soujirou, still watching Akatsuki, evaded it lightly.

Akatsuki stared, admiring the motion, and began to feel strange.

Even now, Soujirou was directing a bone-chilling smile at the murderer and Akatsuki alike. Ordinarily, Akatsuki would have felt enough pressure to make her run straight home.

But she didn't.

There was something here, too, something big that Akatsuki didn't really understand. Soujirou hadn't threatened Akatsuki. He was trying to give her something, and she had grazed it.

Akatsuki felt guilty for not knowing what its true shape was, but, even without knowing, she understood that it was something terribly important.

"Nazuna. Go home ahead of me, please."

"—Understood. We'll await you at the guild hall."

At those words, Akatsuki finally understood that Soujirou had continued to fight a battle he couldn't win against the murderer to protect the girls who'd been rendered helpless. Sensing the barriers that flew at her and Soujirou as a final act of support, Akatsuki felt the others leave. Even as she did so, she and Soujirou began a ferocious attack.

Neither Soujirou's flowing strikes nor the attacks that Akatsuki poured all her special skills into worked against the murderer. They layered on several dozen attacks. The mere fact that they'd managed to last this long against the murderer, with just the two of them, set this battle apart from the man's previous assaults, but of course Akatsuki didn't have the time to register that.

Her strength wasn't enough, but even so, she desperately swung her sword.

She also thought that, as an Adventurer, even if she put herself on the line here, she'd just resurrect in the Temple. What could a cheap life like that change? Even without that, Akatsuki was tiny and weak and slow on the uptake.

Still, she thought Raynesia was doing her best.

Before she knew it, the precious barriers they'd been given as support were gone. Apparently the cold air that blanketed the area wasn't due solely to the winter wind; it was some sort of range attack that radiated from the murderer in front of them. Soujirou had been a direct target for a while now, and his HP was down to about half. There was a limit to how long they could fight this way.

"All right. I'd better give at least a small present to my senior's junior, too."

Soujirou murmured something incomprehensible, then resettled his stance.

Akatsuki had been a kendo girl, and even she thought it was a beautiful middle guard stance: a *seigan* stance, in kendo jargon, with the sword pointing at his opponent's eyes.

"That said, there isn't all that much I can say."

Smoothly, Soujirou stepped out in front of Akatsuki, who was taken aback, and swung his blade. It was a straightforward attack, and on its heels, the murderer's counterstrike cut through space. He'd swung and missed.

"Watch carefully. Listen closely."

This time, the murderer dealt an attack with bone-crushing force. Soujirou intentionally received it, in order to get in an equal blow on his opponent. In the midst of Soujirou's red blood, which froze in midair, the two separated, then closed again.

"Want it badly, and keep thinking about it. Don't give up; keep training."

Akatsuki had leapt out, and she also swung her short sword desperately.

Even though it was something very important, because Akatsuki didn't *understand* its importance, it broke.

That was a terribly bad thing. Sadness filled her chest.

"...It's pitiful, hardly an explanation at all, but... That's everything about the Mysteries."

The murderer spun, with his hips as the focal point. He was a small-scale hurricane.

Not yet, Akatsuki thought. She still didn't understand. She'd touched something, and yet...

She wished hard for just a little longer. It was a feeling of frustrated regret, a feeling Akatsuki didn't normally have.

It was sorrow at parting with "something" that was slipping away from her.

' However, as if to smash those feelings along with her, the roaring, onrushing blade came down.

She felt a longing, as though her fingertips were just about to reach something. However, with an attack that seemed to shatter even that, in the midst of pain they hadn't ever imagined, Akatsuki and Soujirou "died."

▶ 6

The tea party didn't turn into a dress-up tournament every time.

That morning, when they hadn't been blessed with fair weather, the mood in Raynesia's guest room was quiet.

It was safe to say that the atmosphere of the tea party was determined by its members. When Marielle came, it immediately turned bright and lively. When it was only Henrietta, the atmosphere resembled a consultation meeting.

And when it was her and Riezé, the mood was calm and elegant.

Today, apparently, the Crescent Moon League and Roderick Trading Company members wouldn't be coming. Riezé had told Raynesia so, and Raynesia had looked puzzled. She'd welcomed this strategist from

D.D.D., who led a training unit; they'd taken lunch together, then had green tea that was served from a large pot.

Outside the window, the wide, overcast sky threatened rain.

The blond Adventurer who sat on the opposite side of the small reception set gazed through the window into the distance.

She was fairly well acquainted with this female Adventurer, Riezé. The girl was calm and courteous, and she was from the same clan as Krusty-the-menace.

The two of them didn't really converse.

That said, it didn't trouble Raynesia much. Raynesia was the type who generally did care about that sort of thing, and so at first she'd been solicitous and spoken to her about this and that. However, the blond girl had told her clearly that she didn't need to bother, so she'd stopped trying to force a conversation.

Still, it wasn't as though things were uncomfortable, or as if she couldn't talk to her. If they had a good topic, they occasionally had quite long conversations. That was Raynesia's current relationship with the girl named Riezé.

Silence did trouble Raynesia, but she certainly wasn't good at conversation for its own sake. On the contrary, she was aware that she was bad at it. This meant her relationship with Riezé was a pleasant one, as far as she was concerned.

Besides, today, Raynesia wasn't in the mood for that sort of thing either.

A Person of the Earth—and a guard, at that: a being who should have upheld the law in Akiba—had been corrupted and was attacking Adventurers. There had already been several victims. At the thought of her small acquaintance, who'd dashed out toward the town leaving cryptic words behind her, Raynesia's mood grew too painful to bear.

Why did this happen? Why me? The questions never left her mind.

The weather seemed as if it might be trying to exacerbate her depression, and her brow clouded.

"This Tokyo does get quite chilly, doesn't it? I expect this winter will be a cold one."

"Tokyo...?"

The quiet words Riezé had let fall drew Raynesia back to reality.

It was an ancient alv word that meant "eastern paradise." It was said there was a primeval steel plate with the letters "Tokyo" on it in Castle Cinderella, where Raynesia had been born and raised.

"Oh, erm. It's an Adventurer word that indicates the whole area around Maihama, Akiba, and Shibuya," Riezé said.

Hearing that explanation, Raynesia nodded. The statement seemed to be in agreement with her superficial knowledge.

"Was your birthplace warmer than Tokyo, Miss Riezé?"

"It wasn't 'warmer than Tokyo,' it really was Tokyo, but... Yes, I suppose so. Winters weren't this cold. That said, we didn't have much resistance to cold in the first place, so we wore thicker clothes then and stayed shut up in our houses."

...Didn't have much resistance to cold? Stayed shut up in their houses?

Sometimes she abruptly stopped understanding what the Adventurers said.

As Raynesia tilted her head, puzzled, her eyes met Riezé's.

Riezé quietly returned her teacup to the table, then gazed at Raynesia for a little while. Raynesia wasn't sure how to interpret that gaze. Then Riezé began to smile. It was a peaceful, gentle smile, a kind she'd never seen before.

"I was born in a small town in Tokyo."

"Not in Akiba, you mean?"

"That's right. It was a town called Kiyose. Here...it would be the area around Nobidome District, I think. It's the sort of place where you'd expect to find something, but there's nothing."

"But..."

According to Raynesia's memories, Nobidome District was a habitat for water-dwelling monsters. Not only was there no town there, there wasn't a single village.

Raynesia was startled by her own surprise.

"Then you aren't a noble, Miss Riezé?"

She said this because she'd thought Riezé was the child of some aristocratic family, and an influential one at that. All Adventurers were educated to the point where they couldn't be considered commoners. Even among them, Riezé and Henrietta were nobles whose grace and elegance shone through in their interactions with others. It wasn't a matter of superficial etiquette. She thought they were true nobles who'd been raised in an environment where they'd been able to be considerate of others since birth.

It wouldn't have mattered if they weren't, and Raynesia had no intention of discriminating because they were commoners or Adventurers. When she thought about why she'd been startled, that was the answer she reached.

"No, I'm not. I was born into a small, ordinary family, raised as an ordinary child, and sent to an ordinary school."

"……"

"You have schools here as well, correct? They're places where children gather and are made to learn. In the place where I was born, all the children in the area are sent to one school or another. It's mandatory."

She didn't know anything about Riezé.

She didn't know about Akatsuki either, or Henrietta, or Marielle, or Serara, or Nazuna, or Mikakage, or Ranya, or Azukiko.

…Or about Krusty.

In other words, she really knew nothing about the Adventurers.

She'd been made to see this over and over, and yet here it was, happening again. Raynesia felt shame and despair over her own ignorance.

"Let's see… When I was a child, I think I was quite the tomboy. Children's anime… You don't have that here, do you? Fairy tales, I suppose it would be. I adored those, and I dashed around with the boys. That said, I graduated from that sort of thing when I turned ten… After that, let's see… I overreached myself when I tried to become a lady, failed, and was laughed at by those around me. I liked studying, and I was good at it. If I did it, people praised me, so I got good at it. Of course, it didn't take long for that to become only expected, and before long, people stopped praising me…"

"Oh…"

This was something Raynesia knew as well.

She'd been good at smiling and being well-behaved. Sitting so that she looked precociously mature and wise hadn't been difficult for her. She'd done it because she liked being praised. Raynesia had loved her father, mother, and grandparents—her family.

It had become second nature by now, and it was ingrained to the point where she couldn't handle things any other way, but originally, she'd wanted the people who were important to her to smile. She'd wanted them to be happy.

"I was an honor student at school because adults liked me and because I was particularly good at studying. It wasn't that I worked desperately at that; I was simply born that way. The town where I was born had several large hospitals, and there were lots of elderly people. As a result, I was probably more conscious of adults' eyes than I was of children's... In that sense, I'm glad I came here and joined D.D.D. I'd grown conceited, and there are people here who broke me. There are people who taught me, after I'd fallen apart, that it didn't have to mean the end of me. Lots of—"

"I—!"

Raynesia stopped her; her tone was firm.

She couldn't hear this.

She wasn't qualified to hear it.

She'd thought she was a strong woman. Raynesia was embarrassed at having thought Riezé was of noble blood and that she'd been an Adventurer by birth. In the end, didn't that simply mean she hadn't even tried to understand her?

Once she realized this, the world she knew seemed very petty and narrow.

It wasn't that she didn't know about the world because she'd been raised as a princess of Maihama. Raynesia's world was small because she hadn't tried to see the things that were right beside her.

You're working hard, Raynesia.

She finally understood the meaning of the words that had been spoken to her.

They'd meant, "I was paying attention."

Raynesia had been such a child that she hadn't even understood that that was what was being said.

"I was born in the city of Maihama. Since I am a princess, technically, I was raised by a nurse from the time I was small... I don't know many of the games others play. I think I was probably wealthy and happy. I had pretty clothes and plenty of food. I never felt that my life was in danger..."

Raynesia began to speak in a small voice.

"When it came to my studies, there were several teachers in the castle. I think the education I received was above average for a Person of the Earth, but from your perspective, I'm not sure how proud of it I can be…"

Raynesia put the words together, unsure of what she should tell her, or how.

It was a childish ceremony, going on clumsily, just as Riezé had shown her.

"I think I also acted more demure than I really was because I wanted my family to praise me. I…I'm really very lazy. I'd like to spend every day napping and sunbathing, and I don't understand even half of the complicated conversations I hear. When I'm bored, I bite back yawns."

Riezé was thoughtful, and confessing this to her took quite a lot of courage.

However, although Raynesia watched Riezé for reactions, she didn't consider breaking off. After all, that swallow-like girl had probably flown beyond this point.

"I came to this town because I thought I could escape tiresome formalities that way. Even now, I'm bad at business discussions and shouldering responsibility. When I come face-to-face with things I don't understand, it makes me want to cry. I think eating little rice balls and spacing out suits me best. However, I'm… In short, I am a princess, so—I can't do that, and I also think I shouldn't. Truthfully, I don't even know whether that's really the case, but…"

The words wouldn't come out well, and Raynesia began to feel resentful.

Krusty would probably have picked up that feeling for her.

However, that probably wouldn't have been okay.

There was something between her and this blond girl, and the swallow-like girl, that she wouldn't be able to create or connect that way.

She felt as though she'd heard Elissa's admonishing chuckle. Instantly, Raynesia's temper flared, and she continued rather violently, as though wringing the words out.

"I think there's something terribly important somewhere, and because it's important, I have to treat it as though it's important. And so I, um, I think I have to stay a princess. —Only I never have enough strength, so…"

"Yes?"

"I'd like to do things properly with you, too, Riezé. Not only with you, but with Akatsuki as well. And with Marielle. If I don't, I don't think I'll be qualified to be your friend, or to live in Akiba…or to be arrogant enough to think of protecting anything."

"'Do things properly,' was it?"

Riezé laughed a little at the words, but hiding her embarrassed tone with a composed expression, she granted Raynesia's wish for her.

"You're right. This sort of thing is… Well, once one's in high school, it's a little embarrassing. Since we're dealing with each other straight on, you see… In that case, first, a little advice: 'Do things properly' is a difficult way to put it. Too difficult. Let's be friends, Raynesia. I am an Adventurer, but if you don't mind that…"

It was a single fragment of something important, handed to the slacker princess from an entirely unexpected source.

CHAPTER.
4

MARE TRANQUILLIT

-190

-180

-170

-160

-150

▶ AGE: **78**

▶ RACE: **HUMAN**

▶ CLASS: **DRUID**

▶ HP: **7502**

▶ MP: **7363**

▶ ITEM 1:

[SALAMANDER POT HOLDERS]

A PAIR OF COOKING MITTS, A PRODUCTION-CLASS ITEM THAT USES PLENTY OF SALAMANDER SCALES. IMPROVES THE QUALITY AND SUCCESS RATE OF COOKING THAT USES POTS. IT HAS ENDURANCE REGARDING FIRE ATTRIBUTES AND THEIR ACCOMPANYING NEGATIVE STATUS EFFECTS, AND IT'S USED OFTEN IN BOTH COOKING AND COMBAT.

▶ ITEM 2:

[BELDAN HAND-OPERATED KITCHEN TOOL]

A MAGIC KITCHEN KNIFE SHE FOUND IN A CERTAIN DUNGEON. DURING USE, FOUR WIND-BLADES APPEAR AT THE TIP AND SPIN, TURNING IT INTO A HARDWORKING, ALL-PURPOSE KITCHEN TOOL (FOOD PROCESSOR) THAT SLICES, SHREDS, GRATES, WHIPS, AND MIXES.

▶ ITEM 3:

[ANGEL MACARON]

A BERET THAT LOOKS JUST LIKE A MACARON. IT'S A REWARD IN THE "DREAM-COLORED PASTRY CHEF" QUEST, IN WHICH YOU HAVE TO DELIVER A VAST QUANTITY OF HIGH-QUALITY SWEETS. IT ADDS A QUALITY BONUS TO CANDY PRODUCTION. SHE LIKES THIS EQUIP ITEM SO MUCH THAT SHE HAS HER ALRAUNE ASSISTANT WEAR A REPLICA.

\<Thief Tools\>
Obviously meant for
criminal use. In Akiba,
these are sold to
Robin Hood types.

► 1

Shoving her back hard, the line began to move.

Akatsuki had been thinking, but the waves of people pushed her into motion, hurried her on. Whatever she'd been thinking about had vanished. Feeling depressed, the petite young woman walked briskly across an enormous intersection.

On both sides of Akatsuki, behind her and in front of her, tall, black shadows undulated, moving forward. She could hear car horns at point-blank range. They were probably being sounded in irritation by commercial trucks that had shoved their muzzles into the intersection and were now unable to budge. The metallic, shrill sounds echoed, but nobody paid any attention to them.

Was she the only one who shrank into herself, feeling as if she'd been scolded, each time that sound blared out? She wished somebody would do something about it quickly, but in her experience, it had never been resolved, not even once. The human walls that flowed around her were overwhelming. Salarymen. Businesswomen. Students. People of all ages and occupations walked on, mechanically.

Some people were talking loudly. They held their cell phones right up to their lips, conducting business negotiations in yells. Akatsuki ducked her head, frightened of the voices that shouted at their subordinates. Cordial voices, promising dates. Akatsuki knew the women speaking into their cell phones in coaxing voices weren't smiling at all.

That was right: She only "knew" it. She couldn't see the expressions of the people around her. In a crowd like this, it was nearly impossible for Akatsuki to see anyone else's face. There was too little space, and even if she looked up, she couldn't see well.

She only kept walking as if prodded, hurrying, feeling an irritated melancholy, feeling afraid without knowing why.

The town was overflowing with jagged noise. The sound of an emergency vehicle siren, echoing in the distance. Car horns. Exhaust noises, like bad-tempered beasts. The sound of everyone talking away on their cell phones, en masse, rolled in the background like the ocean. Neon lights and music played at all sorts of tempos were mixed in, and the whole mess was plastered over everything like a pizza sauce whose flavor was unidentifiable.

As Akatsuki walked, looking down, she couldn't understand the music that was playing or the content of the conversations. They only ran together, pressuring her ears; sometimes she almost caught a phrase or a scrap of conversation that surfaced, but the avalanche of information washed it away. Yes, this was a violent flood. Akatsuki wasn't drowning, but that was only because she'd learned how to close her mouth, ears, and eyes. She'd been swallowed by the muddy torrent and was being swept along, and in that sense, she wasn't much different from someone who was drowning.

The waves of people that had swallowed Akatsuki passed under the elevated tracks and climbed the sloping road within the urban canyon. Where was this enormous crowd going? Layered structures of glass and concrete bristled as if to pierce the sky, completely burying the ground, and the people went in and out of them. This oppressive state, as if a grotesque giant were chewing and excreting at the same time, was nearly the entirety of the town. Akatsuki and the others traveled in order to be swallowed by buildings, and after being spit out by those buildings, they wandered through this compressed town to be swallowed by different buildings.

The evergreen shrubs caked with red-brown soot were dingy things. They were insignificant plants that only existed to be used as a sort of excuse, an alibi: "This building belongs to a highly-conscious corporation that has taken care to create an abundant natural environment."

Artificial was really the only word for them. Although they weren't quite trampled, they were pressured by the human wave—the one that was currently pushing Akatsuki along—8,760 hours per year, and they drooped, unable even to keep up appearances.

Akatsuki only glanced at them and kept walking. For all the residents of this city, not falling behind the pace of the surrounding black crowd was a survival strategy. Breaking step was nearly synonymous with dropping out.

Asphalt streamed past Akatsuki's eyes. She was walking with her head down, and the asphalt, struck by a great variety of shoes, was the main element in her field of vision. Even though they should have been washed away by the previous night's rain, broken convenience store chopsticks, unidentifiable flyers, plastic bags, cling wrap that had once been silver, key chains that had soaked up muddy water and would no longer be retrieved by anyone, and many other things appeared on the dirty, exhausted road. These were things she was seeing for the first time, of course, and there was no point in really noticing them; they were trampled by the crowd, flowing away into the past as far as the moving Akatsuki was concerned. Still, at the same time, they were unique, and they appeared on the road again and again.

Naturally, any single plastic bag had probably held a product purchased at a store somewhere, but when they appeared on the road as garbage, their individuality was long gone. Now, in every sense, there was no difference between the plastic bag that was stepped on by the crowd and mercilessly shredded and the bag that appeared five minutes later...and this was the same for everyone. Probably for Akatsuki as well.

Time seemed to pass at both a furious pace and as slowly as a snail. The advertising music that was interjected at irregular intervals like sudden, heavy rain sounded like an explosion, and it chopped up Akatsuki's time in ways that had nothing to do with her feelings. It became a pacemaker, controlling Akatsuki's daily life. However, it wasn't that she was too busy to think. On the other hand, in the midst of her thinly sliced time, there was no space for studying or playing, so she inevitably did the things that could be done in small increments.

For the people around her, this seemed to mean talking on their cell phones in loud voices or listlessly buying game items on their smartphones. For Akatsuki, who had no interest in these things, her minced time was a depressing prison of self-awareness. She had to grit her teeth to endure that idleness. The emotion that resembled anger had already cooled completely, decaying into self-loathing. Could she even be called human when she lived a life that was broken down into minimal units like this? Akatsuki thought it was like being livestock. As proof, she had no way to escape this place.

The line stopped, all at once. A traffic signal. It blinked a few times, then turned red, letting traffic that ran at right angles to it move as it did so. The herd of cars rushed by as if pursued by a hunter, setting up a harsh din as it passed in front of Akatsuki. Akatsuki knew that here, in the heart of the city, the distance to the next signal wasn't even fifty meters. Even if that one was green, these cars would probably stop again at the next one, or the one after that. Even though it was such a short distance, the cars accelerated as though they couldn't stand it, spraying fumes around. She couldn't understand what they meant by it. Akatsuki couldn't drive, and possibly it was some secret she didn't know.

The cars charged down the road as though they loathed blank space. As Akatsuki gazed at them without really seeing them, she sneezed. She felt as if she'd been doing this frequently since she began commuting through this town, and she rubbed her nose. A faint regret remained after she'd rubbed it. It wasn't a ladylike gesture, and she was constantly thinking she should stop, but she couldn't seem to correct it. Because of the acrid, acidic car exhaust, Akatsuki's nose was always sneezing.

Akatsuki began walking briskly, moving to the front of the human wave. Even if she had begun to "walk," her steps were short, so it was really closer to a trot.

Abruptly, a doubt welled up inside her: Where was she going? If she was putting herself through this sort of pain to get there, she must have a destination. Not only that, but she was heading there on some sort of schedule, for a meeting or an appointed time. That's right; she'd been heading to—to school. She thought it had been some sort of learning facility. Probably university. However, for some reason, it had vanished from inside of her.

Despair assailed her first, faster than confusion. She felt as if she'd be crushed by a sense of uneasiness with no outlet, here in this town that was like a conveyor belt line. Laughter. Electronic parade noises of the sort that stirred up a fondness for gambling. The scream of car brakes. The echoing rumble of the Yamanote Line going by. Her throat hurt as though there was a lump in it, and her vision blurred. A desire to stop and stand still flooded her, but Akatsuki desperately kept moving, so as not to trouble the people around her. She crossed at a blinking signal, passed by the front of a convenience store, turned the corner at a bank, moving onward, onward, in the midst of a familiar crowd. Going somewhere that wasn't here. Maybe none of the people here had anywhere to go, just like that plastic bag. Not even the replaceable Akatsuki. However, to Akatsuki, she was the only Akatsuki there was, and she needed proof that this was true... Even if that proof didn't exist.

Before she knew it, Akatsuki was running up concrete stairs, taking them two at a time. The dreary emergency stairwell reminded her of the desolate view at a housing development somewhere. It was an extraordinarily familiar view, she knew on sight, but it wasn't distinctive, and so she didn't really know where it was. What was important was that she was running up the stairs, and that there was nothing the least bit thrilling about it: It was an escape, nothing more.

She wasn't clear on what she was running from, but this was because she knew that the moment she specifically imagined it, it would catch her. If she had to say, it was that plastic bag. Akatsuki felt like a plastic bag—trampled by the crowd, clinging as if it were wet, nearly torn—was plastered to her back. Or, no—to the soles of the feet as they struck the stairs, making a rustling noise. But she couldn't hear it, even if she strained her ears. It wasn't really plastered to her; that was a mistake. However, for some reason, Akatsuki kept running, unable even to look at her feet. An unpleasant sense of urgency was rubbing her spine like cold needles.

It felt as though there wasn't much oxygen; she couldn't get enough air, and she was out of breath. She thought this was wrong, but since she didn't know what the right answer was, she couldn't prove it. She ran up the concrete stairs, leapt out onto a landing, doubled back, leaning as though to shake off the inertia, and continued climbing the stairs. The repetition had the absurdity of wasted effort about it, like a rat running in an exercise wheel. Akatsuki fled desperately, spurred on by the sound of concrete excavation echoing from somewhere. It was almost as if she couldn't stand the concrete stairway itself. Still, in order to escape, she had to run up it. How far would she have to go to reach the end of that chain?

Akatsuki didn't know how many dozens—or possibly hundreds—of landings she'd passed, but when she reached the next one, she realized it wasn't a landing at all. Her feet were buried in a creamy gray substance; she lost her footing and fell, dragging the exhaust-stained crowd with her. Car horns. The strident parade. Voices she couldn't understand. As she fell endlessly through screams and violent wind, Akatsuki was sure she saw that plastic bag again.

▶ 2

It was a white beach.

A perfectly clear sky stretched on and on.

A cerulean infinity that seemed to have been sketched lightly in watercolors was full of rippling wavelets.

Akatsuki walked along that shore by herself.

She was alone in that vast space, which was deserted in the way only a winter beach can be.

She felt awed by the sand that crumbled, crisply and easily.

When she looked down, her small toes took another step.

She made one more footprint in the pure, unspoiled whiteness.

Far, far away, she saw a small flying shadow. Was it a seabird?

Crunch, crunch.

All she heard were those quiet footsteps and the sound of the cerulean surf as it lapped the beach.

Hugging her coat around her against the chill, Akatsuki walked.

Slowly, without being rushed by anything.

*   *   *

When she raised her head, the surface of the water sparkled with irregular reflections.

The winter light was simply bright; it held no heat.

Her small footprints and their tiny sound continued across the sandy beach in a chain.

Every time her bare feet touched cerulean, particles of light burst and vanished.

Akatsuki didn't know where this was, but the irritability from a moment before was gone.

This wasn't her destination, but she thought it was a safe place.

Strolling along the quiet beach was a pleasant, calming experience.

How long had she walked?

She approached the water's edge and touched the blue with her bare toes, then pirouetted away.

She dragged her footprints out like a honeybee's dance.

Because she was all alone, Akatsuki did these things seriously.

However, it *was* a little funny, and she gave a tiny smile.

Akatsuki's loyal footprints adored her, following her everywhere.

Even that was fun, like a journal being written.

She had to strain her eyes in order to see into the distance, but she saw a human figure.

It was a tall one, and it was rocking and gazing at the sea as if it was mildly troubled.

Startled by how light her body was, Akatsuki realized belatedly that she'd broken into a run.

She covered what had seemed to be a long distance in so few steps that it surprised her; she slowed her pace.

She wasn't the type to slam into him bodily and hug him.

However, even so, drawn by feelings of longing, she looked up at the man.

Noticing Akatsuki, Shiroe broke into a smile.

Shiroe normally wore an obstinate expression, and whenever Akatsuki saw him smile like that, it made her feel really satisfied.

As if embarrassed, dazzled, awkward...

After Shiroe narrowed his eyes in a smile, he hesitated a bit. Then he turned to Akatsuki, asked her a question with his eyes, and started to walk down the beach.

Akatsuki began to walk with him, as though chasing the tail of his coat.

Shiroe seemed to be walking slowly on purpose.

Akatsuki, who walked wordlessly beside him, did the same.

There was an elegance about the beach, where the only sounds came from the gentle movement of the atmosphere and the waves.

They were both hesitant to break that stillness.

My liege's hands are big.

She thought this as she saw him scratch his head two or three times, then adjust his glasses.

She watched the hand go into the pocket of his white coat, then quickened her steps.

Or, no, would slower be better?

If she fell behind a little, it might give her an excuse to catch the tail of that coat.

As she thought that, Akatsuki's mouth fell into a stubborn line.

The expression she was making wasn't the least bit cross.

To hide her face, Akatsuki twirled at the water's edge.

Her camel-brown coat flared out, and she was sure she was smiling.

Shiroe turned back and waited for her for a little while.

The two of them began walking again, crunching across the sandy beach, which might have been made of spun sugar. They could feel the fragile sand changing shape under their feet. The wind that stroked their cheeks was rather cold, but now it didn't bother them at all. There was a steady warmth in the center of their bodies.

To Akatsuki, everything was novel and fun. Shiroe's big shoes bit into the sand with a crunch. His footprints were deeper than hers; that was fun, too. A mildly strong wind blew through every so often, setting Shiroe's coattail fluttering, and she thought it was cute.

Shiroe's pockets looked five times bigger than Akatsuki's own, and she thought she'd like to stick a hand into one of them, but of course she couldn't. Instead she turned back, saw the way Shiroe's footprints and her own stretched across the beach, and was satisfied.

*   *   *

Something cool brushed Akatsuki's small nose, and her eyes went round.

White snow fluttered down silently, scattering.

It didn't bring the slightest hint of coldness with it, and when she touched it with her fingertip, it vanished, delicately.

Snow had begun to fall.

When Akatsuki looked up to tell Shiroe about it, he nodded, smiling calmly, and she realized that no report was necessary.

Shiroe had pulled the hood of her duffel coat up for her, and she put it over her head and continued walking.

She didn't feel tired, but she thought they'd come quite a long distance.

The turquoise sky grew even clearer, turning a deep indigo, and jewel-like lights appeared in the heavens.

The surface of the water reflected the lights, making everything transparent. It accepted the snow, swaying and pale.

"I didn't think it would be such a quiet place."

As Shiroe murmured, he stopped walking.

Before they were aware of it, they'd reached a small inlet.

"Mm," Akatsuki replied in agreement.

She'd really wanted to respond with something cleverer or more ladylike, but she hadn't been able to think of anything. Still, it didn't seem to have made Shiroe cross. He was gazing at the sea, where night had fallen.

Toom.

Toom.

She thought she heard a sound, as though someone had softly struck a great crystal.

It was as if a distant signal was echoing from beyond the enormous sea.

Suddenly, a new awareness came into being in the back of Akatsuki's mind, but it dispersed the moment she noticed it.

Something inside Akatsuki that was not Akatsuki, something transparent, had blown through and gone.

Even though it hadn't been her, its loss colored Akatsuki's emotions with sorrow.

When a big hand touched her shoulder gently as though to encourage her, Akatsuki realized that Shiroe had felt the same thing. His expression wasn't grim, but it was stern.

Shiroe had taken a box cutter out from somewhere; he lightly ratcheted the blade up, then, awkwardly, cut off a bit of his bangs. The black hair had a mysterious sandy luster to it, and there wasn't enough of it to really call it a "tuft."

Taking the box cutter from Shiroe, Akatsuki cut a little bit off the tip of her ponytail. She had no idea why they were doing this, but she did know it was necessary.

The two of them tossed the hair into the cerulean ocean that moistened the ground at their feet.

Somewhere, as if in acceptance, the crystal sounded, and the snow that held no chill fluttered and danced.

At that, finally, Akatsuki understood that these pale fragments were everyone's memories.

Death doesn't steal people's memories, she thought. *We offer our memories here for a chance to return.* Even if they didn't remember it, she realized, they stood up again because they wanted to.

"Amazing."

The words Shiroe had let fall expressed Akatsuki's feelings exactly.

Just how many thoughts were in the snow that drifted down?

How many people had renewed their resolutions on this shore?

The vast number and weight made Akatsuki feel dizzy.

She was also certain, without reason, that this wasn't a legitimate, guaranteed right, but unbelievably precious good fortune.

…As was the fact that Shiroe was beside her.

"You fell, Akatsuki?"

At Shiroe's words, Akatsuki brooded for a little while, then nodded.

That was right.

She'd died.

By the murderer's blade.

That was all right.

Not because she'd be able to revive in the Temple, although that was all right as well. Akatsuki had fought because she wanted to, and she'd fallen. She had no regrets about that.

However, the awareness that she had died woke Akatsuki's memories. They were memories of dashing out of Raynesia's mansion and racing through the sky, and of the enormous "something" Soujirou had pointed out to her. Of the intent profile of the Kannagi who'd protected him, and of the showy yet serious "something" that Riezé, and Henrietta, and the other women who'd gathered for the tea parties had...

—And that was all.

What is that "something"?

Akatsuki realized that "something" was the only word she had for it. She'd gone through that battle, but she hadn't made any progress at all.

She felt frustrated and guilty over the things she didn't understand, and she couldn't do anything but cry.

She'd touched that important "something." She finally realized that. However, she had absolutely no idea what it was, or what she should do. Even though she knew how valuable and important it was, she hadn't been able to put it to use. Even though it had been a present...

She wanted to explain it to Shiroe.

She wanted to tell him she'd found something really pretty, something wonderful.

Something important had been there. She couldn't be certain, but she thought it was something that had been held out to her.

But she couldn't explain it in specific terms. The words weren't there. The choking regret made Akatsuki cry openly, like a child.

She even felt as though the fact that she couldn't tell him would hurt something important, and she couldn't stand it. She was terrified that the value of that gift might be dulled, all because she was worthless.

Something had definitely been there, and yet.

In Raynesia's eyes.

In Soujirou's invincible smile.

Dying hadn't been a mistake. Akatsuki's mistake had been in failing to grasp *it*, even though she'd brushed it with her fingertips.

...No. Akatsuki thought it might have been right in front of her from the very beginning. In that case, in not having been able to find *it*, she'd piled up countless mistakes. Without having anyone tell her so, Akatsuki was convinced that this was true.

Tears spilled over again at her worthlessness. This was why she'd died without being able to do anything.

"I see. That makes two of us, then. I died."

When Shiroe placed a hand on her head and Akatsuki looked up, he was smiling a troubled, gentle smile. Akatsuki knew he was worrying about her. His reserved, self-deprecating smile was the expression Akatsuki's guild master wore when he spoke to her.

"You, too, my liege?"

"Mm-hmm."

After that, there was silence.

Shiroe moved the hand he'd set on Akatsuki's head as if he was perplexed; Akatsuki thought it was probably because he wanted to say something but couldn't find the words. Shiroe was a bit clumsy that way. Even though Akatsuki didn't mind at all, he was probably trying to be considerate.

"I messed up. My predictions were too naïve. —I didn't believe completely."

They were words of caution directed at himself, more than a complaint.

"I don't understand."

As a result, when Akatsuki responded, she was careful not to complain, either.

"It's funny. I never thought I'd get to meet you here, Akatsuki."

The continuation of the whispered answer came after countless snowflakes had fallen.

When she thought about what Shiroe's words meant, Akatsuki was startled.

He was right: It was very strange. She hadn't seen Shiroe in quite a while now.

Come to think of it, she'd wanted to see him.

She'd really wanted to see Shiroe.

She'd wanted him to pat her head.

She remembered that she'd wanted him to praise her, too.

That alone was enough to make this chance meeting an odd one.

To think they'd be able to meet in a place like this.

Up until just now, she hadn't thought about that, either.

The strangeness of having encountered Shiroe.

Even as Akatsuki didn't understand, she felt that this was not an ordinary place. She was grateful for this miraculous coincidence.

"Yes, my liege. It's funny."

She remembered the pure white sands they'd walked across, and the cerulean sea.

In the midst of a landscape so bright it seemed bleached, Shiroe turned toward her.

When she ran to him and looked up, a big hand stroked her forehead.

It was just a coincidence.

Still, that coincidence blessed Akatsuki.

She wanted nothing else.

No doubt the things Akatsuki hadn't reached were still asleep, still right where they'd been when she'd touched them.

Not only that, but there must be countless things like them. In the shadows, where Akatsuki hadn't seen them. In smiles she'd overlooked until now, because she hadn't tried to find them there.

She'd arrogantly thought that the good fortune she'd acquired was only natural. She'd assumed that good fortune she hadn't obtained didn't exist. Even though it was likely that good luck and encounters and help were waiting all over the world for Akatsuki to find them.

"…And so I'll try one more time," Akatsuki said.

"I'll try again, too, I suppose—Everyone taught me."

Akatsuki caught Shiroe's coat, gripping it hard.

She had a premonition, like the sensation of the fragile sand crumbling under her feet, that this memory wouldn't stay with her.

Because of that, even as she thought she might leave wrinkles in the coat, she squeezed it tightly, tightly.

She and Shiroe would probably be separated again. That was why she wanted to squeeze the coat. However, her wish was in vain: The endless sand dunes, like powdery snow, were growing brighter.

The faint sound of the receding tide held the memory Akatsuki had given it.

The ultramarine sky was growing more jumbled, and she fell into it.

▶ 3

It's all right.

Slowly, smiling at the sensation that lingered in the palm of her hand, Akatsuki let her consciousness surface.

It's all right.

Her palm still held the texture of slightly rough cloth.

It's all right.

However, when she opened her eyes slightly, Akatsuki saw her own small hand, right in front of her face, clenched as if it was holding something.

Akatsuki knew her memories were sifting away, coming undone. As she lay on a hard bier, with tears trickling down her cheeks, she was losing the memory of the dream she'd held inside just a moment ago.

As if to shake off the loneliness and the feeling of guilt that she seemed to have left behind in her shallow sleep, Akatsuki turned her stiff palm into a fist and wiped away her tears.

She got up, then sat on the edge of the plain marble slab.

For some reason, she had the feeling she'd passed through a very strange place.

It had been quiet, lonely, gentle, and transparent.

Akatsuki had traveled there; encountered; realized; and then gotten back on her feet.

She felt as if she'd had some sort of important conversation. If possible, she would have liked to bring it back with her.

Even now, there was a sensation in the palm of her hand. Probably from…cloth she'd gripped. Along with a faint warmth, the sensation was fading rapidly. Akatsuki tried to stop the evaporation of memories that always accompanied dreams, but she knew it was wasted effort.

The sound of the crystal bell was growing fainter.

However, she'd managed to bring back one important thing from that place.

The most important thing.

*   *   *

Akatsuki checked herself over, confirming that none of her equipment had been lost.

She got down from the bier and tried moving, carefully.

It was the first time she'd died since the Catastrophe.

From common sense in *Elder Tales*, and also from rumors following the Catastrophe, Akatsuki knew that resurrection was accompanied by the loss of a certain amount of experience points and memories. She wasn't able to identify any lost memories right away.

She remembered Log Horizon, and Shiroe, and the others. In a general way, none of her memories from the old world—her family and school, her childhood memories—seemed to be missing, either. If she checked carefully, she might find holes, but it would probably take some time.

The lost experience points didn't seem to have left her feeling all that strange physically, either. Since the Catastrophe, people said a loss of experience points—even if it wasn't enough to lower your level—left you feeling fatigued. However, it was hard for Akatsuki to determine whether what she felt now was from losing experience points, or from having gotten stiff from sleeping on marble. It was no worse than that, in other words.

When she took another look around, she saw that she was in the Temple.

The white marble room held several such platforms, and the walls were adorned with unobtrusive carvings.

This was Akiba's Temple. Although she hadn't done it all that often, she'd resurrected in these surroundings when this was a game. Akatsuki began to walk, adjusting the position of her short sword as she went.

There were a lot of things she needed to do.

When she glanced up at the sky from the corridor, the winter sun had risen beyond the clouds.

From the angle, it seemed to be past noon. It had been the middle of the night when she'd begun fighting; had it taken her half a day to resurrect? No, that probably wasn't it. It was likely that, as she'd resurrected, the thread of her tension had snapped and she'd fallen asleep. In that case, she thought, it made sense that she ached all over.

Akatsuki made her way through the Temple zone, which was larger than it looked.

There were things she needed to do.

There were things she absolutely *had* to do.

She couldn't give up just because she'd lost once. Akatsuki had realized just how negligent she'd been up until now. She'd thought she'd been fighting with her entire self. She'd tried to believe she was more desperate than anyone else, but that had been fraud, a mere excuse. There had been lots of things she could have done. Akatsuki had been avoiding the things she really had to do. She'd worked desperately at only the things she *liked* doing, and had tried to convince herself that that was *effort*.

Akatsuki advanced resolutely through the chapel, which was illuminated by stained glass.

Once she descended the staircase, which looked wide to her, she should have been in Akiba in no time.

However, the sight that waited there for Akatsuki was something she hadn't expected.

"Are you all right? You aren't still injured anywhere, are you?"

Akatsuki was boggled: She'd been careless, and so she'd been easily pulled into a hug. "How *sweet!*" Henrietta, melting over the way Akatsuki looked, swung her around, nuzzling her with her cheek. Being able to sweep a girl up that easily—even if she was a small girl—was due to Adventurer strength, but Henrietta didn't seem to have realized this.

"We thought you'd be waking up soon."

Riezé spoke to her; she'd been leaning against the railing on the stone slope. Behind her, she saw Raynesia, bundled up in fluffy clothes and hanging her head apologetically. Behind the princess stood a woman with fox ears, arms folded, smiling a fearless smile. It was the West Wind Brigade Kannagi she'd seen during that late-night battle.

"……"

Akatsuki's lips tightened.

She knew her face was growing darker and grimmer.

It wasn't that she disliked everyone.

She was reaping what she'd sown. Up until now, she hadn't made any friends of her own age and gender, and so she didn't really know how to talk to them. That was all.

Still, she knew she had to do it. That was the one thing Akatsuki had managed to bring back from her lost dream. And so, she squeezed Henrietta's hands, which were over her own stomach, holding her up.

She looked at Henrietta, who'd closed her mouth as if she were startled. At Riezé. At the fox-eared woman. And, most of all, at Raynesia, whose expression seemed troubled.

Once lowered to the ground, Akatsuki simply bowed her head.

"I know this is an impudent request, but I want to ask you for help. Would you teach me about the Mysteries? I want to capture that murderer."

She saw the fox-eared woman startle, and she knew Henrietta, behind her, had gasped. Raynesia's face was sorrowful.

"Master Soujirou was able to use a Mystery, wasn't he, Nazuna?"

Nazuna—the fox-eared woman, a mature-looking beauty—responded to Riezé's questions. "Yeah. That's right."

"But, even so, it wasn't enough."

"Right."

Riezé shifted the conversation back to Akatsuki. "And you want a Mystery, even so. Why?"

Akatsuki bit her lip.

She hadn't managed to explain it well. They'd probably thought she was making a selfish request just because she wanted a Mystery. Regret filled her heart, but she hadn't been able to think of any other way to put it.

"Akatsuki."

However, just then, her eyes met Riezé's.

The girl, who was probably about the same age as her, was gazing at Akatuski with a cool expression.

She was standing firmly as part of a guild so enormous Akatsuki couldn't even imagine it. The woman called Nazuna, and Raynesia, and even Henrietta were all connected to people, going above and beyond simply carrying out their own roles, and they all found the places where they belonged.

Akatsuki remembered her resolution. If she backed down here, things would be just the same as before. Just the same as when she'd given it everything she had and failed, yet consoled herself with the thought that she'd done the best she could. Even so, Akatsuki knew that, in life, there were matches you wanted to win no matter what, and battles you didn't want to lose. There were walls you wanted to get over, no matter who you had to beg or how pathetically you had to plead.

"I want to end that murderer."

Akatsuki appealed desperately. However, sadly, her mouth wouldn't work well for her.

"It isn't just the Mysteries. If there's a way to stop him, no matter what it is, I want you to tell me. Will you let me depend on you?"

"Do you think you can win?"

The blunt question had come from Nazuna. The West Wind Brigade healer who'd supported Soujirou to the very end. A Kannagi with long black hair and traditional Japanese clothes, which she wore carelessly. Akatsuki answered the question almost without plan.

"I don't know. But, even if I win, even if I defeat him, it won't end. If I don't do whatever needs to happen to end it, it won't end...I don't think. We have to try to end it."

Akatsuki went on desperately, trying to shake off the impatience of being unable to communicate.

She resented her own clumsiness.

"Besides, my liege could do it. Probably... So I have to."

Questioning looks pierced Akatsuki.

...Over her words, she thought, *Shiroe could do it.*

Even though she'd already made up her mind, Akatsuki's words accumulated slowly.

"...My liege...isn't here. Not in Akiba."

This was the secret Akatsuki and Log Horizon had been keeping.

Shiroe wasn't here. Since D.D.D. had gone away, they claimed he was buried under a vast amount of work in order to protect the Round Table Council. But that had been a lie. Shiroe had left, probably to do something only he could do. Akatsuki didn't know what that was. She didn't know, but she'd been asked to keep an eye on things while he was away.

And so she had to protect the town from this disaster, which Shiroe would have been able to handle.

She'd promised.

"Nazuna asked whether you could do it."

At Riezé's words, Akatsuki flinched, frightened.

She couldn't make that promise.

She couldn't guarantee it.

She didn't want them to ask her to.

"…I can't do it alone. That's why I want your help. Please, help me."

That was a pain that was hard for Akatsuki to bear. Admitting that she was a child, admitting that she was helpless, was as painful as if she were being physically cut. A feeling like a curse began to take root in her: Was that really all the strength this little body could hold?

Still, before Akatsuki's very eyes, Shiroe had made the same request.

Henrietta's arms tightened around her in a hug, and Akatsuki was startled by their warmth. Seeing her, Nazuna gave a languid smile, as though to say she'd been surprised into giving up the offensive.

"I'd been thinking something like this was going to come up, ever since Souji said he was pulling out. Everyone at Shiroe's place is stubborn. Birds of a feather flocking together, I guess."

"I'd call that a half-passing grade, I suppose. By training unit standards, you need to drill repeatedly. At present, D.D.D. has confirmed eight Mysteries, and is in the process of examining them in detail. Milord has already given his permission. He said to pass them along to you, Akatsuki," the blond-haired girl informed her, calmly.

"I also have something I must do."

Still silent, her face pale, Raynesia nodded.

"…Honestly. To think I came all the way to Theldesia to be a middle schooler again…"

With Riezé's little sigh as the signal, a small, modest subjugation unit was formed.

However, to Akatsuki, it was a very big step.

▶ 4

Mikakage nibbled her onigiri.

These box lunches, delivered by Onigiri Shop Enmusubi, were an incredibly popular meal at RoderLab. They'd never gathered proper statistics, but there was a general rumor that over half the lunches in the guild were supplied by the place.

Behind Mikakage, a friendly People of the Earth girl wearing a triangular kerchief was passing out onigiri with order tags stuck to them, one at a time. Her glossy black hair was cut in an even bob just above her shoulders, and her ever-changing expression was charming. She thought the girl's name was Kaede.

Onigiri Shop Enmusubi was run by approximately twenty People of the Earth, and of them, about five cute girls were treated as idols. They were particularly popular at RoderLab; there was even a fan club. This girl, Kaede, vied for "most popular" with Kuudelya, and Mikakage remembered seeing her on a poster in the cooking building.

No, not that. Now's not the time for that.

Furrowing her brow, Mikakage bit into her rice ball.

Today of all days, she didn't feel like mindlessly thinking about the cute box lunch–girl rankings.

After all, Mikakage was shouldering a small part of this uproar. Of course, it wasn't as though she was responsible for it. Mikakage had only reported what she'd learned from her current investigations and the implications of that knowledge, and she wasn't the least bit responsible for the incident itself. Still, that didn't clear up the murky feelings in her heart.

Allie the Alraune, Mikakage's plant spirit partner, climbed up into her lap, and Mikakage gave her a small onigiri. The Alraune took the perfectly round rice ball in both hands and bit into it. Even as she let the sight soothe her, Mikakage looked around.

The enormous, semicircular, cone-shaped hall she was in was commonly known as "the lecture hall."

Right now, it was filled to about 80 percent of capacity.

For the moment, it was lunchtime, and most of the participants were taking boxed lunches out of their packs or unwrapping the bundles of onigiri that had been delivered.

Ordinarily, more people would have gone outside or to the cafeteria, but due to the content today, movement of that sort was sluggish.

There were both morning and afternoon conferences, but the morning session had been more like presentations by the various research departments than a conference. The afternoon session would probably follow suit.

The RoderLab was a guild that resembled a university. As a result, no matter what they did, conferences tended to end up as reports on research results.

The atmosphere in the tiered classroom was hard to describe.

It certainly wasn't cheerful. It would have been safe to call it depressed. However, rather than simply despairing, it felt as if it was stirring restlessly, hiding confusion and excitement down at the bottom. As a matter of fact, here and there, people with the same major had gathered in groups and were talking in low voices.

Some of these groups had gone beyond gathering by major and were holding quiet, ongoing debates.

That was how shocking some of the content of the morning's presentations had been.

"So hey, there's some good stuff, too, yeah?"

Her colleague Aomori, who was also stuffing his face with onigiri, spoke from beside her.

"Would you call it a good thing?"

"Mmm. Probably?"

Hearing Aomori's noncommittal answer, Mikakage nodded vaguely, a little troubled.

It was true: She couldn't declare that it was a bad thing.

Mikakage had given her presentation during the morning session.

Because of the way it was organized, the RoderLab held many presentation meetings every month. The cooking section to which Mikakage belonged was no exception. However, the cooking section created things that were good to eat, and their presentations almost always took the form of sampling parties. Mikakage had used up all her energy on her presentation that morning.

To her—a Chef whose presentations didn't usually use materials or involve long oral statements—the burden had been a heavy one. Her colleague had pushed it all onto her, and words of resentment coiled within her.

Mikakage kicked Aomori hard, stole the fried chicken out of his lunchbox, and quickly gave it to Allie.

"What was that for?!"

"Is it good, Allie?"

Shy Allie didn't answer the question. She only ate the fried chicken energetically, keeping it hidden from Mikakage. She looked adorable, and Mikakage was relieved.

Little by little, even Adventurers without Chef subclasses were becoming able to cook.

That was the report Mikakage had given.

At present, there were two types of cooking method in this world.

The first was the "menu method." Carrying the materials listed in a recipe you "remembered," you opened the operations menu in the general vicinity of kitchen facilities. Once you selected the desired recipe from the operations menu, the dish was complete.

No matter what kind of dish it was, as a rule, the production time was ten seconds.

There were great advantages to this method. First, the required time was an obvious advantage. Even if it was a stewed dish that took time, or a fermented food, it only took ten seconds.

The economy of the ingredients that were used up was another advantage. At most, recipes only listed five types of ingredients. This included seasonings. For example, when making Meat and Potato Stew, you needed just three types: three potatoes, one beef, and one dark soy sauce. You didn't need onions or carrots, and sweet rice wine wasn't required either. Of course, the finished product looked as though these things had been used. It was as if the materials had been supplied from thin air.

Of course, there was an enormous—a far too enormous—disadvantage as well. This was that, no matter what sort of ingredients had been used or what kind of recipe you'd made, the finished food tasted like bran porridge. One could call it a flavorless flavor. The texture was also like a bland energy bar, and it was nothing that would whet anyone's appetite.

The other method was known as "home cooking."

With this method, it was necessary to cook just as you'd done in the old world. You weren't restricted by recipes, and the taste depended on whether or not the person who was cooking knew how to prepare that particular dish. You had to get all the ingredients together; they wouldn't pop up out of nowhere. In addition, the freshness and condition of the ingredients determined how complete the dish was. In other words, it was very similar to cooking in the real world.

In both cases, the overwhelming difference from the real world was that the person doing the cooking had to have a Chef subclass. It was also characterized by the fact that, with both the menu and home cooking methods, restrictions were applied according to Chef levels.

With the menu method, if the Chef's level hadn't reached the level set for the recipe, the probability that the dish would succeed decreased.

With the home cooking method, it wasn't possible to see the Chef level that was specifically required, but there was a high probability of failure with complicated techniques such as steaming or frying, or with dishes that required lots of steps.

In either case, if they failed, just as in the days when this had been a game, all that was left was a charred wreck or a sloppy mess.

For Adventurers without a Chef subclass, every dish failed. No matter how good at cooking they'd been on Earth, they weren't even able to make salad. Ever since the Catastrophe, this had been common knowledge.

That was slowly beginning to crumble.

Now, even Adventurers without Chef subclasses were able to use simple seasonings and cut up ingredients. At this point, they *could* make salads.

What was happening? No one knew.

They didn't even understand the Catastrophe. There was no way for them to understand what this change meant.

However, it wasn't hard to anticipate that the range it affected would be vast.

Even Mikakage and the other Chefs weren't able to say exactly when this change had taken place. Akiba and the Round Table Council had noticed the subclass restrictions on item creation early on. That had been what had triggered the establishment of the Round Table Council in the first place.

It was safe to say that the way people with the same subclass formed departments at the RoderLab was based on that same discovery. In other words, all the people around Mikakage were Chefs. Not only that, but all of them, Mikakage included, were high-level. In addition, that knowledge was widespread in Akiba, and there was a universal awareness that meals were made by guild Chefs, or that you purchased side dishes from Chefs who were selling them.

That was why they hadn't noticed when this phenomenon began.

According to Mikakage and the cooking section's recent investigation, about half of all Adventurers now had a decent probability of making salad successfully. Even the ones who failed seemed to be feeling a different response than they'd felt before.

They'd managed to verify that the phenomenon was occurring.

However, it wasn't yet clear whether it was the result of each individual's unconscious efforts—a result of the Adventurer's abilities expanding—or whether some game protection was coming undone. They'd confirmed that a similar phenomenon was occurring among the People of the Earth. It had even been possible for Allie, a plant spirit.

What was even more frightening was the fact that the phenomenon wasn't limited to cooking.

For example, the Carpenter subclass had monopolized item creation in the field of construction, while in furniture production, it had been the Woodworker subclass. That had been the way this world was.

However, at the presentation meeting that morning, reports that were similar to the one Mikakage had given on Chefs had shown up here and there.

The techniques of construction and forging weren't as familiar to modern people as cooking techniques, and so even when they tried to conduct surveys, the sample sizes were too small, and they couldn't get conclusive evidence. Even so, from a handful of cases, there had been clear reports that the old experience rule was wavering.

Mikakage wasn't the only one who was disturbed.

Aomori, her other friends in the hall, and everyone at the RoderLab had a premonition of something.

At the sudden hush, Mikakage looked up.

The eyes of the people around her were focused on Roderick, who stood on the platform. Since it was still the middle of the lunch break, the nearby companions who'd been stuffing their mouths with onigiri and sandwiches were gazing at Roderick with expressions full of questions.

The man wore his white coat casually, and there was fatigue in his ordinarily calm, easygoing face. Scratching his head, he began to speak.

"Uh. I'm sorry to interrupt your meal, but I was waiting on news regarding an investigation; that's come in, and it looks as though we'll have to switch gears this afternoon, so let me cut in here. We'll extend lunchtime by an hour. In addition, when I say 'switch gears,' I mean we'll be shifting to countermeasures."

At the words *shifting to countermeasures,* a stir ran through the hall.

Half was surprise at the fact that it was on a level where countermeasures were necessary. Half was due to the fact that the cautious Roderick had decided to actively contribute.

"You can keep eating, so do listen. There are three concerns I need to report. The first has to do with the Appearance Reset Potions and the difference in genders going back to the days of the game. According to many cases...or rather, to nearly all cases, we reported earlier that physical bodies influence character, and it appears as though voices are influenced as well. It isn't clear whether or not the vocal cords have a mechanistic role, but the voices of Adventurers who currently have female bodies are gradually growing feminine...even if the player happens to be male."

A pen rolled, making an awfully loud noise.

The lecture hall was so silent there wasn't a single cough to be heard.

"The next has to do with visual observations... Erm. We haven't actually confirmed this matter. We're measuring again, but it's still uncertain. That said, I think it is a fact. The distance between the town of Akiba and Fuji seems to be expanding. Or rather, the space between two arbitrary points is growing, albeit slightly."

This report seemed to have struck most of the crowd in the venue as a bolt from the blue.

"Excuse me…"

One timid-looking Blacksmith raised his hand. When Roderick gave him permission, the question he asked gave voice to everyone else's doubts.

"Is that true everywhere, do you think? In other words, is Yamato… growing?"

"We believe so."

At Roderick's answer, the entire venue gulped.

"The final matter has to do with the results of a survey request we received from an external party, but I think I should share them… It's in regard to the flavor text set for items. For some items, we have confirmed that this text has effects."

Mikakage's eyes went round.

Flavor text with effects? What did that mean?

For example, say there was a certain magic weapon: "Damage +5%, Additional Flame Damage 180 to 216 Points, [STR] Boost +15." This was the strength of the magic. Special magic effects accompanied normal weapon stats, making the weapon more powerful.

In comparison, "flavor text" indicated text like this: "This weapon, Mighty Inferno Spear, was bestowed on distinguished knights by the regular army of Ancient Westlande. It is decorated with Fire Dragon fangs and holds the power of flames. In antiquity, Loga Zari used this spear to inspire courage in his subordinates." In other words, it explained the item, detailing its origins and features. It was information you could read as a result of appraising the item, but in terms of the game, it was meaningless. It was text that existed to enliven the atmosphere.

In any case, the "flavor" in flavor text meant just that: to add flavor. That was all.

There were no effects. Not having effects was what made it flavor text…or that was how it should have been.

But there *were* effects?

Mikakage didn't understand right away just what that meant.

Because she didn't know, she looked at Aomori.

Aomori didn't know either. He looked back at Mikakage uneasily.

Most of their companions were doing the same thing.

Roderick closed his eyes briefly and gave a deep sigh. On seeing him, everyone braced themselves, finally realizing that something troublesome had happened.

"We don't think these are isolated phenomena. It's impossible to think that phenomena such as these could happen at a time like this, one after another, without any connection to each other. In other words, we feel they are related cases. At present, we believe this world is in the midst of ongoing, large-scale changes. The Catastrophe has not ended. I propose that we gather information regarding this matter to the greatest extent possible."

Roderick's words rolled around the dumbstruck hall, unanswered.

Almost none of Akiba's residents knew of these changes yet.

▶ 5

In a busy office, Akatsuki and Raynesia were both kneeling formally.

In front of them were Riezé and Henrietta. Lots of maids were bustling around them, and for some reason, Nazuna was kicking back and eating a strawberry *daifuku*, a dumpling made of mochi and stuffed with jam.

Akatsuki had been marched straight here from the Temple, and after she'd been fed a combination breakfast/lunch served with the words "for now," they'd decided to ask her about the circumstances in detail.

Akatsuki had thought that being asked for "the circumstances in detail" would be a problem, and she kept shooting glances at Raynesia. Prompted by Henrietta, Raynesia sat down neatly beside Akatsuki.

The pile of the luxurious carpet was long and fluffy, so her knees certainly wouldn't get sore; but Akatsuki lived in a Japanese-style room normally and so had absolutely no reluctance with regard to kneeling formally. However, what about Raynesia? She didn't seem used to kneeling that way at all; she was just copying Akatsuki, with a terribly serious expression on her face.

*   *   *

"We've heard the general outline already. The murderer is actually a Person of the Earth. A member of the Kunie clan, at that. Those combat abilities are thanks to mobile armor. The city's defensive magic circle supplies the magic, and he has acquired fighting power equal to that of a small-scale raid boss."

At Riezé's words, Raynesia hung her head.

Apparently Raynesia had explained the circumstances to the female Adventurers who gathered for the tea parties.

This startled Akatsuki.

A Person of the Earth was killing Adventurers.

Raynesia had been terribly frightened and worried about that situation being discovered. Even so, as she knelt formally next to Akatsuki, looking at Riezé and Henrietta, her expression was a resolute one, not one of dejection.

However, that might have been only natural. Come to think of it, the People of the Earth princess Akatsuki had thought she wanted to support had ridden a griffin and soared through the sky in order to recruit heroes for the Zantleaf siege.

"—If this incident is discovered, the relationship between Adventurers and People of the Earth in Akiba will sour. If suspicion toward the Kunie clan grows, cracks may begin to appear in city life itself. That's what you two thought. You were concerned about that situation, Akatsuki, and so you tried to resolve the incident, instead of killing the murderer. Is that correct?"

Still sitting, Akatsuki thought for a little while, then nodded.

Put into words, that was probably what it was.

Akatsuki was aware that she'd dashed out into the nighttime streets without thinking much at all. She'd only wanted to tell somebody that Raynesia hadn't made a mistake. She'd felt that if she stopped the murderer, that would get across. No: She was only able to understand that because she was thinking about it after the fact. If she remembered that time honestly, she might have been simply acting out her frustration for no good reason. She thought she'd just been venting her irritation at the world, which didn't even try to understand her or Raynesia.

However, she was hesitant to put that into words, and she only gazed at Riezé silently.

"I can understand why you would have thought that. I don't think it's an incident that can be kept hidden to the end, but even so, resolving it quickly will be a big part of calming the uproar."

"Plus there've been all these victims."

Nazuna, who'd taken sweet sake out of her pack, poked fun at Riezé, who was speaking like a lecturer.

"...Will the West Wind Brigade make this matter public, then?"

"Nah. Soujirou said he'd pull out. We won't make it public or retaliate. The guild members will probably have something to say about it internally, but Soujirou will handle that somehow. That's the sort of guild we are. I'm the one who cleans up the mess... Although whatever happen now is up to you two."

"That's..."

"Enough of the roundabout review. Just lecture 'em already."

At Nazuna's words, Riezé and Henrietta sighed.

It wasn't that they couldn't deal with Nazuna, but they would have preferred her to go through the proper procedures, yet Nazuna didn't seem to care one bit. Depending on how you looked at them, her licentious, traditional Japanese clothes also seemed untidy. White skin wrapped in a chain mail undershirt bulged from the open neck of her clothes, and as she sprawled on the sofa, she vividly resembled not a fox but a big cat.

Her current appearance didn't match her stern, tense atmosphere in battle. However, to Akatsuki, she looked natural. This version of her might be the real one.

But maybe there's no such thing as a "real version"...

Akatsuki thought that the Shiroe who patted her head was her real liege.

However, he was her liege when he was at his wits' end over documents as well, and the one who arranged for reinforcements on the battlefield was her real liege, too.

It made a slight pain race through her chest, but the lieges who praised Minori and smiled at Marielle were also real.

Just as the Raynesia next to her didn't look elegant and fragile as usual—or limp and tired. Instead, she wore an intent expression rife with determination.

Essentially, it was likely that none of it was a lie.

In the midst of a world that had grown just a bit wider and more vivid, Akatsuki realized this for the first time.

There were lots of "reals."

"In short, is this what it was?"

In front of Akatsuki and Raynesia, Henrietta folded her arms and spoke to them softly.

"You thought you could do it all on your own and tried to look impressive. You knew you really should have discussed it with us, didn't you? Akatsuki and Raynesia, haven't you gotten a bit conceited? Aren't you patronizing the people around you?"

Henrietta's eyes held none of their usual mischief.

She wore a truly serious expression.

Akatsuki had no way to respond. She was right.

This incident wasn't the worst it could have been. She could excuse herself by saying the blood had rushed to her head and she'd dashed out.

But she'd hidden in Shiroe's shadow all this time, and there really was no way to excuse that.

In the end, she hadn't tried to relate to other people: She'd considered it too much work and had cut them off, thinking she didn't need them. Sage Nyanta and Naotsugu were one thing, but hadn't she been stingy with her words with Minori, Touya, and the others, the younger members of her own guild?

Of course she'd supported their efforts. She'd guarded them silently, provided materials. She'd reconnoitered and chosen hunting grounds. However, she'd avoided speaking with them directly and traveling around with them. There hadn't even been a good reason.

She'd used evasive words, saying that that wasn't her role.

The realization that she'd dimly understood this tormented Akatsuki.

"How long do you intend to stay on your own? Don't you think it's spoiled of you to assume that, provided Master Shiroe is there, that's enough?"

At Henrietta's reprimanding voice, Akatsuki drooped.

She had no words. Everything was as she'd said.

Because she'd been entirely dependent on her liege, the moment that liege was gone, she'd stopped being able to do anything. She'd wanted to at least carry out her liege's request, but she hadn't even been able to do that. Even though it was a mission Shiroe had given to her alone…

"Did you visit this manor with the intention of acting as a guard?"

Feeling as though her thoughts had received a response, Akatsuki raised her eyes.

"Visiting Water Maple Manor and assisting its security system—that duty wasn't given to you alone, Akatsuki. It was mine as well, and Riezé's."

This time, Akatsuki turned bright red with shame and pain.

Come to think of it, that was only natural. Raynesia was currently one of the most important women in Akiba, and Akatsuki wouldn't have been assigned as her only guard. Raynesia's tea parties were being held on Shiroe's instructions. If she'd given it just a little thought, she would have known.

Even the thought that Shiroe was counting on her had been self-important.

That was so sad and frustrating that it made tears well up.

Now wasn't the time to cry, though. Akatsuki had definitely thought that she would protect Raynesia. However, she hadn't wanted to protect only her life, as a bodyguard. That day, at that time, she'd wanted to protect the wish and the nobility of this girl, who bore a heavy responsibility as the representative of the People of the Earth.

"Akatsuki is, um…m-my—"

Raynesia broke in, speaking with what sounded like great difficulty. However, Riezé stopped her.

"But I still want your help. I need it."

Akatsuki desperately strung pleading words together.

"Yes, of course. I will help, and so will Riezé. Just as we promised a moment ago. However, to whom are you directing those words?"

That question was incredibly difficult for Akatsuki.

To whom? To Henrietta and Riezé? To Nazuna? To Mikakage and the others who weren't here?

But who was that? Who should she rely on? Did she have any right to rely on anybody?

Still, there was definitely something there.

It was only that Akatsuki couldn't find the right words. The *gift* was there.

Akatsuki had realized that in the dream she'd lost.

The thing she'd let fall in the faint light of dawn tormented her.

She was sure she'd been holding it tightly, along with Shiroe's coat, but when she'd opened her eyes, her hand had been empty.

She hadn't been able to bring it back from the dream.

There was an unbearable impatience in her chest.

The words she was sure she'd had wouldn't come out.

They had to be there, properly, inside her heart, but she couldn't communicate them to everyone.

Akatsuki thought, quite seriously, that if it made it possible to convey these feelings and wishes—the ones she thought were really, truly important—to everyone, she wouldn't mind splitting her own chest open.

However, even if she'd split her chest open, they couldn't have seen them.

At the thought of the worthlessness of her clumsy self, Akatsuki's expression twisted, and she found herself on the verge of tears.

"Akatsuki is my friend."

Having shaken off Riezé's restraint, Raynesia declared this; her face was angry. Akatsuki gazed at her with an expression of blank amazement.

Inside her, something was born.

It was the words she hadn't managed to hold on to, and the door she'd been pretending not to notice. The *key* to that door.

Hearing those words from the silver princess—words she'd never thought she'd say—warmed Akatsuki and gave her strength.

"Raynesia is doing her best, so… I want to help her. Everybody… *With* everybody. Because, um…we're friends…"

She couldn't put it into words well.

Feelings of embarrassment and helplessness and depression flooded her.

Even so, the strong determination that she had to push through was there as well.

As if to break through that irritation, Akatsuki took half a step forward.

It was an advance so small you really couldn't call it a step.

Inside her mouth, the word *friends* seemed about to become hoarse with hesitation.

Inside Akatsuki, a slow understanding came together.

The Raynesia who wore a peaceful smile and seemed to be somewhere far away was real, but the Raynesia who was getting angry beside Akatsuki was real as well. The Henrietta who always toyed with Akatsuki was real, but so was the Henrietta who was taking Akatsuki to task. The Riezé who carefully inspected the dresses the People of the Earth wore and the Riezé whose profile was that of a battle commander were both real.

When she looked at them properly, straight on, there were all sorts of people around Akatsuki who worried about her.

Even if Akatsuki looked uncool, it wouldn't make her a fake. The Akatsuki she couldn't forgive was still the real Akatsuki.

There were this many people who were worried about the Akatsuki who'd messed up and been killed.

She thought she understood why Riezé had mentioned middle schoolers. This really was middle school level. To think she'd have to learn something like this so late in the game... *I'm lower than Minori,* Akatsuki thought. Still, there was no gut-wrenching anxiety in the idea. It was probably true that she was lower than Minori. Besides, right now, there were people right here in front of her who were worried about her.

"Understood. In that case, I have a plan. A plan to put an end to this matter. I've contacted the Round Table Council and requested that they set a ban on going out at night. Three days from now, let's bring down that murderer."

At Riezé's words, Akatsuki felt her heart relax. This time, she wouldn't get it wrong.

▶ **6**

Henrietta looked out over Akiba from the landing on the stairs.

Most of the town's trees were deciduous, but there were some evergreens as well. The verdant accents within the gray town were gentle on the eyes. The Crescent Moon League's home was in this guild center, so she was used to the scenery itself. However, at the moment, the altitude was different.

Her guild home was on the fifth floor of the center. This landing was on the tenth. She was headed for the top level of the same building—in other words, for the Round Table Council.

Henrietta kept walking. Viewed from a real-world perspective, climbing up and down a high-rise building with dead elevators time after time would be torture, but Adventurer bodies were high-performance. She could make the entire round trip without any trouble, even when carrying a wooden crate.

The walls of the stairwell were exposed concrete, but she reached the floor she wanted without the cold posing much of a problem.

Greeting a Person of the Earth girl whom she knew by sight, Henrietta entered the Staff Office. This was the core of the Round Table Council. The true "Round Table Council" indicated the council composed of the leaders of the eleven guilds that represented Akiba, but the plans they settled on were administered by this Staff Office.

Many loud voices had said that technically, in some way, the eleven guilds had a hand in setting Akiba's policies, and it was probably a bad idea not to give them space in which to do that, so each of the eleven guilds had been given an office inside the Staff Office. That said, most of the eleven guilds were big enough that it wasn't odd for them to be representing Akiba. Most of the guild masters had offices within their own headquarters and conducted a variety of business there. Although it was a midlevel guild, the Crescent Moon League was the same in that respect, and Marielle had a fancy office that reflected her tastes.

As a result, it was typical for guilds to put someone in their Staff Office offices to hold the fort and use them as places where they could be contacted. However, unfortunately, the Crescent Moon League didn't have that many people. This meant that Henrietta stopped by regularly to organize the materials and correspondence that had piled up.

Many People of the Earth worked here, too.

This was partly with the goal of commissioning them for simple office work, and partly an operational test to see whether or not they could work together in the same space. It might have been all right to ask them to handle the role of contact, but they were letting the current situation stand. Even without being assigned jobs like that, the People of the Earth staff had all sorts of work, such as handling contacts and negotiations for Akiba's several hundred guilds.

Having greeted them, Henrietta reached the office, then let out a groan. The work desk was overflowing with documents again. This happened all the time, and just looking at it depressed her. Of the eleven guilds, the Crescent Moon League had things comparatively easy, and even *it* was like this. She didn't even want to think about the other guilds.

As she quickly sorted the files, Henrietta poured them into the crate she'd brought along. It looked like a huge amount, but most of it was reports and confirmation documents. When files weren't important enough to take back to the guild house, she just signed them to show they'd been looked over and tossed them into the furnished "approved" box.

As she performed this simple work, she thought back over the past few days.

After that day, things had moved quickly.

Riezé's supervision had been brilliant, but the other participants hadn't fallen behind. Come to think of it, even though they were women, Nazuna, Kyouko, and Azukiko had participated in raids before the Catastrophe. Organized action was probably their forte.

Raynesia's sitting room had become a temporary strategy headquarters, and a work desk Riezé had brought in from her guild had been installed there. That room was a scene of pandemonium to rival this one. Vast amounts of written memos overflowed in the processes of correction and the creation of clean copies. Henrietta and the other Adventurers had been raised in real-world Earth's paperless society, and the sight made their heads ache.

The participants in the antimurderer strategy called the initiative "the arrest strategy," "the recapture strategy," and similar things.

Because they were using Raynesia's manor as the strategy's headquarters, the only participating members were the women who'd been invited to Raynesia's tea parties. Which meant that, of course, Henrietta and Marielle were participating as well.

There were two central figures: Akatsuki and Raynesia. Unfortunately, not only were both of them unused to this sort of exercise, they didn't even have any aptitude for it. Their eyes had gone wide at this string of "firsts," and they were running around in confusion. As the ones who'd proposed the plan, the two of them were key, but as far as group action was concerned, they couldn't be counted upon. As a result, Riezé and Henrietta were handling the actual administrative duties.

They'd had to.

Growing tired of organizing, Henrietta sat in a leather-covered armchair and looked up at the ceiling. As long as they weren't summoned, no staff other than Crescent Moon League members would enter the office. It was probably inevitable that her posture looked more deflated than usual.

At the guild, she was surrounded by Marielle and the other cheerful, noisy members, and she couldn't think properly. Henrietta gently pushed her glasses up, gave a quiet sigh, and took a single card out of her well-used mini commuter pass case.

It was a brusque card, with nothing but a few lines of letters written on it in plain handwriting.

The card was a bank account.

A card that showed an account at the only banking organization in *Elder Tales*, which was annexed to the guild center. It was an access card, something that hadn't existed until now.

Before the Catastrophe, *Elder Tales* had been a game. Its "bank" hadn't been like a bank on Earth: It was a nonprofit organization that was there to hold players' cash and items. Actually, it hadn't even been a nonprofit organization. It had been one of the game functions.

The moment game characters were born—in other words, the instant they began the game—they automatically had a bank account. Procedures to open one weren't required. Guilds were the same way: The instant they were formed, they had one bank account. It was an automatic process, and in exchange for being no trouble at all to open, you couldn't refuse to have one. That was the long and short of what it had been. Naturally, there hadn't been any cards or bankbooks. After all, the game system identified individuals with absolute precision and managed everything without those things.

However, the card in front of her was different.

It was one of the three cards the three committees on the Round Table Council would soon have the right to own. The account it showed belonged neither to an individual nor to a guild. It was a possibility no one in Yamato had considered.

"...Because of this, I'd really prefer to stay quiet just now."

Henrietta spun the card around and around between her fingertips and closed her eyes.

She'd had a vague hunch that Shiroe wasn't in Akiba. No one had explicitly told her so, but she'd guessed as much when Shiroe had asked her to take care of this card.

The card didn't have any meaning; not yet. There was no money in the account, and it wasn't linked to any action. At present, it was just a blank account that had been set up.

However, the future possibilities were dizzying.

Henrietta knew this. Just thinking of how it would be used gave her a faint chill.

The matter of the account hadn't been made public because the card was currently still meaningless. In other words, at this stage, they were still verifying the possibilities, and it wasn't yet time to announce them. At the very least, that was how it had been explained to Henrietta. Meanwhile, Henrietta had also guessed the circumstances that hadn't been explained.

Shiroe had probably avoided announcing it because he'd taken information leakage into account.

Akatsuki's behavior in hiding the fact that he wasn't in Akiba also supported this idea.

Krusty, Shiroe, and Michitaka were thinking about problems that might come up in the future. The existence of enemies was probably one of those problems. To make matters worse, they thought they'd have to assume they might exist within the Round Table Council as well.

Henrietta felt that Plant Hwyaden was in the west, watching Akiba. Although a minority, the Odysseia she'd begun hearing about were eerie as well.

The idea that, if we only die enough, we'll be able to return to Earth...

Their incomprehensible claim made Henrietta sigh. The worry was too heavy for the accountant of a midlevel guild. She couldn't possibly shoulder it. However, in that case, who would carry it? It would be easy to say Shiroe could do it and leave it to him. However, would that be all right? From Henrietta's perspective, Shiroe was younger than she was.

That's right. He's younger. That pitch-black gentleman. Honestly...

Shiroe probably didn't have any particular interest in Henrietta as an individual. No matter what he was doing, he wasn't doing it for Henrietta's sake. Still, she felt as though it wouldn't do to say, "Shiroe can handle it" and detach herself, as though it were someone else's problem. She felt as if that would be the same as giving Shiroe up.

Since she thought this way, Henrietta was convinced that she really did need to be involved with the murderer incident.

If Riezé was advising Akatsuki with regard to combat, Henrietta should probably be involved with the matter from a different angle. She'd provide cover fire for that obstinate Shiroe. Henrietta thought it would be rather nice to pitch in and help for that reason.

Ever since the ball at the Court of Ice, where she'd danced with Shiroe, Henrietta had thought that she didn't mind supporting him. She thought it suited her to support Akatsuki and Shiroe from the shadows.

Riezé, meanwhile, was drilling Akatsuki and training the other members of the task force in teamwork.

Until dusk, they practiced the Mysteries. There were several interested people involved besides Akatsuki, so their information regarding the Mysteries would probably expand a bit.

Then, after dinner, they'd assemble for a meeting, and after that, Akatsuki, Riezé, and the rest of the combat unit would scatter throughout Akiba, in order to keep an eye on a wide area and capture the murderer.

Having heard the detailed circumstances from Akatsuki and Nazuna, Riezé had apparently determined that the murderer wouldn't show himself for several days. Henrietta had agreed with her, and it was good to have that time. The murderer had taken ferocious attacks from Soujirou and Akatsuki, and had sustained more damage than ever before. It would probably take some time for those wounds to heal. Since he wasn't an Adventurer, it would certainly take more than a night.

Henrietta had negotiated with the Round Table Council and had a ban on going out at night put in place for Akiba.

This was a trick she'd settled on after discussing the matter with Riezé, both for damage control and to draw out the criminal. These days, Akatsuki and the others who were on guard continued patrolling until dawn, then slept for a short while when the sun came up.

Now was the time for Henrietta to do her job as well.

Putting together a mental list of people who needed to be persuaded, Henrietta stood. She scooped the documents on the work desk into the crate without sorting them, then contacted Hien via telechat.

Michitaka first. Then Calasin, then the members of the eleven guilds. This persuasion work would serve to provide a smoke screen for Shiroe's operation as well. She didn't know how far Shiroe had anticipated, but Henrietta smiled, feeling a bit spiteful.

"It may not go the way you've predicted, Master Shiroe. Especially... the determination within the girls."

CHAPTER. 5

RAID BATTLE

▶ AGE: **14**

▶ RACE: **HUMAN**

▶ CLASS: **ROSE GARDEN PRINCESS**

▶ HP: **1147**

▶ MP: **695**

▶ ITEM 1:
[POMEGRANATE FLYING-SWALLOW CHOKER]

A GLOSSY DARK-BLUE NECKLACE, MADE FROM DEEP SEA ROCK, REMINISCENT OF A SWALLOW. DRAWN TO ITS SHAPE AND COLORS, RAYNESIA BOUGHT IT EVEN THOUGH SHE KNEW IT WOULDN'T LOOK GOOD ON HER. NOW SHE IS THINKING OF GIVING IT TO SOMEONE WHO WOULD WEAR IT BETTER.

▶ ITEM 2:
[BLANKET WITH POCKETS]

A LAP ROBE WITH POCKETS, WOVEN FROM COLD-RESISTANT MATERIAL. WHEN YOU PUT POCKET HEATERS IN, IT'S SLIGHTLY WARM, AND IF YOU'RE NOT CAREFUL, YOU'LL WANT TO GO LIMP AND LAZE AROUND. ACCORDING TO THE PRINCESS, "IT ISN'T A MAGIC ITEM, BUT IT DOES FEEL AS THOUGH IT'S HAD A SPELL CAST ON IT."

▶ ITEM 3:
[WHITE ROUND RABBIT FUR]

A PURE-WHITE COAT MADE FROM THE FUR OF THE WHITE ROUND RABBITS THAT LIVE IN EZZO. IT WAS A PRESENT FROM A CLOTHING AND ACCESSORIES GUILD IN AKIBA. ALTHOUGH IT HAS NO DEFENSIVE POWER, IT'S CUTE AND VERY POPULAR AMONG WOMEN. BECAUSE STAINS STAND OUT ON WHITE CLOTHES, ELISSA IS CAREFUL WITH IT.

\<Dresser\>
It stores all kinds
of clothes, and from
the perspective of
a rabid thief, it's a
treasure trove.

▶ **1**

In the sticky darkness, a man stirred.

Slowly, he pulled his creaking body up out of the mud.

The sound of a trickle of muddy water echoed from somewhere. This might be a sewer, but it wasn't like the sewers of modern Tokyo on Earth. The area where the man had made his den was no more than an underground labyrinth with rivulets of muddy water thinner than fingers running here and there.

Standing up from his bed, which was just a messy pile of old clothes he'd stolen from the Adventurers, the man slowly ran his fingers over his abdomen. The rough, rust-like matter that clung to his fingers was dried blood. Inside his shredded jet-black coat, the hot wounds had already closed.

Apparently his wounds had healed.

The interior of the iron helmet, which looked a bit like a mask, glowed faintly. It was a magic effect that granted the ability to see in the dark.

Mobile armor was an indestructible magic tool that had existed since ancient times. Even the words *magic item* and *artifact* didn't go far enough: It was phantasmal, a memento from a vision.

Its abilities surpassed the current People of the Earth civilization, the Adventurers' magic civilization, and even that of the Kunie clan. It was a concentration of lost technology.

In his pale green field of vision, the man inspected his body.

His wounds had healed.

The man's physical abilities were advanced. Mobile armor dramatically improved his entire body's motor functions, and its effect on strength in particular was outstanding. In terms of HP, his was probably three times what it had been before he'd equipped the armor. However, on the other hand, it didn't reinforce his recovery abilities all that much. It had never assumed situations in which the wearer would sustain damage. The defensive abilities of mobile armor could negate most attacks, and if you didn't take damage, there was no need for recovery abilities. These injuries had exposed an unexpected weakness in the mobile armor. As far as the man was concerned, that had been a significant humiliation.

However, the gear wasn't his only weapon now.

In the tall man's hand, Hail Blade Byakumaru looked rather small. It was rattling in its sheath.

This mystical blade was said to have been used by Lugurius, the hero of the ice cliffs, and it granted its owner the qualities of a hero. Apparently, the more blood he let Byakumaru, the White Snow Devil, drink, the further his body adapted to its powers. The muscles in his arms, which had grown to easily twice their size, spoke of this eloquently. The mystical blade rattled in its sheath, hungry for more sacrifices.

Giving a low grunt in the darkness, the man left without a single look back at his den.

In any case, he didn't really think of this sewer as his headquarters or stronghold. Any place that would hide him and wasn't noisy was fine. This underground cavern was the space behind a collapsed floor. The air did move, so it was probably connected to something aboveground at some point, but as far as he knew, there were no passages left that were large enough to let people enter. He could use teleportation, so this wasn't a problem, but if ordinary People of the Earth or Adventurers wanted to break in, it would require a large-scale construction operation.

In his mind, the man visualized the town of Akiba. It was a place he'd guarded for a long time, and he had its layout memorized. Lately, the Adventurers had been reconstructing and expanding the buildings one after another, but the streets were basically unchanged.

He jumped to one of the teleportation destinations he remembered. Immediately, he was surrounded by empty, windblown air.

The wintry night wind buffeted him, trying to freeze him, but it was blocked by the mobile armor's cold resistance, and it didn't affect the man in the least. On the contrary, it was the perfect aperitif, and it brought premonitions of the coming feast.

From a ruin that seemed set to crumble any minute, the man looked down over a deserted huddle of street stalls.

A few lights shone deep in the darkness. At the sight of that fragile, unreliable glow, the man couldn't keep from smiling. Trembling with joy, he leaned his hunchbacked body out as far as he could, licking his lips.

When the light and noise of the day had gone, the town of Akiba grew still, looking like a young girl lying quietly in the depths of the darkness. During the day, she'd been an extremely stubborn, haughty woman, but in the dark of night, she was no more than a girl, as frightened as a rabbit.

The lean man drew his sword from its sheath.

The freezing winter air swirled around him, losing its edge.

As if his soul was crystallizing, in the midst of pain and delight the man gave a twisted laugh.

He was the winter.

The freezing cold air was the man himself. Just as the raging blizzard felt no cold, the man stripped off his black coat in the darkness and flung it away.

Illuminated by the lights from Akiba far below, the man's silhouette showed dimly, an unbalanced shape. His lean body was taut, but nothing that really looked like muscle showed on the surface. The man wore leather pants and a black tank top that hugged his torso, and metal armor—gauntlets and body armor—on his lower arms and legs only. The sizes of the components were so different they seemed to belong to someone else. Having cast off his stained coat, which fell toward the street like an ominous black bird, the man was a fiendishly trained weapon.

The enormous metal shells were packed with brownish-gray fibers that stored magic and mitigated shocks. Supplied with magic from the magic circle, the fibers soundlessly began to run. Multiple barriers formed around the man's arms and legs, and a force field was deployed around his body.

Memories of fighting giants on the frozen plains of the north country rose inside the man.

He was one of Akiba's People of the Earth, and the memories didn't belong to him.

They belonged to the hero Lugurius.

Lugurius had fought as an Ancient, and as a Knight of Izumo. For a whole century he'd driven the wicked giants back, to protect the smiles of the people of Susukino. He'd chased the monsters into the Jade Garden, deep in the mountains of Ouu, and had been just a step away from sealing them. That had been the achievement of Lugurius, the hero of Ezzo.

That fierce pride blustered inside the man like a raging blizzard.

If Sutu Inaw, the Maiden of the Japanese Elms, hadn't betrayed him, if she hadn't murdered him with a dastardly poison, he would still have been celebrated as the hero of the North and an immortal Ancient. If it hadn't been for that fragile girl's treachery...

As if to freeze everything, rampaging wind laced with snowflakes seeped out of the mouth of the sword's sheath. The mystical blade was responding to the man's anger; it wanted to work its cursed ice magic.

Lugurius's grudge screamed that he wanted to gather crowds of people, make them kneel, and make their lives his own.

The man shook his head.

He wasn't Lugurius.

He was a Person of the Earth, of the Kunie clan. The proud guardians who protected Akiba. However, they weren't honored. They were scorned as pseudohuman automatons. Although their abilities surpassed even the Adventurers, their status was, at best, security devices, and they were essentially treated as nothing more than accessories for the town. They were a tribe of dogs. Truly a clan of slave-warriors, offered up as sacrifices, just as the characters in the name *Kunie* implied.

Recalling his own circumstances, the man saw a blazing, pitch-black resentment in them. That resentment twined around rage that was frozen into pure white. *That's how it is. That's why I was chosen by Lugurius*, the man thought.

In order to destroy the human who'd betrayed him, the Maiden of the Japanese Elms.

Showing no hesitation, the man fell from the building, crashing into the ground feetfirst without any particular plan. The barriers around the man's body didn't even flicker at a mere six-story drop. On top of that, most of Akiba's streets weren't paved. They were soft black dirt, with mossy roots crawling across them. Having landed, shattering twisted branches and tree roots as he did so, the man realized there were barely any signs of life.

There was no prey.

The murderer was suspicious. He also wondered whether they'd all run away.

The man had excellent combat abilities, but he wasn't omnipotent. There were countless things he wasn't good at, and one of them was searching for enemies. In the first place, the clan's guards were ordinarily stationed in the security facilities during their shifts. When the facilities detected a crime in town, guards in mobile armor rushed to the scene and apprehended the criminal.

Detection and searching for enemies were functions of the security facilities, and individual guards didn't have them. Naturally, as magic equipment from ancient times, the mobile armor didn't have the ability to strengthen these functions either.

As a result, the man's senses weren't good enough to grasp all of Akiba, but even so, the night was far too empty. Going to bed when the sun went down was common sense in this world, but things were different in Akiba. Possibly because of their advanced combat abilities, Adventurers tended to go to bed later than People of the Earth. This was because they were able to defend themselves from nocturnal monsters.

Maybe as a result, even late at night, it was rare for the streets of Akiba to be entirely empty of Adventurers. This was the sort of person the man had sacrificed repeatedly to his mystical sword.

However, right now, he could sense no one.

* * *

The man swung Byakumaru in irritation. A spiral blizzard was released, freezing a patch of briars. He kicked them apart, then headed north on the central avenue, searching for sacrifices.

The mobile armor's teleportation abilities were only compatible with the zone of Akiba.

The armor received its teleportation magic from the ancient magic circle said to have been built under the city. As a result, if Akiba's Adventurers had evacuated from the city, he couldn't leave the city to pursue them.

In addition, the teleportation wasn't able to cross zone boundaries.

Isolated, closed spaces sometimes formed small enclosures known as zones. The rooms at inns were one example. The existence of a door made a small area that could barely hold two beds a separate space, shutting it off from the outside world by magic. It was in the town of Akiba, but it wasn't considered part of Akiba.

The same was true for the magic facilities known as guild halls that the Adventurers used. Each of the numerous headquarters inside the buildings, seemingly made of obsidian, functioned as separate spaces, or so he'd heard. Most of the buildings the Adventurers had rebuilt were also used as separate zones now.

The man wasn't able to invade spaces like these with teleportation. Even if he walked to them directly, the zone magic carefully identified the people who were allowed to enter or leave, and would exclude him.

Because of this, hunting prey that had shut themselves up in zones was difficult.

Holding a hand to his throat, the man chuckled.

In other words, this was a siege.

Frightened of the military might of this man, this hero, the Adventurers had finally admitted defeat and shut themselves away. Laughing softly, the man wandered, searching for prey. Peering into alleyways, destroying signs, and swinging the mystic sword was almost unbearably fun. He would probably never have admitted it, but the man was behaving like a murderer drunk on blood.

He didn't have to wait long.

A small shadow appeared, blocking his path.

The lean man's mouth twisted into the shape of a crescent moon.

How small. What soft-looking meat.

As the small shadow came toward him, trailing the faint scent of camellia oil, the murderer intercepted it. The blade of ice and snow groaned, demanding a sacrifice. Together, they would smite this town with a hero's rage and hunger.

▶ 2

At the feel of the clash, Akatsuki steeled herself.

Her opponent was a monster. She couldn't afford the slightest bit of carelessness. Or rather, forget carelessness: What she was most keenly aware of was the probability of her loss.

In any case, she wasn't a tank, specialized toward drawing enemy attacks. She was an attacker, designed to inflict damage.

During this operation, Akatsuki was third in the priority order for this position. In other words, there were two members who were better suited to direct combat than she was.

Which meant that the fact that Akatsuki was now crossing blades with the murderer was half coincidence. The town of Akiba was two kilometers square. It wasn't vast, but it certainly wasn't small. In addition, one unit was too small to build a network to guard against a murderer who could appear anywhere. However, there were circumstances which kept them from deploying a large number of personnel.

For that reason, the strategy Riezé—the raid leader—had chosen took the form of a patrol conducted by squads. Dispersed action by squads of between three and six members created a net that was sparse but still widespread.

One other reason lay in Akatsuki's subclass and combat experience. Her subclass, Tracker, had several types of special skill that investigated conditions across a wide range, including presence detection and searching for enemies. The range she could monitor alone was equivalent to the area four squads could cover. Her discovery of the murderer had been coincidence, but that hadn't been all it was.

Wordlessly, Akatsuki unleashed a blade from the left.

Quick Assault released a silver light that seemed to split the night into horizontal halves. Knowing she couldn't take this guy down with an attack of that level, Akatsuki threw herself forward, using the momentum from her slash. Quick Assault's special characteristics had increased her leg strength and agility, and she'd spotted a safe area by the murderer's side.

However, cold air and an impact that was enough to make her shudder burst from the short sword that struck at her back.

Akatsuki had known, but she still gave a bitter groan. She tumbled forward, then picked herself up.

She'd thought she'd leapt into her opponent's blind spot, but she'd been forcibly chased out of it.

"Akatsu... Eep!"

Struck by a cold, violent gust of wind, Marielle covered her face. Even so, a faintly sparkling recovery effect shimmered on Akatsuki's back. It was response-activated recovery. Like the Druid Pulse Recovery and the Kannagi Damage Interception, this was a class-specific recovery magic effect, the type that distinguished the three recovery classes from each other.

Feeling the ripples of that recovery like the palm of Marielle's warm hand, Akatsuki stepped forward. Evading the tip of the blade that bore down on her, dodging right and left with her small body, she pressed forward, forward.

Before her was the demonic murderer, the one she'd been no match for that day.

The core of the incident, the thing she had to defeat.

With a faint smile, the man waited for Akatsuki's charge. The ominous armor he'd equipped was mobile armor... Or parts of it, anyway. Akatsuki and the others already knew that. Its defensive power was probably equal to that of fantasy-class magic armor. However, she was undaunted.

In the blink of an eye, a blizzard began to rage on Akiba's wide avenue in the dead of night, freezing the soil.

When Akatsuki looked across the avenue, she saw the ordinary, unchanged walls of the buildings. Even as she fought, Akatsuki's mind raced. The range of the blizzard was about five meters, ten at most. The katana the murderer brandished was its origin; it was gushing cold air.

As she evaded new attacks she hadn't been able to take in the previous battle, Akatsuki thought about countermeasures. That had been the first thing Riezé had taught her: Size up your opponent. Watch them and clarify what they can and can't do. No matter how tough the fight you're in, you mustn't give up on that. Akatsuki bit her lip and observed that lesson.

That said, she couldn't go on the defensive. Right now, Marielle was behind her. Marielle, the leader of the Crescent Moon League, and her bright smile. Her liege's friend. She couldn't let her get hurt. Not as a ninja, and not as a gamer.

Marielle was a healer. In order to let healers do their jobs, the vanguard had to draw the enemy. Even if she wasn't a dedicated tank, right now, Akatsuki was the only one who could fill that role. That meant she had to focus the enemy's hate on herself.

The feeling of anxiety was strong enough to tear her limbs off.

It made Akatsuki want to cry out, but she bit the urge back and swung her blade.

One. She threw in an Accel Fang. She knew it wouldn't reach him.

Using the recoil, another Accel Fang. It scraped her opponent's gauntlet slightly. The grating noise of slashed metal, a scorched smell. Feinting with one more Accel Fang that drew nearly the same trajectory, Akatsuki dropped low, almost as if she was hugging the ground.

The former Akatsuki would probably have leapt up.

She'd been desperate to put power behind her attack, and had wanted to be as far above her opponent as possible. However, this time was different. Her body was already small; if she rolled, ducking, her opponent's own limbs would act as a blind and he'd lose sight of her. This attack method used her own small size to her advantage, and it wasn't an advantage she'd had in the past.

Akatsuki had received this strategy from the others.

She unleashed a Death Stinger, as if to pry him open. Unfortunately, the attack she slammed into the back of his knee didn't add continual damage. However, it had thrown the murderer slightly off-balance, and she struck at his brute-force attack with her Kiln-Turned Tenmoku Sword.

*   *   *

The sound of clashing steel echoed loudly through Akiba's night.

Unable to hold out against his force, Akatsuki had jumped back about five meters, and she was already sweating. The series of exchanges and its tension had raised her temperature, even in the face of the cold that blasted at her from the murderer. Her arms hurt, too. Although she normally held her short sword with her left hand, she set her right hand on the hilt as well, timing her move to match her opponent's attack. She'd realized that if she didn't do it, she wouldn't make it through.

However, the reality was that, even with both hands in play, she took great damage.

That was only to be expected. According to the *Elder Tales* specs, if your timing matched exactly, an effect that made the attacks cancel each other out would occur. However, this wasn't something you could do intentionally as a rule, and even if it did occur, it wasn't the sort of effect that would reduce the damage to zero. It only meant that you could weaken your opponent's attack slightly. Powerful attacks surpassed the cancellation and wounded the opponent directly…just as the murderer's attack, with its extraordinary force, had punched through Akatsuki's cancellation.

Even so, Akatsuki had a little smile on her lips.

Her arms felt puffy, as though they were inflamed, but a golden, sand-like sparkle had enveloped them and was healing them. Response Activated Recovery was a spell that automatically recovered HP in response to damage inflicted by enemies. This healing power provided support through five or ten attacks. The spell automatically recovered health with each enemy attack, and its effect was enormous. Akatsuki and Marielle were beginners at raids, and the breathing room casting a spell beforehand gave them was a nearly unparalleled merit.

However, it did have weaknesses. Recovery conducted after damage had been taken—recovery after the fact—wouldn't let you avoid fatal injuries. It couldn't handle the sort of powerful attacks that severed arms and sent them flying in one blow. Besides, Marielle's Response Activated Recovery was less experienced than the sort used by, for example, a Cleric affiliated with D.D.D. Even if it actually was recovering, Akatsuki's HP was far from fully healed.

Even so.

Akatsuki ran.

She charged as if falling: Trick Step. She twisted her right leg by force, turning halfway around. In a mesmerizing movement, she ran past her opponent, inflicting Paralyze Blow as she did so.

Because, after all, Akatsuki wasn't dead.

"Akatsuki!"

The murderer's attack grazed her yet again. She could feel her armor being slashed. The attack had been a blast of death that passed over Akatsuki's heart.

But she was alive.

Her fighting spirit was blazing. A week ago, she hadn't been able to fight without hiding behind Soujirou. True, the situation was bad. Even with a normal healing spell layered over Response Activated Recovery, her HP was still falling. However, that was only natural. She was up against a murderer, one who was clearly a raid-class enemy. Akatsuki was a hastily trained member of a weak guild, and this monster wasn't the sort of opponent she could take on. As proof, even Soujirou, leader of the West Wind Brigade, had gone down under his attacks. There was a reason she was able to tackle that opponent, if only for a limited time. The reason gave her courage.

Morning Star Catcher was wrapped around her right arm, the one she'd thrust out. This production-class gauntlet had been made for her by the Lucky Dice sisters. The matte bracer generated a force field, and it had greater defense than its appearance suggested. Even if the blizzard whittled away the defense on her right arm, Ink-Feather Garb gave off a faint glow of magic, forcibly creating a tiny gap in time to allow her to twist her body.

As she used her natural agility to slide through these gaps, Akatsuki was grateful for her new defensive gear. Even though her silhouette had gained attribute defense and increased abilities several times greater than what it previously had, there had been barely any increase in weight. They were all presents from the girls who gathered for those tea parties.

"Could you use something like this?"
"The size is all wrong. Here, I'll fix it for you."

"You can eat those strawberries. Those are everyone's."
"I've got some fan-tas-tic materials. Hee-hee-hee!"

The girls had smiled at her, taking care of Akatsuki almost as if they'd gotten a new little sister. They might have been more than half teasing her, but they'd given her unstinting support.

Most of the equipment that was protecting Akatsuki now had been presents from them.

The durability of her old equipment had deteriorated too far in her fight with the murderer, and it had been clear that it wouldn't be able to stay with her in her new battle.

She'd known all the women's faces, but she'd never spoken to any of them for more than half a minute or so. Whether or not they'd heard the explanation about the murderer that Akatsuki had given or the circumstances surrounding Akiba's crisis, they spoke encouraging words to her and gave her sweets.

It whipped up the old familiar feelings of irritation in Akatsuki's heart. It was a conditioned reflex: She didn't want to be treated like a child. Still, on the other hand, there was a comfort in it that she'd never felt before.

Akatsuki had gone down on her knees and begged for their help. That meant that, in a way, she couldn't get around being treated like a child. Giving up on her repulsion, Akatsuki thought: *It's because I'm not strong enough.* Begging everyone for help was admitting defeat.

However, even so, not being strong and losing certainly weren't meaningless.

She thought there were some things you could only understand by admitting weakness.

One of them was probably the peace she felt in her heart.

When she calmed down and thought about it, Akatsuki understood right away that the many people who'd spoken to her hadn't had any particular ill will. They were only treating her with kindness, plain and simple.

Most of the people she'd rejected and bared her fangs at hadn't had the slightest intention of making fun of her.

Of course, it had been a very embarrassing experience, but there was nothing about it that she couldn't accept.

Strangely, Akatsuki was very focused as she fought.

The HP bar, where she could see her HP edging downward, didn't bother her.

She struck with another attack, hitting the murderer with the biggest movement reduction effect she could manage. This was an expression of trust in a confirmed tactic, more than it was a way to prolong her own life.

"Ten more... Five!"

At Marielle's voice, which was almost a scream, Akatsuki gave a small smile.

Come to think of it, Marielle had said this was a first for her, too.

Right now, Akatsuki and the others were fighting their first-ever raid.

▶ 3

Having been contacted by telechat, Riezé immediately passed on the content to the other team leaders.

"Target acquired. He's currently traveling on foot down the central avenue in the direction of Old Ogawamachi. Akatsuki's unit made first contact. A two-man cell, with one healer. Team D move; all others stand by."

As she relayed the telechat in a yell, Riezé also broke into a run.

The raid had finally begun.

Riezé sent telechat after telechat. There were currently twenty-four Adventurers in Akiba under her command. According to the standard formulas of party organization, they should have formed four parties of six members each. When those were joined together, they'd have a twenty-four member full raid. However, this time, they hadn't been able to use that formation: Four parties wouldn't be able to patrol all of Akiba. They'd had to split up, or in other words, organize into smaller teams. Although she hadn't announced it, the twenty-three people currently under Riezé's command were split into irregular parties of two or three members. There were more than ten of these.

Riezé was part of the group as well. Kyouko was trailing along behind her. She was a level-90 Guardian, and had been one of the victims during this incident. Riezé herself was a Sorcerer.

Their formation was far too fragile. Even if Team D, which she'd contacted, joined up with Akatsuki's team, there would only be four members. They really wouldn't be able to keep a large-scale class enemy in check.

Riezé and Kyouko had been over by the canal, and they ran under the elevated tracks, hurrying toward the central avenue. Unfortunately, the action was a long ways away. They'd have to cut clear across Akiba on a diagonal. The distance was probably a little less than a kilometer. However, with their sturdy Adventurer bodies, they could probably reach their destination in about two minutes.

They detoured around the decayed skeleton of a billboard, dashing down a path covered by underbrush.

"It's Akatsuki?"

"Yes. Are you all right, Kyouko?"

"Of course. To be honest, I *am* scared of that guy. Still, I'd fight him again before I'd put him in front of Master Soujirou. I'm not an athletic type for nothing!"

"That's the spirit!"

"We're absolutely going to win this!"

Although Riezé didn't respond to those words aloud, she nodded firmly as she ran. Akiba's volunteers had leveled the ground in the plaza in front of the station, to make the outdoors more pleasant; the two of them cut across it with strides that were practically long jumps and ran into the guild center, dashing up the concrete stairs as though they'd sprouted wings.

Riezé bit her lip and reviewed the current strategy.

Most of the mysteries had been solved. It was probably safe to say that she understood most of how it was done as well.

The enemy was the dead warrior Lugurius.

Or rather, something that resembled Lugurius.

He was a raid enemy and quest boss in Decayed Exploit, which had been packaged with Sacred Heart, the tenth expansion pack. Since Decayed Exploit had been fully raid content, it was meant to be played with twenty-four people, but the difficulty level wasn't all that high. Things had been different at the outset, when they hadn't had enough information, but after that, she didn't remember the combat content being difficult at all. In any case, the Decayed Exploit quest had been an introduction that acted as a gateway to a bigger quest, the Nine Great Gaols of Halos. Its difficulty really *couldn't* be that high.

Even as an enemy raid boss, the fallen warrior Lugurius, who was said to have died in the Ezzo Empire, had haunted Hokkaido. Riezé had no idea why he was attacking the town of Akiba now. She didn't worry about it, either. Worrying about reasons wasn't her style. To Riezé, reasons were meaningful only at the stage when you were examining ways to deal with something, and at this point, handling the situation by force was the only way to turn it in their favor.

Riezé had conducted exhaustive interviews of all the victims who had been attacked by the murderer so far. As a result, she had inferred that the culprit was Lugurius, or someone who had tendencies and powers that resembled Lugurius's. It had taken time because, at first, the murderer hadn't been able to exercise his abilities completely, or had been trying to hide them.

It was also because the murderer wasn't simply the raid monster Lugurius: He also had the combat power of mobile armor. He was a monster who could use two different types of strength, and when the incident had first occurred, these two types had camouflaged each other.

The hint that had decisively revealed the truth had been that the murderer's weapon was Hail Blade Byakumaru.

Akatsuki, who had fought the murderer last, had declared that it was.

As weapons, short swords were on the small side, and it was hard to tell them apart. Riezé wasn't confident that she could look at an equipped one and guess its name. However, if a girl who also used short swords had declared it, then Riezé concluded that she must have been certain.

After that, things had moved quickly. The name Hail Blade Byakumaru had reminded Riezé of the tale of the hero Lugurius, who had been fond of that sword and had used it to fight for Ezzo, and of the quest to subjugate the now-fallen warrior.

* * *

A cursed weapon.

It seemed ridiculous, but that was what Hail Blade Byakumaru was.

From a report Mikakage had delivered, Riezé knew that flavor text was being eroded. The hero who had died filled with bitterness had written his feelings of rage and resentment into the explanatory text of his beloved sword. That cursed text had taken physical shape and attacked its bearer.

That's absurd!

For the several hundredth time, Riezé bit her lip in a spasm of irritation. Flavor text had taken shape and attacked someone.

That situation awoke a visceral terror, as though a nightmare had slipped out of the realm of dreams and tried to tear its dreamer apart.

However, in a territory separate from that horror, the brain that was entrusted with D.D.D.'s training unit had set to work on tactics. If the murderer had Lugurius's abilities, there were roughly three of them.

One was a great increase in HP. Lugurius's maximum HP changed drastically depending on the number of people in the zone. In Decayed Exploit, a quest in which he'd been faced in a subterranean graveyard, he'd kidnapped more than fifty People of the Earth and had had them in the zone with him. That alone had raised Lugurius's HP to three times its minimum.

If Akiba had stayed as lively as it was ordinarily, his HP capacity would probably have soared, swelling to more than several hundred times its normal size. No one would be able to take down a monster like that, not even the West Wind Brigade or D.D.D.

And so Riezé had come up with a plan. She'd worked with Henrietta, who wasn't here right now, to get a ban put in place on going out at night. Just as they'd evacuated the People of the Earth from the zone in the raid quest, they'd make the town of Akiba a battle zone that was empty of everyone but themselves. That was the minimum requirement for fighting Lugurius.

The second was that all his abilities increased in response to the number of people who were nearby. All of Lugurius's abilities—his attack power, evasive power, defensive power, and hit rate—increased in response to the number of Adventurers within a fifty-meter radius. This had been part of Lugurius's secret, the one that had defeated even Soujirou. It was also the reason Riezé had divided her raid into the smallest groups possible.

It had been the same in the Decayed Exploit quest. They'd left only the six strongest, while the remaining eighteen had evacuated the People of the Earth, simultaneously routing the vengeful ghosts that had been attracted by Lugurius's grudge. By doing so, they'd been able to weaken Lugurius to the point where he was an enemy that could be defeated.

The last was the range attack that used ice. The area in front of Lugurius turned into a blizzard, decreasing visibility. No doubt there would be cold-air damage as well. On its own, the ability was a simple one, but precisely because it was simple, equipment with attribute defense was the only way to deal with it.

The more living people there were in the area, the greater his abilities would become. He could freeze all living things. These abilities existed to express the background for Lugurius, who had died swallowing his resentment.

These were exceptional abilities, given to him as a dramatic background because he was a raid quest boss.

These three abilities were Lugurius's secret, and the factors that made this battle hopelessly difficult. In Akiba, which overflowed with people, a gimmick that had made for a mere warm-up as level-90 raid content became the worst possible ability.

In particular, the combination with the mobile armor's teleportation ability was lethal.

Lugurius could run at any time, and he could aim for a place and time when there were lots of people in Akiba. So far, the murderer had chosen to attack the town only at night, but that might not last forever. It might be because the combat time in the original quest had been night, or it might be the murderer's own preference. It could even be coincidence.

Riezé could think of another "worst."

It was the inability to declare the murderer who had Lugurius's abilities as an enemy NPC. According to eyewitness testimony, the murderer was a Samurai named Enbart Nelles. In that case, he was cursed, and at the same time, he had a human mind. In other words, he had the ability to learn.

Raid quests were game content. True, they were designed to be hard enough that you'd get wiped out several times, but that was only because the administrators had made them that way, in order to let you enjoy the sense of achievement when you eventually did conquer them. Riezé knew this precisely because she belonged to the biggest raid guild on the Yamato server. There had been an invisible trust relationship, rather like the one shared by good rivals, between players who enjoyed harsh raid content and the administrators.

However, this was no longer the *Elder Tales* game, and Riezé and the others weren't game characters. There was a possibility that this raid hadn't been designed in such a way that they'd be able to conquer it eventually. On the contrary, the possibility that it hadn't was much greater.

And wouldn't that possibility continue to grow? Once Riezé and the others fought him once, the murderer would know their strategy. It was possible for him to attack Akiba in ways that were craftier and more lethal. The teleportation ability and Lugurius's resentment went together far too well. The only thing Riezé could imagine beyond that union was hell.

Of course she'd thought of countermeasures. Riezé had a shot at success.

However, even so, there was no proof.

After the Catastrophe, this world had lost the reliability of a game, and there was no guarantee whatsoever that any plan would succeed. The realization made Riezé shiver. Just having put something obvious into words, inside her mind, made her feel as if an ice-demon had suddenly seized her spine. Riezé shuddered with chills that wouldn't stop.

Neither the title of operation commander nor the pride of being training unit captain did her any good.

On the contrary: They only made her terror all the greater. With those titles, Riezé could make mistakes that would take others' lives along with her.

Her knees had gone oddly weak. She scolded them and kept moving.

It was a terrible thing. Riezé finally knew the terror that came with the responsibility of involving other people in her decisions. She thought of the silver-haired princess, wondering if she'd known that terror since she was born. The thought that she'd dashed into the lords' conference and ridden on a griffin with Krusty when she knew that terror gave Riezé a feeling that was close to awe.

That princess was really something.

...As was Krusty. And Shiroe. And the eleven guild masters. And Akatsuki.

What a terrifying thing it was to try to change matters, even though there was no guarantee of success.

She was ashamed of herself for having made fun of it, calling it a middle schooler's journal. She'd just looked down on them from a place she'd assumed was safe and spouted her ever-so-valuable opinions.

Riezé was embarrassed by her own ugliness. However, for that very reason, she couldn't turn back.

There were nine ways the strategy she'd prepared could end. She'd explained this to everyone as "taking the proper steps as the occasion demands," but not having been able to narrow it down to one way was proof that she was an incompetent strategist.

Still, even so...it was better than losing.

"We're here!"

The steel door—which Kyouko had opened by practically breaking it down—led to empty, moonlit space. What spread below them were broken concrete beams, evergreen treetops that half-covered their field of vision, and, far below them, Akiba's station-front plaza.

This place, where the wind roared, was the fifteenth floor of the guild center, the obsidian fortress that was Akiba's pride. It was the shattered top floor of a former high-rise building that seemed to have been smashed by a blow from a giant.

"Be careful, Riezé."

The wind, which was freezing cold because it was perfectly clear, billowed Riezé's mantle, trying to snatch it away. Instantly, Riezé stiffened, but Kyouko grabbed her belt firmly, and the two of them hid themselves in the shadow of a pillar.

Opening their telechat menus again, Riezé and Kyouko plunged into the midst of yet another battle.

▶4

In that same guild center, in a room somewhere underground, a different sort of battle was approaching its conclusion.

The combination of faded indigo wallpaper and dim, indirect lighting made the room feel like the ocean floor at night. Remembering the labyrinth she'd come through to reach this reception room, Raynesia gulped. This was not polite behavior for a princess, but endless timidity welled up inside her, and she couldn't help it.

She'd met with all kinds of aristocrats before.

She'd always thought it was a pain in the neck, but she'd never felt this uneasy. For the first time, she realized what it was like to be swallowed up by a mood, rather than by the content of the conversation. It felt as if she was about to be engulfed in an eerie atmosphere completely unlike the awe she felt with her grandfather Sergiad or with Krusty-the-menace.

She concentrated on relaxing the hands that were clutching a handkerchief in her lap.

If she wasn't careful, it felt as if she might cling to even that thin cloth.

A warm hand gently touched her shoulder. It was Henrietta, one of Akiba's most accomplished ladies. At the reassuring touch, Raynesia almost turned around involuntarily and thanked her, but through sheer willpower, she forced herself to refrain.

Right now, she had to prioritize her conversation with Kinjo, the man sitting on the sofa opposite hers.

The young leader of the Kunie clan was smiling the faintest possible smile. He seemed so at ease, it was tempting to believe that the meek expression with which he'd apologized to her at Water Maple Manor had been just her imagination.

It wasn't fearless. It wasn't taunting, either.

Raynesia was convinced that this was this man's natural expression. He might have been pretending to be demure during their previous meeting. Elissa was always pointing the same thing out to Raynesia, and Raynesia didn't feel like calling him on it, but even so, she braced herself again.

*　　*　　*

"You're certain you want us to interrupt the magic channels from the magic circle?"

"Yes," Raynesia answered.

They'd been repeating this exchange ever since she arrived at this subterranean mansion, the Kunie clan's headquarters in Akiba. Kinjo had already accepted her request and given his agreement. His black-coated Kunie attendants had gone to initiate the interruption.

This question was probably the final confirmation.

"If we stop the supply of magic, the magic circle that serves as the city's defense will also lose its abilities. It will take decades to bring it back into operation."

His gaze was questioning. Raynesia nodded firmly.

"Yes. I understand."

"The guard system that protects Akiba will stop."

"Yes, it will."

"The city will be defenseless."

"Yes."

Raynesia answered without hesitation.

Was she uncertain? —Absolutely.

Of course she was. Even in this moment, when she was feigning calm, she was very close to bursting into tears from regret and fear.

Why me? she thought.

And also: *Why is this happening?*

If she could have run, she would have, no matter what apologies she had to make.

That was obvious. Only natural.

But she'd made up her mind. She'd resolved to make this request.

When she thought back now, she understood what Kinjo had done to her that day.

This young man had come to leave the decision in her hands. He'd set the whole burden down at Raynesia's feet and gone home... Probably wearing this same faint smile. No doubt it had been premeditated.

Coward, Raynesia thought. *Don't toy with me.* This failure had been caused by the Kunie clan. Why shouldn't *they* make the decision and bear the responsibility? She thought that the Kunie clan, and no one else, should resolve the incident immediately and pay for the damages.

If no such convenient resolution method existed, as the person in charge, Kinjo could at least have stopped the magic circle on his own. Then, if the citizens of Akiba saw it as a problem, they could throw rocks at *him*… That was what she thought.

However, come to think of it, that was exactly what Raynesia had been thinking of doing.

When Raynesia had learned of this incident, she'd thought of contacting her grandfather, Duke Sergiad. She'd also considered begging Krusty in tears. Wouldn't that have been forcing all the responsibility for the decision onto them? She couldn't say she'd never done anything like that. In fact, up until now, that was practically all she'd done.

Kinjo was exactly like Raynesia.

And the girl in black had flown off into the town.

At the time, Raynesia had thought:

Oh, how convenient.

Of course, if notable Adventurers got wind of this incident, there was danger of a serious confrontation between the People of the Earth and the Adventurers. As a daughter of the Cowen family, and as a noble of Yamato, she absolutely had to prevent that. However, on the other hand, when she hung her head in the usual way, the Adventurer girl had leapt into the incident on her own, and an inkling of a solution had conveniently appeared. Not only that, but she'd eavesdropped, and the situation had progressed without Raynesia having to make a decision.

It was true that, for a moment, she'd thought that way.

That was what had made her see it: The responsibility Kinjo had shifted onto Raynesia was the responsibility Raynesia had constantly shifted onto those around her, from the time she was born until now. The irritation she felt regarding the young man in front of her was the exact emotion Raynesia should have turned on herself.

Of course she'd discussed this issue with Riezé and Henrietta. Through them, the matter had been reported to the Round Table Council as well. However, Raynesia was the one who'd made the decision. She couldn't just pass the responsibility Kinjo had foisted onto her on to the Round Table Council. The fact that she hadn't liked having it done to her wasn't the only reason.

No matter how you tried to gloss it over, Kinjo was a Person of the Earth, and so was Raynesia. They couldn't very well just shift things onto the Adventurers, could they?

Adventurers and People of the Earth were different beings.

In blunt terms, People of the Earth were weaker than Adventurers. However, precisely because that was the case, there was a line they couldn't yield. If they left everything to others, saying it was because they were weak, it would be admitting that they weren't simply weaker but inferior as well. In that case, they'd never be able to join hands. They wouldn't be able to be friends.

Elissa's words rose again in her ears.

Dropping all pretenses, Raynesia glared at Kinjo.

"This incident wasn't solely the Kunie clan's mistake. The fault lies with all People of the Earth. We blundered in being unable to provide sufficient defense. We must admit that, clearly and plainly. As that is the case, I have decided that cutting off the supply of magic is the best policy we can implement at this time."

"……"

"We must do what we can in order to apologize to the Adventurers. This time, that means stopping the magic circle."

"It may cause a greater nuisance."

On having this pointed out to her, Raynesia didn't know what to say.

Of course. As an individual, she didn't have the power to bear responsibility for all the consequences that might arise from this incident. Was there anyone or anything that *could* bear that responsibility? The responsibility for a decision that used a great number of irreplaceable human lives as the wager? Raynesia silently murmured the word *gods*. It was a cheerless, lonely word.

Still, *nobles* were people who bore unbearable responsibilities.

Even if it meant their crucifixion, nobles showed courage.

Raynesia had learned this from the grandfather she respected.

Just like faith in the gods, this teaching had no physical form, but inside Raynesia, it was a truth with a solid feel to it. Moving her head as though it needed oiling, Raynesia nodded a few times. It was an unbecoming gesture.

"There's no need to worry."

As if to encourage Raynesia, Henrietta spoke from behind her. She wore a cape over the uniform that marked her as a senior envoy of the Round Table Council, and she spoke in a clear voice.

"The Round Table is already aware of this incident. Please assume that you have our consent with regard to stopping the magic circle."

"You have patrons in the Round Table Council, then."

"They aren't a patron. They are simply cooperating in efforts to bring the situation under control, as fellow residents of Akiba. I presume 'fellow residents' includes the Kunie clan as well. Am I mistaken?"

"Is that Lord Shiroe's rhetoric?"

Henrietta's voice stiffened. "No."

Raynesia didn't know what the exchange meant, but she glared at Kinjo the whole time, determined not to yield a single step.

"…Understood. No matter what the cause of this incident was, it's true that the Kunie clan failed in its defense. We have left a blot on our proud, centuries-old history of defense and the administration of the magic circle. We were distracted by the natural disaster that has come from the continent, and we have consistently underestimated the threat of the West. The blame for these sins lies entirely with me."

"…Master Kinjo?"

The young man in front of Raynesia spoke with his head bowed, but Raynesia wasn't able to understand most of what he said. The words were enigmatic, and they gave her a premonition of something, but the greater part of it slipped through her fingers.

This man… The Kunie clan… They're different from the People of the Earth somehow…

"It's just as you say. I expect we must also do what it is in our power to do. Not rejection, but a new step. I apologize for testing you earlier. I will place us in your debt with regard to this matter, Lady Raynesia."

When he raised his head, Kinjo wore a solemn expression. It was something Raynesia had never seen before. However, shifting into that enigmatic smile, he bluffed, "That said, I would like to repay that debt to someone else."

Apparently Kinjo had tested her.

Raynesia finally came to that realization. That previous meeting had been a test Kinjo had set her. She understood this, although she didn't know its objective or the results. That was a terribly trouble-some thing. Even though she truly wasn't suited to it, this Kinjo and the mind-reading menace and that white devil with glasses were all scheming to make her shoulder heavy burdens.

"It appears everything is ready."

A young member of the clan whispered in Kinjo's ear, and he informed Raynesia as well.

To answer him, for the first time, Raynesia looked up at Henrietta, over her shoulder. Shaking her honey-colored hair, the intelligent woman with glasses wore a distinctive expression, as though she was gazing off into the distance. She murmured a few words in a small voice.

"In ten...five... Understood. In one minute."

On seeing Henrietta—who'd probably just awakened from a telechat—nod, Raynesia spoke in a firm voice.

"All right. Then consider this my formal request: Please interrupt the magic supply circuits to the magic circle that defends Akiba."

One minute later, a ripple like a small sigh from a giant spread through the town of Akiba.

The absolutely invincible guard system had shut down.

▶ 5

"Ten meters...five meters... Engage!"

A sweet voice echoed over the road.

Akatsuki dodged the gigantic stone figure that abruptly appeared as if she'd known it was coming. The golem, which looked like a locomotive made of gray granite, swung down a stout arm that was roughly the size of a car.

Apparently even the murderer didn't decide he was able to take that attack: He evaded magnificently. Although the golem's attack was penetrating and had a wide range, it wasn't all that fast; dodging it was easy.

However, Akatsuki had included that in her calculations.

As the murderer evaded the golem's attack, she aimed for his side: Fatal Ambush. This technique, which was crowned with the term "ambush," had a long activation time, or "charge time." It was hard to hit a fast opponent with this particular special attack skill. She activated the attack from his blind spot in a combination that used the golem as a screen.

Her reward for having struck home with a difficult attack came in the form of damage to the murderer.

The sword guard howled with rage, and Akatsuki twisted away, evading a blizzard. A slight evasion of a few dozen centimeters. It really wasn't enough to dodge the blizzard range attack, and what covered for her, as expected, was the golem. Akatsuki lasted through the cold air by ducking into its giant shadow.

However, as the penalty, the golem began to freeze over with a cracking sound.

The golem boasted a huge body, and as its appearance suggested, it had lots of HP. However, it was only "a lot" in terms of the minions Summoners could summon. These minion-class summoned creatures had about a third of the combat strength of an Adventurer at the same level. That meant they also had one-third the HP. Even if the golem was slanted toward defense and toughness, its HP didn't even equal Akatsuki's.

However, it was possible for it to last five seconds against the murderer's attack, and with those five seconds, Akatsuki and the others could shift into their next action.

"Pulse Recovery... There ya go!"

Holding a rod that resembled a broom, Mikakage cast the unique Druid healing spell, Pulse Recovery, on Akatsuki from behind the wrecked hood of a decaying microvan. A vivid green glow began to pulse over Akatsuki's heart, guarding her. Her HP gradually replenished itself in time with its rhythm.

At Mikakage's feet, Allie, a little girl whose gestures exactly mimicked Mikakage's, was also casting a spell. Alraune, plant spirits, were able to help out in combat just like the other summoned minions, but more important, they had a special ability that boosted the effect of their summoner's recovery spells. Shy Allie squeezed her eyes shut and brandished a tiny ladle. This wasn't out of fear: She was desperately, heroically trying to help her mistress.

After the Pulse Recovery spell came a ranged recovery spell, then an instant recovery spell. Mikakage cast more healing spells on Akatsuki, one after another. She was using the unique Druid healing work, which combined several recovery spells, in an attempt to heal Akatsuki, who'd been wounded during the fierce battle. This devoted act, which ignored her remaining MP, recovered Akatsuki's HP to about 80 percent.

Akatsuki didn't thank her. She didn't have the time for that.

Her current mission was to draw all the murderer's attacks to herself, and to sprint down the central avenue. The only way for her to express her gratitude was to carry out that mission perfectly. Her mind was more focused than ever before, and Akatsuki understood this very well.

The range of her senses widened, growing as clear and calm as the surface of water, grasping the state of her surroundings.

Marielle, who was running along behind her, was continuing to chant Response Activated Recovery so that the spell wouldn't be interrupted. The Monk girl who was acting as a mobile attacker and her Cleric partner were from the West Wind Brigade.

Feeling a sizzling, burning sensation on her skin, Akatsuki leapt in the opposite direction from the Monk girl.

Byakkou, the Summoner who'd created that opening for her by summoning the golem earlier, had summoned Lance Dísir from an enormous magic circle. Clad in pure white dress-style armor, the spirit hurled a shining spear that had seven branches. It was a sub-variant spell of Combat Skill Summoning—Sword Princess. It was the Summoner's greatest attack spell, and yet it was unable to do lethal damage to the murderer. That was only natural: Raids weren't so easy that they could be finished up with an attack spell from one person, no matter how strong. However, the continuous attacks were wearing a hole in the rock.

As Mikakage and Byakkou cast attack spells and recovery spells one after another, Akatsuki's group dashed through the pair's area. They couldn't stop. Akatsuki and the others had to lead the murderer to the target location, and besides, if Mikakage and Byakkou kept casting spells at that rate, they'd burn through their MP in less than two minutes.

"You can do it!!"

A bright cheer that wasn't at all suited to a scene of mortal combat reached her. As the murderer bore down on her with a face like a demon, over his shoulder, she saw Mikakage waving so hard it seemed as if her arms might come off. Akatsuki's chest grew warm. It wasn't just due to Pulse Recovery.

"Update! Ten more meters!"

With Marielle's supporting voice at her back, Akatsuki danced through space as if to cut out the moon. They'd passed through the Mikakage-and-Byakkou area. There were ten meters until the next area. It was like a winter parade that traveled through a variety of attractions. Lugurius's abilities increased in response to the number of Adventurers who were within fifty meters of him. This meant they could only station a few people within a fifty-meter range.

However, if the combat time dragged on, those few people would burn through their MP and grow exhausted. In addition, with only a few people, they wouldn't have enough damage output, and combat time would inevitably be drawn out. As a result, they'd wear down much faster. It was a vicious cycle.

In order to break through that, Riezé had come up with this raid tactic. They'd set up several circular areas with fifty-meter radii in several places around Akiba, distributing them so that they didn't overlap. The squad with Akatsuki at its center would lead the murderer through these areas, using the firepower and recovery abilities of the members stationed in the areas to recharge and attack at the same time.

As Akatsuki ran, she thought of the remaining areas.

She swore she'd keep running until morning if she had to.

She knew that Marielle's encouragement had been growing less frequent for a while now. Akatsuki was an attack class, so she could watch her remaining MP and be stingy with her special skills as she fought. The damage itself would probably drop, but that only meant the battle would drag on longer. However, Marielle was a recovery class, and things were different for her. If Marielle was stingy with her recovery spells, it would lead directly to Akatsuki's death.

For that very reason, precisely because she was leaving that heavy responsibility to others, Akatsuki wanted to protect them. She didn't want to lose. The equipment that hugged Akatsuki's body, the protective spells that supported her, the various arts that healed her—none of these were hers.

In order to repay the treasures she'd borrowed, Akatsuki charged ahead, rushing onward.

Seeking sharper steps, faster slashes.

Inside Akatsuki, something clicked into place.

Lowering her body into a slight crouch, she stopped breathing for a moment. The image that rose in her mind with that stance acted as a trigger, activating a special skill: the Tracker's "Hide Shadow." Ordinarily, the special ability could be activated only from the command menu, but Akatsuki had added conditions to her martial arts and trained until she could activate it.

Almost as if her life force was draining away, the sense of presence evaporated from her black-clad body. Akatsuki was fading.

Even Akatsuki stopped knowing where she was. As the demon sword flew toward her, its attack stood out sharply in her fixed field of vision. Akatsuki was leaving herself open to an attack that would strike home. However, there was another Akatsuki watching the scene from somewhere else. "Hide Shadow" had evolved to "Shadow Lurk," and the separated life force was traveling straight across the battlefield.

Akatsuki ran through the murderer's attacks, which whipped up a freezing blizzard.

The shadow that looked like Akatsuki and Akatsuki's own perspective were in different places.

As proof, her shadow flickered and blinked, blurring as though the blizzard was erasing it, and, like a phantom, it negated every attack.

In the midst of overwhelming acceleration, Akatsuki reached the murderer's back.

She wasn't able to hold this state for long periods.

The special skill was active for only a brief time, while Akatsuki

stopped breathing and froze her heart. A skill that could take an ability that was ordinarily used for infiltration work or evading monsters' senses and forcibly activate it during combat: This was the Mystery Akatsuki had acquired.

Pointless.

With the speed of a swallow in flight, Akatsuki swung her short sword.

The attack, which had come at the murderer suddenly from behind, left a shallow cut on his neck. To think that even when she'd launched an attack on a vital spot from that illusion, he'd been able to avoid a fatal wound. The power of the demon sword was limitless. But...

Pointless.

There was no delight at having a wish fulfilled in Akatsuki's heart.

She held her breath and activated Shadow Lurk again. The shadow double appeared immediately, and she used it as camouflage to leap out of the way of a triple thrust from the demon sword.

Evading the large pellets of ice that accompanied the thrusts, Akatsuki sped up even further, dancing over the murderer's sword.

The Mystery she'd acquired was the same as that demon sword.

A skill that operated on external logic that went beyond *Elder Tales.*

The power Akatsuki had wished for was the same as that blizzard-crazed demon. The young innocence that had longed for it seemed terribly embarrassing to her now.

A green pulse dwelled in Akatsuki's chest, and a cloud of powdery golden scales surrounded her.

There was power in the gauntlets on both her hands, and the black clothes she wore protected her.

More than that, the hands that had been waved so hard they'd seemed in danger of coming off... The words that had been spoken to her. These small affirmations warmed Akatsuki.

Mysteries—or Overskills, as some called them—were a state beyond the changes of the Catastrophe, reached through individual effort after understanding the system in *Elder Tales.* They were insignificant tricks, and they were also the result of training. In the end, although Riezé had instructed her in the eight Mysteries D.D.D. had grasped, Akatsuki hadn't been able to learn a single one. Just as, for example, Nyanta's cooking was a combination of Nyanta's Chef subclass and his own, real skills, every Mystery required awareness and study on the part of the person in question in order to be complete.

They weren't something you could learn how to use simply by having someone explain them to you.

They weren't the sort of thing you could acquire in an instant, the way you could level up if the game system granted permission.

You didn't try to acquire Mysteries. You simply worried endlessly and trained, and the Mysteries lay beyond that.

"The real lesson is that you can say the Mysteries don't mean much," Nazuna had said. Those words had engraved themselves into Akatsuki. These weren't powers that existed so you could boast about being a high-class Adventurer. They were more important: fragments of the "something" Akatsuki had brushed against that day.

In order to demonstrate this, Akatsuki ran. To vanquish her own naïveté, which had wished for power, she slid her short sword from its sheath. Even if it tore her apart, she had to shatter that demon sword.

The true form of Akatsuki's Mystery, Shadow Lurk, was her Tracker subclass's Hide Shadow. It was a special movement method that she shouldn't have been able to activate during combat, but which she'd forcibly activated in this real, post-Catastrophe world, using it in combination with Road Mirage and Trick Step to create doubles. It was a set of wings Akatsuki had made for herself, wings that were hers alone.

With a sharp report, the swords bit into each other.

Even with all those support spells, even with all this assistance, the murderer's power still far outstripped Akatsuki's. Even as she was showered by long breaths crazed with the scent of blood, as their swords locked and pushed at each other, the murderer leaned on Akatsuki, overpowering her.

I have to get some distance and drop out for one attack.

Having reconfirmed the strategy, in order to evade the lean man in front of her, Akatsuki released Stealth Blade in pinpoint mode. She'd shown the murderer this skill many times; he'd dodge with the left half of his body, and she'd use that opportunity to get some distance... Or that was what should have happened. But.

"Like this? Huh, like this?"

The murderer had let her pierce his side without defending, and he smiled with an expression of intolerable delight. The demon had lost HP in order to close the gap, and hellishly cold air was seeping from him. In a mere moment, the blizzard solidified, becoming ice, and the murderer froze his own wound, and Akatsuki's sword along with it.

Having lost her only weapon, Akatsuki took a hard blow from the arm the man swung at her.

▶ 6

"I'm okay."

Akatsuki got up.

The momentary carelessness had pushed her HP to death's door. She didn't even have 5 percent left… But she was still alive.

Marielle had come running up to her, but even her recovery magic had little effect. Her MP was very low.

"I'm sorry. Really… I'm sorry."

Marielle's strained voice hurt Akatsuki's heart. Marielle hadn't done a single thing wrong. Even though this was her first raid, just because she'd been put on a team with Akatsuki, she'd had the role of main healer pushed onto her; that was all. Akatsuki wanted to comfort Marielle, but she couldn't think of the right thing to say… And so she repeated herself, putting all the feeling she had into the words:

"I'm okay."

The words were a bluff, but that wasn't all they were. They were based in her sincere wish to reassure someone she liked. She wasn't putting on a bold front; Akatsuki had wanted to express her gratitude to Marielle. There was no way even to confirm whether that short exchange had gotten the message across. As Akatsuki broke into a run, as if to shake free of the exchange, someone flung a short, spinning, sticklike object at her.

"Great timing. Take that with you."

A twenty-fifth girl, who'd poked her head out of her workshop, pushed her goggles up as she spoke to Akatsuki.

The sheath was still warm when she caught it. In Akatsuki's hands, which were growing numb with cold in the blizzard, heat surged from the blade, as though it had just been born.

"…Ringing Blade Haganemushi."

"Nope. Haganemushi—Tatara. Reforged."

When she looked closer, the length was different. So was the grip. It was designed for Akatsuki. More than that, the flavor text shown in the item appraisal was different.

"I can't…pay this much—"

"Win."

Tatara, the Amenoma Swordsmith, spoke over Akatsuki, who looked as if she was about to cry. It wasn't the merchant's usual absent, sleepy voice. It had a strong ring to it.

"Defeat that thing with my sword."

She pointed: Kawara of the West Wind Brigade, who'd been acting as a guerrilla, was fighting.

Even as a mad dance of snow and ice sliced her up, even as she was smeared with bright blood, she yelled bravely, fighting courageously. The murderer's primary target was Akatsuki. Even now, his eyes were turned toward her. However, in order to protect the fallen Akatsuki from the murderer, the girl was making fine use of her Monk skills.

"Akatsuki. You're all set, hon."

Marielle, who'd continued casting recovery spells on Akatsuki, nodded. It was time.

No words were necessary now.

Like an arrow shot from a bow, Akatsuki ran across the earth in a straight line. She sent her Shadow Lurk doubles flying for one attack. She switched her grip on her new short sword and swung it: Accel Fang. The murderer went on the defensive with Hail Blade Byakumaru, and the sword locked with Haganemushi Tatara. Under a storm of iron, in which the blades grated against each other with a tearing sound, Akatsuki blurred and vanished.

Appearing behind the murderer's back, she launched a Venom Strike at his head. The man deflected the poison-laced strike with the side of his head, then forced his body in and swung his certain-kill blade at Akatsuki, who was still in midair.

That attack could only have inflicted a fatal wound, but Akatsuki evaded it easily, as if she had a foothold. Help had arrived.

"That weak endgame of yours is just like Shiroe's."

Nazuna had leapt in like a bullet.

Half-turning her body in a splendid motion that made it impossible to believe she was still wearing tall wooden clogs, she leapt into the air. She curled up, kicked the murderer's blade up, then got some distance and began running parallel to Akatsuki. Possibly because she'd felt eyes on her glamorous body, her expression twisted, but there was no carelessness in her gaze.

"Okay. If you're Shiroe's junior, you're pretty much my junior, too. I'll pitch in and help so Soujirou won't worry."

Akatsuki nodded.

The demon was chasing them down the central avenue with the force of a tank, and when they turned, they were in a gap between buildings where the bricks on either side seemed to press in on them. The blizzard was compressed by the narrow space. As they scattered it with Nazuna's barrier spell, Akatsuki and the fox-eared beauty sprinted away.

"What's the matter?"

At the words, which were so gentle it was hard to believe they were being chased by a monster, Akatsuki looked up at Nazuna. She wore a smile that was mischievous, and also kind. "Well, you're crying," she told her, and Akatsuki wiped the outer corners of her eyes. She couldn't say it was nothing. She was happy.

Even though she'd been so close to death, even though she was still being chased by a terrible enemy, Akatsuki no longer felt the terror of losing something. Right now, surrounded by a crowd of friends, she was fighting her first raid. For the first time in her life, she felt the warmth of comrades she could stand with as equals.

Akiba's night was a battlefield now.

It was a stage for Akatsuki, Raynesia, and the other Water Maple girls.

It was also stirring enough to renew her longing for Shiroe. Of course Akatsuki had loved the gentle, intelligent young man she'd chosen as her liege before, but she was confident that her feelings for him were even stronger now. Preparing a place for someone else to belong was a noble thing. Making a place where someone could spend their days happily was very difficult. And Akatsuki's liege, who'd known both the difficulty and the importance of it, was someone worthy of her affections.

"Engage!"

At that scream, Nazuna and Akatsuki leapt up at the same time. From the front of the narrow passage, countless arrows cloaked in electricity pierced the murderer. Coming from an Assassin who specialized in sniping, this Assassinate attack seemed to have inflicted damage on a completely different scale from Akatsuki's, whose style focused on attacking from the shadows and on the number of attacks.

Pulling away from their pursuer, who was bellowing as if he'd gone mad, Nazuna and Akatsuki ran through the air. Under their feet floated several thin, pale blue slabs fifteen centimeters square. This was Nazuna's Mystery, Celestial Passage.

It was a skill that set the basic Kannagi spell, Purification Barrier, in open space. The Damage Interception spell barrier was deployed as Nazuna dictated. These paperback-sized force fields, which would have had a difficult time stopping even the smallest attack, were a spell meant for defense and recovery that had been converted for use in movement. They were, literally, "footholds" generated in empty space.

They reached Akiba's central plaza, practically tumbling into it. It would have been safe to call this place—Akiba Station and its elevated lines, surrounded by elevated walkways and several enormous buildings—the heart of Akiba. Having reached the space, Akatsuki turned around in front of a jet-black building, waiting for the murderer.

The deep breath of frigid winter air she'd drawn in burned her chest. It hurt her lungs, but the cold air cooled Akatsuki's head and cleared her mind.

Possibly because he'd realized Akatsuki had stopped, the murderer advanced into the plaza slowly, his gleaming metallic armor clanking. Akatsuki's HP was down to 20 percent. The murderer's was also close to that HP. The absolute value was about a hundred times greater than Akatsuki's, but Akatsuki leveled her new favorite sword, preparing to engage the enemy.

She held it pointed at his face, a position she'd repeated several thousand times, or maybe several tens of thousands of times, since the Catastrophe.

"So you're not running anymore?"

At that question, delivered with a rictal smile, Akatsuki nodded.

"Then go ahead and—" As if to shake off the rest of the sentence—*die*—the murderer closed in, bringing down Hail Blade Byakumaru, made enormous with ice and the freezing blizzard. When they hung in Amenoma, the two weapons had seemed to be about the same size, but now they looked as different as a twig and a huge tree.

However, as he raised Byakumaru high, a gigantic mass attacked it from far up in the sky, like a waterfall.

In Akatsuki's mind, she could see her friends, surrounding this plaza. Her enemy detection ability sensed a wide range of people, and it told her about them. If they got within fifty meters of the murderer, they'd instantly reverse all the work they'd done to get here. Fifty meters was wider than the range of all magic attack spells and recovery spells. In other words, her friends outside that range couldn't take part in the combat.

That had been a blind spot.

More than fifteen stories above the ground, just a little more than fifty meters in altitude…

At the very edge of the range Akatsuki could detect, there was Riezé, using Kyouko's hold as a lifeline. Freezing Liner was a Sorcerer's wide-range attack spell designed to sweep enemies away with a stream of ice-studded water. When used in dungeons or fields, the spell's firing range wasn't even twenty meters, but it had been sent down in free fall from the top of a huge building to strike the murderer.

The attack devoured the phenomenal cold air the murderer radiated. It used that frigid temperature as fuel, and the instant it showered over the murderer, he began to freeze.

"Wha—!!"

The murderer twisted his body, trying to run. However, his legs from the knees down and the huge gauntlets that held the sword were already being encased in a pillar of ice. The fact that he'd raised his sword to slash through the girl in front of him also worked against him: Byakumaru was pointing straight into the deluge of cold water that fell from the sky.

The damage itself wasn't all that great. He probably hadn't even lost 1 percent of his maximum HP. However, when he was trapped by this much ice, it was hard to avoid having his movements restricted. Not liking this, the murderer tried to teleport, then found himself aghast.

There was no way he could know it, but Raynesia, who'd returned from the basement of the guild center, was staring fixedly at the scene.

His remaining HP was irrelevant.

They'd led the murderer this far in order to whittle down his combat abilities, see the cards he held, and make him fall to arrogance.

The curly-haired strategist's tactics had used the murderer's abilities against him, rendering him unable to move. With light steps, Akatsuki approached him.

The first attack was a straightforward Deadly Dance. It was launched from a low stance, as if scooping up, and was a special skill meant for close combat. It wasn't that powerful, but the recast time was incredibly short: just one second. And, if you struck home with it several times in a row, it got stronger and stronger.

The serial attacks struck at Byakumaru, which jutted out of the coffin of ice as though to reshape it.

To begin with, Ringing Blade Haganemushi had been a high-performance transferable raid weapon with a special ability that reduced the durability of any weapon it struck. It was a short sword with advanced capabilities and a weapon destruction ability that displayed its effect in hand-to-hand combat. Haganemushi Tatara was a reforged version of Ringing Blade Haganemushi. Its abilities weren't fantasy-class, but even so, it was beyond comparison with Akatsuki's previous weapon. However, what had encouraged her wasn't the attack power.

Something more ephemeral, something smaller and more important, was protecting Akatsuki.

Tatara, Swordsmith of Amenoma, retempers this just for its taciturn, unsociable bearer. Let that too-serious girl move forward without breaking or warping. Let it repel wicked curses and the miseries of the world. Let the person support the blade, and the blade the person.

The flavor text written in the history, those "meaningless" words, protected and warmed Akatsuki.

The meaning in them, and the feelings; the history, the lineage, the legends:

There wasn't a single meaningless thing about them.

They were inside the person who read them, important from the start. They were irreplaceable things. And precisely because they were so, a tragedy had happened to the murderer, and Akatsuki had been saved.

The clash of crossed swords echoed powerfully in the ultramarine dawn.

With the single-mindedness of a swallow that had found a place to return to, she dealt out more than twenty intensely focused attacks.

Even in the dawn, before the sun was visible, Akatsuki and her friends no longer doubted their victory.

Mikakage, who came running up. Azukiko, and Henrietta, and Marielle. Riezé, whose nose was red at the tip, possibly because she'd bumped it on something. Raynesia, who was clinging to Kyouko, who carried her. They gathered around the shattered cursed sword, which had been broken in front of them, and the crumpled murderer, catching their breath.

There were no victory cheers. Instead, a relieved murmur spread, and the girls looked at each other, smiling bashful smiles. Everyone had complained and leaned on their friends during this difficult fight. Many girls had made a sorry display of themselves.

Even so, this had been the Water Maple girls' first real battle.

Their small, modest subjugation unit had completed its mission.

Their victory was the bell that announced the beginning of the Second Catastrophe in Akiba, but more than that, it was a new blessing as they took a step toward the future.

The girls should have been tired, but—in an epilogue only Elissa knew—they occupied Raynesia's guest rooms and office and partied in their pajamas late into the afternoon.

<Log Horizon, Volume 6: Lost Child of the Dawn—The End>

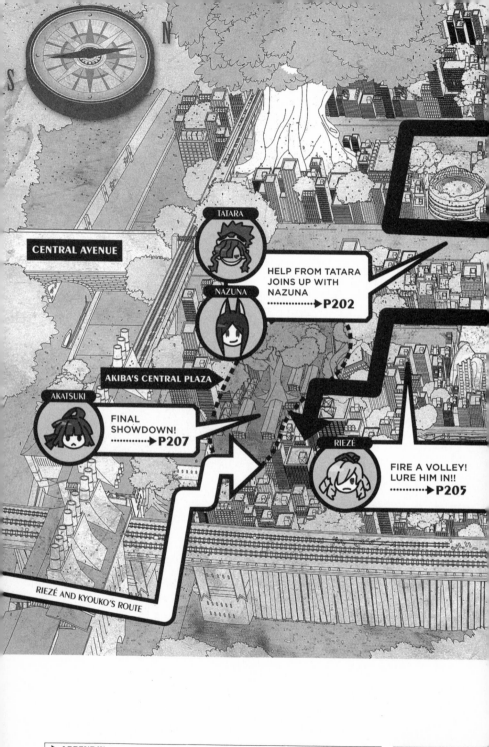

CENTRAL AVENUE

TATARA

HELP FROM TATARA
JOINS UP WITH
NAZUNA
·········►P202

NAZUNA

AKIBA'S CENTRAL PLAZA

AKATSUKI

FINAL
SHOWDOWN!
·········►P207

RIEZÉ

FIRE A VOLLEY!
LURE HIM IN!!
·········►P205

RIEZÉ AND KYOUKO'S ROUTE

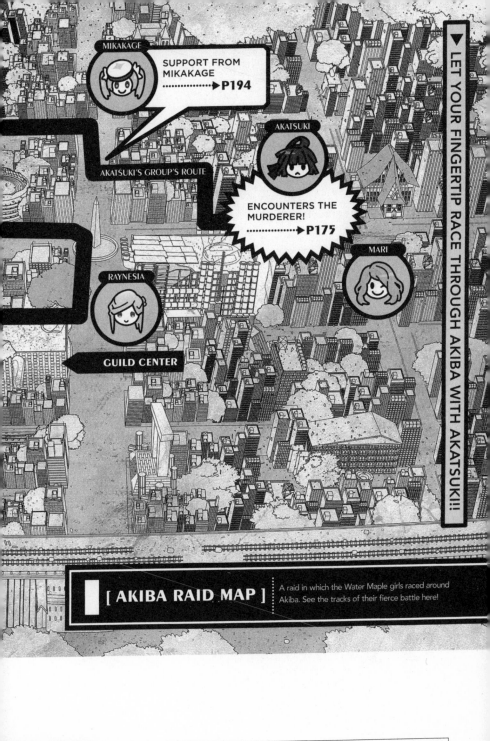

MIKAKAGE

SUPPORT FROM
MIKAKAGE
·········►**P194**

AKATSUKI'S GROUP'S ROUTE

AKATSUKI

ENCOUNTERS THE
MURDERER!
·········►**P175**

MARI

RAYNESIA

◄ GUILD CENTER

▼ LET YOUR FINGERTIP RACE THROUGH AKIBA WITH AKATSUKI!!!

[AKIBA RAID MAP]

A raid in which the Water Maple girls raced around Akiba. See the tracks of their fierce battle here!

[GUILD ORGANIZATIONAL CHART]

From combat and production to small and midsized: How are the guilds operated?

LOG HORIZON

[MEMBERSHIP]
8 people

The guild's important matters are decided at the Dinner Council (?) held every day. However, for the most part, there are no real problems, so the daily routine usually turns to Nyanta's "I'll take care of that" and Shiroe's "Please do." They're recruiting new members, but Shiroe is shy, so the recruitment isn't going anywhere.

[DINNER COUNCIL] EVERYONE PARTICIPATES

[SHOPPING/COOKING DUTY] CAPTAIN NYANTA

[CLEANING/REPAIR DUTY] MINORI & TOUYA

[ROOFTOP KITCHEN GARDEN & STOCK MANAGEMENT] ISUZU & RUNDELHAUS

[COMBAT LEADER] NAOTSUGU

[GUILD MASTER] SHIROE (※Plus all remaining jobs)

[SPY] AKATSUKI

THE CRESCENT MOON LEAGUE

[MEMBERSHIP]
61 people

A domestic, midsized guild led by Marielle. There's a strong sense of community life about it, and aside from doing their own jobs, everyone spends their life in Akiba in harmony with one another. It's run by a team of two women: Henrietta, who's in charge of the guild's budget, and Marielle, who's always smiling.

[TREASURER] HENRIETTA

[ACCOUNTANT] HENRIETTA

[SHOPPING DUTY] EIZEL

[GUILD CARETAKER] ASUKA

[MEAL TEAM CAPTAIN] GIROF

[COMBAT TEAM] SHOURYUU

[NEWBIE CARETAKER] SERARA

[CHEER TEAM] MARIELLE

[MARIELLE'S CARETAKER] HENRIETTA (adtl. post)

[GUILD MASTER] MARIELLE

D.D.D.

[MEMBERSHIP]
1,500
people

Akiba's biggest combat guild. Since it was built on a foundation of community matching in raid battles back in the days of *Elder Tales*, it's characterized by its large membership and by the completeness of its training for new raid combatants.

Positioned as an autonomous organization, it has raid chiefs who lead twenty-four-member full raids; legion leaders, who lead legions (108 members, including reserves); and raid generals, who supervise four legions. Each of the raid battle groups is organized to be capable of acting independently, even when Krusty is away.

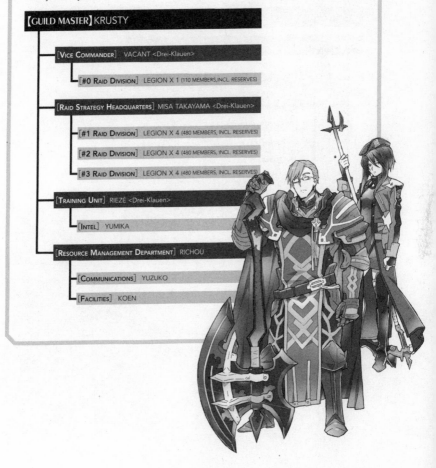

【GUILD MASTER】KRUSTY

[VICE COMMANDER] VACANT <Drei-Klauen>

[#0 RAID DIVISION] LEGION X 1 (110 MEMBERS,INCL. RESERVES)

[RAID STRATEGY HEADQUARTERS] MISA TAKAYAMA <Drei-Klauen>

[#1 RAID DIVISION] LEGION X 4 (480 MEMBERS, INCL. RESERVES)

[#2 RAID DIVISION] LEGION X 4 (480 MEMBERS, INCL. RESERVES)

[#3 RAID DIVISION] LEGION X 4 (480 MEMBERS, INCL. RESERVES)

[TRAINING UNIT] RIEZE <Drei-Klauen>

[INTEL] YUMIKA

[RESOURCE MANAGEMENT DEPARTMENT] RICHOU

[COMMUNICATIONS] YUZUKO

[FACILITIES] KOEN

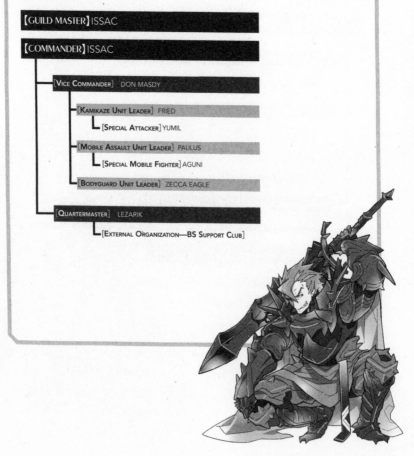

THE WARRIOR'S COMBAT GROUP

KNIGHTS OF THE BLACK SWORD

[MEMBERSHIP]
180 people

A major combat guild that professes to have the most actual ability in Akiba. It technically has an organization and an org chart, but because the group moves mostly through the moods and enthusiasms of its members, they don't mean much. Because things are like that, Lezarik used to work hard to maintain and manage the asset books and similar things all by himself, but a support organization of People of the Earth has been created recently, and he's finally able to get some rest. The group's slogan is "Hit it hard." That said, it meticulously carries out policies such as making matching mantles, and it's popular with its members.

[GUILD MASTER] ISSAC

[COMMANDER] ISSAC

    [VICE COMMANDER] DON MASDY

        [KAMIKAZE UNIT LEADER] FRIED

            [SPECIAL ATTACKER] YUMIL

        [MOBILE ASSAULT UNIT LEADER] PAULUS

            [SPECIAL MOBILE FIGHTER] AGUNI

        [BODYGUARD UNIT LEADER] ZECCA EAGLE

    [QUARTERMASTER] LEZARIK

        [EXTERNAL ORGANIZATION—BS SUPPORT CLUB]

THE WEST WIND BRIGADE

[MEMBERSHIP]
64
people

A female-centric combat guild famous for being a "harem guild." In terms of scale, the West Wind Brigade is midsized, but there's also an ingeniously duplicated organization, Unofficial Organization SFC. Since the SFC is an informal organization, it's impossible to tell the full extent of its membership, but many People of the Earth belong to it, and its total numbers are rumored to be over three figures. A lively, showy daily routine winds intricately between the two organizations, and apparently they live boisterously, holding bucolic chicken races and black market publicity photo exchanges, and hearing the day's activity reports.

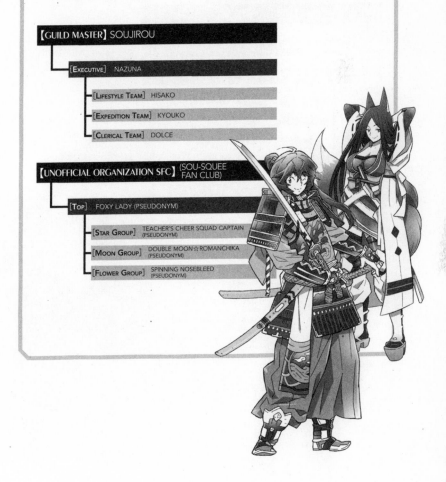

【GUILD MASTER】 SOUJIROU

[EXECUTIVE] NAZUNA

[LIFESTYLE TEAM] HISAKO

[EXPEDITION TEAM] KYOUKO

[CLERICAL TEAM] DOLCE

【UNOFFICIAL ORGANIZATION SFC】 (SOU-SQUEE FAN CLUB)

[TOP] FOXY LADY (PSEUDONYM)

[STAR GROUP] TEACHER'S CHEER SQUAD CAPTAIN (PSEUDONYM)

[MOON GROUP] DOUBLE MOON☆ROMANCHIKA (PSEUDONYM)

[FLOWER GROUP] SPINNING NOSEBLEED (PSEUDONYM)

THE MARINE ORGANIZATION

[MEMBERSHIP] 5,000 people

Akiba's biggest production guild. With over five thousand members, its scale isn't much different from that of a manufacturing corporation. It's been highly organized in order to make all sorts of production and operations possible. The guild's long-term operating policy is determined at the guild general meeting, which is usually held every other month, but individual matters are handled by the divisions, which stay in contact with each other as they work through them. At present, they don't stop at simple item production. They're also developing techniques involved in civil engineering and construction, and the fields in which they're active continue to expand.

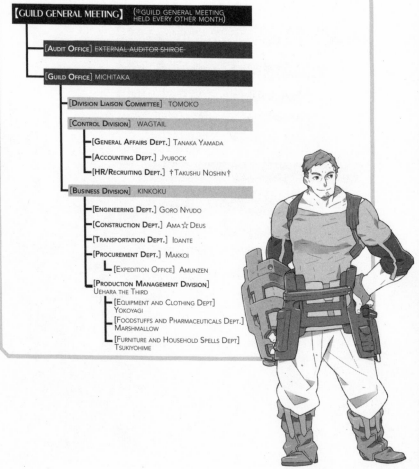

[GUILD GENERAL MEETING] (✱GUILD GENERAL MEETING HELD EVERY OTHER MONTH)

[AUDIT OFFICE] EXTERNAL AUDITOR SHIROE

[GUILD OFFICE] MICHITAKA

[DIVISION LIAISON COMMITTEE] TOMOKO

[CONTROL DIVISION] WAGTAIL

[GENERAL AFFAIRS DEPT.] TANAKA YAMADA

[ACCOUNTING DEPT.] JYUBOCK

[HR/RECRUITING DEPT.] †TAKUSHU NOSHIN†

[BUSINESS DIVISION] KINKOKU

[ENGINEERING DEPT.] GORO NYUDO

[CONSTRUCTION DEPT.] AMA☆DEUS

[TRANSPORTATION DEPT.] IDANTE

[PROCUREMENT DEPT.] MAKKOI

[EXPEDITION OFFICE] AMUNZEN

[PRODUCTION MANAGEMENT DIVISION] UEHARA THE THIRD

[EQUIPMENT AND CLOTHING DEPT] YOKOYAGI

[FOODSTUFFS AND PHARMACEUTICALS DEPT.] MARSHMALLOW

[FURNITURE AND HOUSEHOLD SPELLS DEPT] TSUKIYOHIME

THE RODERICK TRADING CORPORATION

[MEMBERSHIP]
1,900
people

Akiba's second-largest production guild. It's been a major guild since the days of *Elder Tales*, and since it was established with the goal of collecting all the recipes, after the Catastrophe, it has continued to center its activities on research into "new discoveries." Compared to its fellow production guild, the Marine Organization, it places emphasis on research and development, and its production and sales abilities are weak. Its organizational structure results in long rows of stations known as "departments" and "sections" which have anywhere from a few to several dozen members. This makes it look like a university, and as a result, the atmosphere in the guild house is more like that of a campus than a trading company.

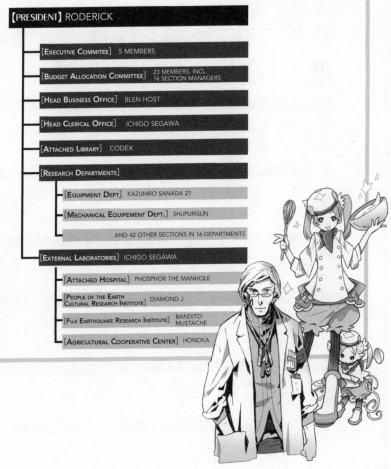

[PRESIDENT] RODERICK

[EXECUTIVE COMMITEE] 5 MEMBERS

[BUDGET ALLOCATION COMMITTEE] 23 MEMBERS, INCL. 16 SECTION MANAGERS

[HEAD BUSINESS OFFICE] BLEN HOST

[HEAD CLERICAL OFFICE] ICHIGO SEGAWA

[ATTACHED LIBRARY] CODEX

[RESEARCH DEPARTMENTS]

[EQUIPMENT DEPT] KAZUHIRO SANADA 21

[MECHANICAL EQUIPEMENT DEPT.] SHUPURISUN

AND 42 OTHER SECTIONS IN 16 DEPARTMENTS

[EXTERNAL LABORATORIES] ICHIGO SEGAWA

[ATTACHED HOSPITAL] PHOSPHOR THE MANHOLE

[PEOPLE OF THE EARTH CULTURAL RESEARCH INSTITUTE] DIAMOND J

[FUJI EARTHQUAKE RESEARCH INSTITUTE] BANDITO MUSTACHE

[AGRICULTURAL COOPERATIVE CENTER] HONOKA

►*ELDER TALES*

A "SWORD AND SORCERY"—THEMED ONLINE GAME AND ONE OF THE LARGEST IN THE WORLD. AN MMORPG FAVORED BY SERIOUS GAMERS, IT BOASTS A TWENTY-YEAR HISTORY.

►THE CATASTROPHE

A TERM FOR THE INCIDENT IN WHICH USERS WERE TRAPPED INSIDE THE *ELDER TALES* GAME WORLD. IT AFFECTED THE THIRTY THOUSAND JAPANESE USERS WHO WERE ONLINE WHEN *HOMESTEADING THE NOOSPHERE*, THE GAME'S TWELFTH EXPANSION PACK, WAS INTRODUCED.

►ADVENTURER

THE GENERAL TERM FOR A GAMER WHO IS PLAYING *ELDER TALES*. WHEN BEGINNING THE GAME, PLAYERS SELECT HEIGHT, CLASS, AND RACE FOR THESE IN-GAME DOUBLES. THE TERM IS MAINLY USED BY NON-PLAYER CHARACTERS TO REFER TO PLAYERS.

►PEOPLE OF THE EARTH

THE NAME NON-PLAYER CHARACTERS USE FOR THEMSELVES. THE CATASTROPHE DRASTICALLY INCREASED THEIR NUMBERS FROM WHAT THEY WERE IN THE GAME. THEY NEED TO SLEEP AND EAT LIKE REGULAR PEOPLE, SO IT'S HARD TO TELL THEM APART FROM PLAYERS WITHOUT CHECKING THE STATUS SCREEN.

►THE HALF-GAIA PROJECT

A PROJECT TO CREATE A HALF-SIZED EARTH INSIDE *ELDER TALES*. ALTHOUGH IT'S NEARLY THE SAME SHAPE AS EARTH, THE DISTANCES ARE HALVED, AND IT HAS ONLY ONE-FOURTH THE AREA.

►AGE OF MYTH

A GENERAL TERM FOR THE ERA SAID TO HAVE BEEN DESTROYED IN THE OFFICIAL BACKSTORY OF THE *ELDER TALES* ONLINE GAME. IT WAS BASED ON THE CULTURE AND CIVILIZATION OF THE REAL WORLD. SUBWAYS AND BUILDINGS ARE THE RUINED RELICS OF THIS ERA.

►THE OLD WORLD

THE WORLD WHERE SHIROE AND THE OTHERS LIVED BEFORE *ELDER TALES* BECAME ANOTHER WORLD AND TRAPPED THEM. A TERM FOR EARTH, THE REAL WORLD, ETC.

►GUILDS

TEAMS COMPOSED OF MULTIPLE PLAYERS. MANY PLAYERS BELONG TO THEM, BOTH BECAUSE IT'S EASIER TO CONTACT AFFILIATED MEMBERS AND INVITE THEM ON ADVENTURES AND ALSO BECAUSE GUILDS PROVIDE CONVENIENT SERVICES (SUCH AS MAKING IT EASIER TO RECEIVE AND SEND ITEMS).

▶THE ROUND TABLE COUNCIL

THE TOWN OF AKIBA'S SELF-GOVERNMENT ORGANIZATION, FORMED AT SHIROE'S PROPOSAL. COMPOSED OF ELEVEN GUILDS, INCLUDING MAJOR COMBAT AND PRODUCTION GUILDS AND GUILDS THAT COLLECTIVELY REPRESENT SMALL AND MIDSIZE GUILDS, IT'S IN A POSITION TO LEAD THE REFORMATION IN AKIBA.

▶LOG HORIZON

THE NAME OF THE GUILD SHIROE FORMED AFTER THE CATASTROPHE. ITS FOUNDING MEMBERS—AKATSUKI, NAOTSUGU, AND NYANTA—HAVE BEEN JOINED BY THE TWINS MINORI AND TOUYA. THEIR HEADQUARTERS IS IN A RUINED BUILDING PIERCED BY A GIANT ANCIENT TREE ON THE OUTSKIRTS OF AKIBA.

▶THE CRESCENT MOON LEAGUE

THE NAME OF THE GUILD MARI LEADS. ITS PRIMARY PURPOSE IS TO SUPPORT MIDLEVEL PLAYERS. HENRIETTA, MARI'S FRIEND SINCE THEIR DAYS AT A GIRLS' HIGH SCHOOL, ACTS AS ITS ACCOUNTANT.

▶THE DEBAUCHERY TEA PARTY

THE NAME OF A GROUP OF PLAYERS THAT SHIROE, NAOTSUGU, AND NYANTA BELONGED TO AT ONE TIME. IT WAS ACTIVE FOR ABOUT TWO YEARS, AND ALTHOUGH IT WASN'T A GUILD, IT'S STILL REMEMBERED IN *ELDER TALES* AS A LEGENDARY BAND OF PLAYERS.

▶FAIRY RINGS

TRANSPORTATION DEVICES LOCATED IN FIELDS. THE DESTINATIONS ARE TIED TO THE PHASES OF THE MOON, AND IF PLAYERS USE THEM AT THE WRONG TIME, THERE'S NO TELLING WHERE THEY'LL END UP. AFTER THE CATASTROPHE, SINCE STRATEGY WEBSITES ARE INACCESSIBLE, ALMOST NO ONE USES THEM.

▶ZONE

A UNIT THAT DESCRIBES RANGE AND AREA IN *ELDER TALES*. IN ADDITION TO FIELDS, DUNGEONS, AND TOWNS, THERE ARE ZONES AS SMALL AS SINGLE HOTEL ROOMS. DEPENDING ON THE PRICE, IT'S SOMETIMES POSSIBLE TO BUY THEM.

▶THELDESIA

THE NAME FOR THE GAME WORLD CREATED BY THE HALF-GAIA PROJECT. A WORD THAT'S EQUIVALENT TO "EARTH" IN THE REAL WORLD.

▶SPECIAL SKILL

VARIOUS SKILLS USED BY ADVENTURERS. ACQUIRED BY LEVELING UP YOUR MAIN CLASS OR SUBCLASS. EVEN WITHIN THE SAME SKILL, THERE ARE FOUR RANKS— ELEMENTARY, INTERMEDIATE, ESOTERIC, AND SECRET—AND IT'S POSSIBLE TO MAKE SKILLS GROW BY INCREASING YOUR PROFICIENCY.

▶MAIN CLASS

THESE GOVERN COMBAT ABILITIES IN *ELDER TALES*, AND PLAYERS CHOOSE ONE WHEN BEGINNING THE GAME. THERE ARE TWELVE TYPES, THREE EACH IN FOUR CATEGORIES: WARRIOR, WEAPON ATTACK, RECOVERY, AND MAGIC ATTACK.

▶SUBCLASS

ABILITIES THAT AREN'T DIRECTLY INVOLVED IN COMBAT BUT COME IN HANDY DURING GAME PLAY. ALTHOUGH THERE ARE ONLY TWELVE MAIN CLASSES, THERE ARE OVER FIFTY SUBCLASSES, AND THEY'RE A JUMBLED MIX OF EVERYTHING FROM CONVENIENT SKILL SETS TO JOKE ELEMENTS.

▶THE TOWN OF AKIBA

ONE OF THE MAIN ADVENTURER TOWNS IN THE YAMATO REGION. IT'S BUILT ON THE SITE THAT AKIHABARA OCCUPIES IN REAL-WORLD JAPAN.

▶ARC-SHAPED ARCHIPELAGO YAMATO

THE WORLD OF THELDESIA IS DESIGNED BASED ON REAL-WORLD EARTH. THE ARC-SHAPED ARCHIPELAGO YAMATO IS THE REGION THAT MAPS TO JAPAN, AND IT'S DIVIDED INTO FIVE AREAS: THE EZZO EMPIRE; THE DUCHY OF FOURLAND; THE NINE-TAILS DOMINION; EASTAL, THE LEAGUE OF FREE CITIES; AND THE HOLY EMPIRE OF WESTLANDE.

▶CAST TIME

THE PREPARATION TIME NEEDED WHEN USING A SPECIAL SKILL. THESE ARE SET FOR EACH SEPARATE SKILL, AND MORE POWERFUL SKILLS TEND TO HAVE LONGER CAST TIMES. WITH COMBAT-TYPE SPECIAL SKILLS, IT'S POSSIBLE TO MOVE DURING CAST TIME, BUT WITH MAGIC-BASED SKILLS, SIMPLY MOVING INTERRUPTS CASTING.

▶ MAIN CLASSES

[WARRIOR CLASSES]

GUARDIAN
BOASTS THE HIGHEST DEFENSE. ABLE TO ATTRACT ENEMIES WITH TAUNTS.

SAMURAI
USES JAPANESE EQUIPMENT AND TECHNIQUES WITH POWERFUL EFFECTS.

MONK
A BALANCED TYPE. SHORT ON WEAPONRY, BUT HAS FANTASTIC EVASIVE SKILLS.

[WEAPON ATTACK CLASSES]

ASSASSIN
A FOCUSED ATTACKER. SKILLED WITH A WIDE VARIETY OF WEAPONS.

SWASHBUCKLER
A VERSATILE, MOBILE FIGHTER. USES TWO SWORDS.

BARD
A LIGHTLY EQUIPPED WARRIOR. USES A WIDE RANGE OF "SONGS" WITH MAGICAL EFFECTS.

►MOTION BIND

REFERS TO THE WAY YOUR BODY FREEZES UP AFTER YOU'VE USED A SPECIAL SKILL. DURING MOTION BIND, ALL ACTIONS ARE IMPOSSIBLE, INCLUDING MOVEMENT.

►RECAST TIME

THE AMOUNT OF TIME YOU HAVE TO WAIT AFTER YOU'VE USED A SPECIAL SKILL BEFORE YOU CAN USE IT AGAIN. THIS RESTRICTION MAKES IT VERY DIFFICULT TO USE A SPECIFIC SPECIAL SKILL SEVERAL TIMES IN A ROW. SOME SPECIAL SKILLS HAVE SUCH LONG RECAST TIMES THAT THEY CAN BE USED ONLY ONCE PER DAY.

►CALL OF HOME

A BASIC TYPE OF SPECIAL SKILL THAT ALL ADVENTURERS LEARN. IT INSTANTLY RETURNS YOU TO THE LAST SAFE AREA WITH A TEMPLE THAT YOU VISITED, BUT ONCE YOU USE IT, YOU CAN'T USE IT AGAIN FOR TWENTY-FOUR HOURS.

►RAID

THE TERM FOR A BATTLE FOUGHT WITH NUMBERS LARGER THAN THE NORMAL SIX-MEMBER PARTIES THAT ADVENTURERS USUALLY FORM. IT CAN ALSO BE USED TO REFER TO A UNIT MADE UP OF MANY PEOPLE. FAMOUS EXAMPLES INCLUDE TWENTY-FOUR-MEMBER FULL RAIDS AND NINETY-SIX-MEMBER LEGION RAIDS.

►RACE

THERE ARE A VARIETY OF HUMANOID RACES IN THE WORLD OF THELDESIA. ADVENTURERS MAY CHOOSE TO PLAY AS ONE OF EIGHT RACES: HUMAN, ELF, DWARF, HALF ALV, FELINOID, WOLF-FANG, FOXTAIL, AND RITIAN. THESE ARE SOMETIMES CALLED BY THE GENERAL TERM, "THE 'GOOD' HUMAN RACES."

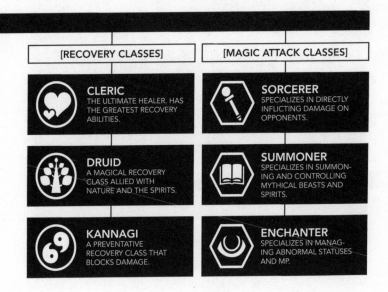

[RECOVERY CLASSES]

CLERIC
THE ULTIMATE HEALER. HAS THE GREATEST RECOVERY ABILITIES.

DRUID
A MAGICAL RECOVERY CLASS ALLIED WITH NATURE AND THE SPIRITS.

KANNAGI
A PREVENTATIVE RECOVERY CLASS THAT BLOCKS DAMAGE.

[MAGIC ATTACK CLASSES]

SORCERER
SPECIALIZES IN DIRECTLY INFLICTING DAMAGE ON OPPONENTS.

SUMMONER
SPECIALIZES IN SUMMON-ING AND CONTROLLING MYTHICAL BEASTS AND SPIRITS.

ENCHANTER
SPECIALIZES IN MANAG-ING ABNORMAL STATUSES AND MP.

CHARACTER POPULARITY POLL

RESULTS!!

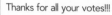

Thanks for all your votes!!!

The top five characters are shown on the opening illustration page, all dressed up. Wallpapers of the top five characters can also be downloaded from the Mamare Touno official site (http://mamare.net).

This was a poll conducted for the Japanese audience. Yen On's results are listed on page 224.

1ST AKATSUKI ▶ 1186 votes

[REASONS] I like black hair / I like her stealth action scenes / Quiet and little and cute / She got me with her feelings for Shiroe

2ND SHIROE ▶ 852 votes

[REASONS] A completely new type / He looks good when he's thinking / The gap between his enthusiasm and his craftiness

3RD NYANTA ▶ 541 votes

[REASONS] Reliable retiree / Soothing / Because he's a dashing, dignified gentleman

4TH MINORI ▶ 450 votes

[REASONS] I was touched by her devotion / I like how she's trying to catch up to Shiroe

5TH RUNDELHAUS ▶ 209 votes

[REASONS] I was moved by his struggle against destiny / Handsome / I like hotheaded dumb guys

6TH HENRIETTA ▶ 186 votes

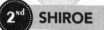

[REASONS] Because she's a reliable, sophisticated lady with glasses / I like how she's secretly a little sad

7TH MISA TAKAYAMA ▶ 158 votes

[REASONS] Because she's cool and awesome / She's my type / Her character illustration is epic

8TH NUREHA ▶ 154 votes

[REASONS] She's just gorgeous / Way too sexy / I want to go with her

9TH KRUSTY ▶ 134 votes

[REASONS] The way he has slim glasses and is cold-blooded / The contrast with Shiroe is fun

10TH RAYNESIA ▶ 127 votes

[REASONS] She and Krusty make a neat team / I like how she's really a slacker

1 Vote → The girl from Cocoa Brown / The farmers of Choushi / The one Adventurer who read the atmosphere and told them where Krusty was on p. 187 of Vol. 4 / Krusty's cat / The newbie Crescent Moon League girl who says "Ma'am" / The innkeeper's daughter in Choushi / Kazuhiro Hara / Demiquas / Marquis Kilivar / Coppelia / The group in navy blue overcoats with undyed tomoe crests who responded to Raynesia's plea first / The pretty waitress at Linguine / The middle school guy who confessed to Akatsuki in the real world / Everyone at Tsubakiya Design Agency / The Adventurer who said, "S-somebody get out here! Hey, whoever's in charge! I know you're listening!!" / The three Adventurers who stood up to help the Linguine waitress in her crisis / Akatsuki before the Catastrophe / Simurgh / The Goblin General / The Summoners from the Knights of the Black Sword who visited the new Log Horizon guild building / Akatsuki's little sister / The griffin mounts / Rondarg / Griffin / Shoji Masuda / The newbie Bard girl who staggered and got supported by Touya on p. 39 of Vol. 2 / The huntsman who spotted the horde of Goblins at the beginning of Vol. 3 / The Goblin King / Garnet Dragon / The caretaker at the village where Shiroe's group stopped on the way back from Choushi / The young men of Choushi who took up arms to protect the villagers after they'd evacuated from the Sahuagin / Naotsugu's Griffin / The apprentice of the huntsman who spotted the horde of Goblins at the beginning of Vol. 3

COMMENT FROM MAMARE TOUNO

You sent in 5,090 votes! Thank you so much! Akatsuki took first place. The heroine's the strongest.

Gloomy Shiroe also got into the top ranks and managed to hang on to his dignity somehow.
Thank you for voting for me and Sister Touno, too!

11th	Touya	119 votes
12th	Naotsugu	116 votes
13th	Shouryuu	100 votes
14th	Marielle	89 votes
15th	F——ta	88 votes
16th	Calasin	77 votes
17th	Isuzu	67 votes
18th	Isaac	63 votes
19th	Roderick	47 votes
20th	Michitaka	41 votes
21st	William Massachusetts	37 votes
22nd	Sister Touno	37 votes
23rd	Lezarik	35 votes
24th	Soujirou	25 votes
25th	Elissa	18 votes
26th	Ains	13 votes
27th	Serara	12 votes
28th	Leonardo	10 votes
29th	Li Gan	9 votes
30th	Mamare Touno	8 votes
30th	Riche	8 votes
30th	Rouge Vermillion	8 votes
33rd	Riezé	5 votes
34th	Sayaka (Krusty's little sister)	4 votes
35th	Kushiyatama	3 votes
35th	Kanami	3 votes
35th	Hiyoko	3 votes
35th	The guy who bawled while he ate a Crescent Burger	3 votes
39th	Nazuna	2 votes
39th	Duke Sergiad	2 votes
39th	Woodstock W	2 votes
39th	Akaneya Ichimonjinosuke	2 votes
39th	The Crescent Moon League Chef	2 votes
39th	The old Person of the Earth man at the beginning of Volume 2	2 votes

THANK YOU!

The Japanese audience's *Log Horizon* character poll inspired Yen On to see who our readers love the most. We thought it would be fun and interesting to see how our rankings differ! And without further ado, here are the results!

1ST SHIROE
18.63%
▶ 122 votes

2ND AKATSUKI
14.96%
▶ 98 votes

3RD NYANTA
11.15%
▶ 73 votes

4TH KRUSTY
7.94%
▶ 52 votes

5TH RAYNESIA
5.8%
▶ 38 votes

Rank	Character	%	Votes
6TH	Rundelhaus	5.65%	37 votes
7TH	Naotsugu	4.89%	32 votes
8TH	(tie) Marielle, Henrietta, Soujirou	3.82%	25 votes each
11TH	Minori	3.51%	23 votes
12TH	Isuzu	3.36%	22 votes
13TH	Isaac	2.29%	15 votes
14TH	William Massachusetts	1.98%	13 votes
15TH	Li Gan	1.83%	12 votes
16TH	Serara	1.53%	10 votes
17TH	Misa Takayama	1.37%	9 votes
18TH	Shouryuu	1.22%	8 votes
19TH	Michitaka	0.76%	5 votes
20TH	Touya	0.61%	4 votes
21ST	(tie) Calasin, Ains	0.31%	2 votes each
23RD	(tie) Roderick, Woodstock W, Duke Sergiad	0.15%	1 vote each

TOTAL VOTES ▶ **655**

Each voter nominated up to four characters, and even though the stealthy yet adorable Akatsuki crushed him in the Japanese poll ranking, the Machiavelli-with-glasses, Shiroe, came out on top in ours! We all love the gentlemanly Nyanta, and even Raynesia made it into our top five. Thank you to everyone who voted in our poll! We enjoyed seeing which characters you love! We hope you'll continue supporting the English releases of the *Log Horizon* novels and the manga, *Log Horizon* and *Log Horizon: The West Wind Brigade*!

AFTERWORD

Hello for the first time in a year and a half. This is Touno Mamare.

…Wow. I'm really sorry this is so late. I sort of got lost, body and soul. The writer's the "lost child," not Akatsuki. Common sense would dictate ritual disembowelment. To all the readers I kept waiting: I'm terribly sorry. I plan to get myself back in gear.

Thank you very much for buying *Log Horizon, Vol. 6: Lost Child of the Dawn*. It's cold every day, but by the time this gets to you, the water will probably have started to warm up a bit. All sorts of things have been happening. They made *Maoyuu—Demon King and Hero* into an anime. Stuff has been on the radio constantly. I got to meet lots of different people! I'm really grateful.

All right: The *Log Horizon* novels have entered their second season, and as previously announced, I'm changing the heroine of the afterword from Sister Touno to my editor, F——ta.

Why the heroine change, you ask? The popularity poll that was held in *Log Horizon, Vol. 4* (Thank you for all your votes). In that poll, Sister Touno came in twenty-second, and my editor F——ta came in fifteenth. Fifteenth place… That's Kawarimi Senbei (from the Relaxing Character Popularity Poll). —I couldn't really feel the awesomeness in that.

Well, if it had been Lady Yukari Yakumo (Touhou Character Popularity Poll), the awesomeness would have gotten through to me. My sister, in twenty-second place. That's an overwhelming difference in combat power.

I'm quick to spot opportunities, and on seeing this, I decided to bet on a winner and switch the heroine. It wasn't because I messed with Sister Touno a bit too much and have become the target of serious mental attacks. That isn't it at all, but I'd like to note that, when you're an adult, it's important to avoid unnecessary risk.

Okay, since I bet there are lots of you who won't know who I'm talking about if I just throw the name "F——ta" out there, F——ta is the supervising editor of *Log Horizon*. She's a talented lady editor with glasses, but she's really small. About the size of a soft drink bottle. In terms of race, she's a Fairy of the Koropokkuru variety. Carnivore. During meetings, she usually kneels formally on the tabletop. When things get lively, though, she jumps. She's a terribly cute, talented editor, but she is a carnivore.

I don't mean "carnivore" figuratively. She really *is* a carnivore.

One day, after a meeting, we'd decided to go to a family restaurant to eat. I knew my meat-loving editor, so I casually attempted to establish rapport—"They're holding a hamburger steak fair, you know?"—and she got mad at me: "Ground meat isn't meat! Hisss!" Whenever I try to order bean sprout *namul* at a *yakiniku* restaurant, she says, "I don't eat grass. Hisss!" According to F——ta, all women love meat. Come to think of it, Sister Touno seems a bit like that, too.

One day, F——ta and I were talking:

"Apparently there's someone who wants to make a *Log Horizon* anime."

"Oho."

"NHK."

"Sounds fishy."

"It really does, doesn't it? I thought so, too. They'd never make an anime out of that."

"Let's just ignore them and work on another job."

"Sounds good. Want to leave it alone and go eat meat?"

And so we left it alone for about six months, and then they settled on it formally. That's called "dry-aging." They say it's going to start airing in autumn 2013. That's half a year away, but the production work is already in full swing. By the time this book comes out, they'll probably be releasing information about it, little by little. It's going to be aired nationwide, so please do watch, if you feel like it. If possible, I'd be really happy if you watched it with your brothers and sisters or as a family. We should be launching all sorts of projects, too, so look forward to that.

The *Log Horizon* publishing team celebrated at a pub a little bit early. To be honest, I don't really believe they're making an anime yet, so I'd like to go out for a meat banquet once things are more settled.

And, with that report on recent events, this has been *Log Horizon 6*.

In the world of television, "All I need is the one" is a line that you hear all the time, but lately I've been thinking that "Just the one" is pretty difficult in real life. Maybe you want to get involved with one person, but that person has a pretty big society inside them. Family, comrades, friends. I think you have to get involved with all of it, and then you'll finally reach the person you wanted to connect with in the first place.

Akatsuki, who wants to be linked to one person (Shiroe), may have come up against that limit. This story was about how, at times like that, the people around you may be what you have to face. In other words, this story belonged to the girls. There are bonds that are created by doing your very best, and this was that sort of story. Apparently all girls like meat.

The items listed on the character status screens at the beginning of each chapter in this volume were collected on Twitter in February 2013. I used items from 291to230, carduus06, ebius1, hakuhai, hpsuke, kane_yon, kuroyagi6, luck_29, makotoTRPG, mizu_to, momon_call, ro_ki_, root425, sawame_ja, tepan00, and yamaneeeeee. Thank you very much!! I can't list all your names here, but I'm grateful to everyone who submitted entries. There were lots of submissions from new readers this time. Once the anime starts, I may get to meet all sorts of new readers!

For details, and for the latest news, visit http://mamare.net. You'll find information about Touno Mamare that isn't *Log Horizon*–related as well. Look for information on the comicalization projects there, too! Hara, Motoya Matsu, Koyuki, and Kusanaka are making it possible to read fantastic *Log Horizon*s, and I'm really happy.

Finally, Shoji Masuda, who produced this volume as well; the illustrator, Kazuhiro Hara (Allie was thanks to Tensai Design); Tsubakiya Design, who handled the design work; little F——ta of the editorial department! And Oha, I'm in your debt yet again! Thank you very much! I'm really, really sorry to have been so late.

Now all that's left is for you to savor this book. *Bon appétit!*

Mamare "Looking over the storyboards for
Episode 1 of the Log Horizon *anime" Touno*

▶LOG HORIZON, VOLUME 6
MAMARE TOUNO
ILLUSTRATION BY KAZUHIRO HARA

▶TRANSLATION BY TAYLOR ENGEL
COVER ART BY KAZUHIRO HARA

▶LOG HORIZON, VOLUME 6:
LOST CHILD OF THE DAWN

▶FIRST PUBLISHED IN JAPAN IN 2013 BY KADOKAWA CORPORATION ENTERBRAIN. ENGLISH TRANSLATION RIGHTS ARRANGED WITH KADOKAWA CORPORATION ENTERBRAIN THROUGH TUTTLE-MORI AGENCY, INC., TOKYO.

▶ENGLISH TRANSLATION © 2016 BY YEN PRESS, LLC

▶YEN ON
1290 AVENUE OF THE AMERICAS
NEW YORK, NY 10104

▶VISIT US AT YENPRESS.COM
FACEBOOK.COM/YENPRESS
TWITTER.COM/YENPRESS
YENPRESS.TUMBLR.COM
INSTAGRAM.COM/YENPRESS

▶FIRST YEN ON EDITION: NOVEMBER 2016

▶YEN ON IS AN IMPRINT OF YEN PRESS, LLC.
THE YEN ON NAME AND LOGO ARE TRADEMARKS OF YEN PRESS, LLC.

▶THE PUBLISHER IS NOT RESPONSIBLE FOR WEBSITES (OR THEIR CONTENT) THAT ARE NOT OWNED BY THE PUBLISHER.

▶LIBRARY OF CONGRESS CATALOGING-IN-PUBLICATION DATA
NAMES: TOUNO, MAMARE, AUTHOR. | HARA, KAZUHIRO, ILLUSTRATOR.
TITLE: LOG HORIZON. VOLUME 6, LOST CHILD OF THE DAWN / MAMARE TOUNO ; ILLUSTRATION BY KAZUHIRO HARA.
OTHER TITLES: LOST CHILD OF THE DAWN
DESCRIPTION: FIRST YEN ON EDITION. | NEW YORK : YEN ON, 2016. | SUMMARY: "THE UNTHINKABLE HAS HAPPENED— MURDER IN THE CITY OF AKIBA. THE LIBRA FESTIVAL'S EVENTS HAVE LEFT AKATSUKI DISPIRITED. DESPAIRING AND CONFUSED, SHE WANDERS THE CITY IN SEARCH OF THE MURDERER AND A CHANCE TO GAIN THE POWER AND RECOGNITION SHE CRAVES—BUT FEELINGS ALONE WILL NOT BE ENOUGH. A NEW CHAPTER IN THE LOG HORIZON EPIC BEGINS!"
IDENTIFIERS: LCCN 2016027921 | ISBN 9780316263870 (PAPERBACK)
SUBJECTS: | CYAC: SCIENCE FICTION. | BISAC: FICTION / SCIENCE FICTION / ADVENTURE.
CLASSIFICATION: LCC PZ7.1.T67 LOL 2016 | DDC [FIC] —DC23 LC RECORD AVAILABLE AT HTTPS://LCCN.LOC.GOV/2016027921

ISBN: 978-0-316-26387-0

10 9 8 7 6 5 4 3 2 1

▶LSC-C

▶PRINTED IN THE UNITED STATES OF AMERICA

▶AUTHOR: **MAMARE TOUNO**

▶SUPERVISION: **SHOJI MASUDA**

▶ILLUSTRATION: **KAZUHIRO HARA**

▶AUTHOR: MAMARE TOUNO

A STRANGE LIFE-FORM THAT INHABITS THE TOKYO BOKUTOU SHITAMACHI AREA. IT'S BEEN TOSSING HALF-BAKED TEXT INTO A CORNER OF THE INTERNET SINCE THE YEAR 2000 OR SO. IT'S A FULLY AUTOMATIC, TEXT-LOVING MACRO THAT EATS AND DISCHARGES TEXT. IT DEBUTED AT THE END OF 2010 WITH *MAOYUU: MAOU YUUSHA* (*MAOYUU: DEMON KING AND HERO*). *LOG HORIZON* IS A RESTRUCTURED VERSION OF A NOVEL THAT RAN ON THE WEBSITE *SHOUSETSUKA NI NAROU* (*SO YOU WANT TO BE A NOVELIST*).

WEBSITE: HTTP://WWW.MAMARE.NET

▶SUPERVISION: SHOJI MASUDA

AS A GAME DESIGNER, HE'S WORKED ON *RINDA KYUUBU* (*RINDA CUBE*) AND *ORE NO SHIKABANE WO KOETE YUKE* (*STEP OVER MY DEAD BODY*), AMONG OTHERS. ALSO ACTIVE AS A NOVELIST, HE'S RELEASED THE *ONIGIRI NUEKO* (*ONI KILLER NUEKO*) SERIES, THE *HARUKA SERIES*, *JOHN & MARY: FUTARI HA SHOUKIN KASEGI* (*JOHN & MARY: BOUNTY HUNTERS*), *KIZUDARAKE NO BIINA* (*BEENA, COVERED IN WOUNDS*), AND MORE. HIS LATEST EFFORT IS HIS FIRST CHILDREN'S BOOK, *TOUMEI NO NEKO TO TOSHI UE NO IMOUTO* (*THE TRANSPARENT CAT AND THE OLDER LITTLE SISTER*). HE HAS ALSO WRITTEN *GEEMU DEZAIN NOU MASUDA SHINJI NO HASSOU TO WAZA* (*GAME DESIGN BRAIN: SHINJI MASUDA'S IDEAS AND TECHNIQUES*).

TWITTER ACCOUNT: SHOJIMASUDA

▶ILLUSTRATION: KAZUHIRO HARA

AN ILLUSTRATOR WHO LIVES IN ZUSHI. ORIGINALLY A HOME GAME DEVELOPER. IN ADDITION TO ILLUSTRATING BOOKS, HE'S ALSO ACTIVE IN MANGA AND DESIGN. LATELY, HE'S BEEN HAVING FUN FLYING A BIOKITE WHEN HE GOES ON WALKS. HE'S ALSO WORKING ON THE *LOG HORIZON* MANGA ADAPTATION PROJECT, AND *LOG HORIZON*, VOL. 1 (FAMITSU CLEAR COMICS) IS ON SALE AND REALLY POPULAR. IT'S ALSO RUNNING ON COMIC CLEAR'S WEBSITE, WHERE IT'S POPULAR AS WELL.

COMIC CLEAR SITE: HTTP://WWW.FAMITSU.COM/COMIC_CLEAR/SE_LOGHORIZON/

Adventurer, you whose weight is borne by your winged soul! The mystical world of Theldesia is home to dragons and giants, magical beasts, and demihumans. Fragrant green winds blow across this new yet ancient land that opens before you like a blank page. Fill it with your life.

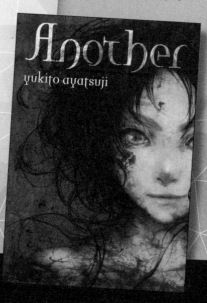

Dive into the latest light novels from *New York Times* bestselling author REKI KAWAHARA, creator of the fan favorite *SWORD ART ONLINE* and *ACCEL WORLD* series!

©REKI KAWAHARA ILLUSTRATION.Shimeji

©REKI KAWAHARA ILLUSTRATION.abec

And be sure your shelves are primed with Kawahara's extensive backlist selection!

SWORD ART ONLINE Light Novels

©REKI KAWAHARA ILLUSTRATION.abec

SWORD ART ONLINE Manga

©REKI KAWAHARA/
TAMAKO NAKAMURA

©REKI KAWAHARA/TSUBASA HADUKI

©REKI KAWAHARA/
NEKO NEKOBYOU

©REKI KAWAHARA/KISEKI HIMURA

ACCEL WORLD Manga

©REKI KAWAHARA/HIROYUKI AIGAMO

ACCEL WORLD Light Novels

©REKI KAWAHARA ILLUSTRATION.HIMA

YEN ON

Yen Press

www.YenPress.com